D1608149

The First Thing Coming

SHORT STORIES BY KEITH ABBOTT

COFFEE   HOUSE   PRESS   ::   MINNEAPOLIS   ::   1987

OESTERLE LIBRARY, NCC
NAPERVILLE, IL. 60566

ACKNOWLEDGMENTS
None of these characters exists, except in my fiction. I have played
with certain historical facts, altered a few buildings, and had a good
time with my photographic imagination. The story "Spanish Castle"
is dedicated to the following three people: 1.) David Katz, who gave
me both HIGHS IN THE MID-SIXTIES, whose liner notes are quoted,
and THE HISTORY OF NORTHWEST ROCK, Vol. 4, whose cover, a
photo of Spanish Castle, sparked off the story; 2.) Peter Howard, bookman, for the bound copy of a 1963 Tacoma *Yellow Pages* in good condition; 3.) Charlie Seluzicki, bookman, for finding a mint copy of the
1956 Tacoma Town Directory. I am grateful to John Knoll for the
loan of his reference books on rock and roll. Some of these stories have
appeared in different forms in *The Berkeley Poetry Review, Number,
Poetry Project Newsletter,* and *Big Deal* magazines.

Copyright © 1987 by Keith Abbott.

Cover watercolor by Gaylord Schanilec.

The publishers thank the National Endowment for the Arts, a federal
agency, for a Small Press Assistance Grant, United Arts of Saint Paul
for a grant from their Arts Development Fund, and the Dayton Hud-
son Foundation, for a grant from Dayton's and Target stores.

Coffee House Press Books are available to bookstores and libraries
through our primary distributor: Consortium Book Sales & Distribu-
tion, 213 East Fourth Street, Saint Paul, Minnesota 55101. Our books
are also available through most other small press distributors and
through all major library jobbers. For personal orders, catalogs, and
other information, write to: Coffee House Press, Post Office Box
10870, Minneapolis, MN 55458.

Library of Congress Cataloging-in-Publication Data
Abbott, Keith, 1944–
    The first thing coming.

    I. Title.
PS3551.B26F5 1987   813'.54   87-18190
ISBN 0-918273-31-5 (pbk. : alk. paper)

813.5
Ab2f

This book is for John Veglia and Persephone

OESTERLE LIBRARY,
NORTH CENTRAL COLLEGE
NAPERVILLE, ILLINOIS

CONTENTS

The Northwest Sound
Take a loud, sloppy, grungy band, give 'em an old R&B riff like "Louie Louie" or any Little Richard song, add a vocalist who has mastered the blood-curdling visceral scream and an inept but deranged guitarist conditioned to spring into action at the words "Let's give it to 'em!" and record the whole thing in some teenage nightclub in suburban Oregon or Washington and you've got the prototypical Northwest disc.

It became a matter of pride for the bands to outdo one another in greasy crudeness.... The Northwest had a standard of sonic integrity beyond that which prevailed elsewhere. The best Northern bands...hit realms of intensity unmatched by anybody, anywhere, anytime.

—Liner notes to Pebble's *Highs in the Mid-Sixties, Volume 7*: The Northwest (Archive International Productions).

We are a coast people
There is nothing but ocean out beyond us. We grasp
The first thing coming.

—Jack Spicer, *Book of Magazine Verse* (White Rabbit Press, 1963).

I
HIGH SCHOOL

The First Thing Coming

OUT IN THE WOODS it was possible to imagine that no one had been there before. It was possible to see himself as the first one there. He came to believe it, simply because there was no one else around. Yet he found it exciting to prowl among the remains of his older brother's two camps out in the woods: a few orange crates sinking into the ground and a board nailed across a birch tree with some words fading on it, and a three-cornered shack without a roof, nailed up between three pines. These signs meant that someone else had been there and left, leaving little that would not rot. Somehow, no matter how much or how little he found, he had the sense that he was the first one seeing it. When he thought of himself, he had the sense of light fading. In the woods there was no one to name the trees for him or even give a name to the ridges and mountains and rocks. He came to believe that the names rotted too. He delighted in sitting in the woods and feeling the wind go through him. If he sat still enough, he could feel it happen. And then too, the animals came out and went around as if he were not there. To him, not being there was the first step to being the first one there.

Out on the Res

WHEN PETE DWYER turned into a teenager, there was not a lot for him to do. From the movies, Pete knew what teenagers were supposed to do, only they seemed to be doing it in lush and sunny California parks. In Washington all Pete had were vacant lots, cow pastures, and a small section of pine trees and prairie rock along the highway south from Tacoma that had been given the name Parkland. There were no parks in Parkland. According to the movies, teenagers also hung out around the town soda fountains. But since Parkland was a collection of failing businesses, dying back from the highway, the only soda fountain had closed soon after Pete turned thirteen.

What Pete needed was a car, because he knew that three big things were going to happen to him in cars: his first sex, his first trouble with the law, and his first brush with death. Any of those could make a guy famous.

Pete's baseball hero, Sean Kingsley, had ended up on the front page of the *Tacoma News Tribune*. He was a switch hitter, had a great arm, and wore his hair in a perfect curled flattop cut. Enshrined in Pete's memory was the newspaper story of the wreck. The photograph was taken from the rear, so all that showed was Sean's head resting on the back seat. Next to his photograph was a diagram of how the car had swerved and hit another head on. Sean had died on a double date.

Dave gomm's father was a mechanic, and he had several old cars parked around the house. He didn't care that Dave drove, because he said that the sixteen-year-old age limit was a bunch of horseshit. After school, Rob O'Rourke, Hubie Cooper, Ray Steen, Jamie Gordon and Pete would go to Dave's and ride in the speckled blue 1936 Dodge. The Dodge always reminded Pete of the big roasting pan that his mother cooked the Thanksgiving turkey in.

Dave's house had a circular driveway, and he would ease the Dodge out to the road, look both ways for the county sheriff, and then race around the corner and back into the driveway. There was always that thrill as the car hit the street and made them all fugitives from the law.

They began to sneak out to Lovers' Lane, since during the day no police patrolled it. Lovers' Lane was a stretch of rocks, scrub pine, Scotch broom, and gravel roads to one side of the McCord Air Force Base. Cars and sex went together, so to drive illegally where sex had taken place was about the best thrill they could imagine.

But that got tame fast, and they risked runs out a back road going from Lovers' Lane to the military reservation. Out on the res was where they could roar through the scotch broom, knocking over small trees and scattering rocks.

Once they turned sixteen, everyone got driver's licenses, and some bought cars, and so the runs out to the res were forgotten.

Even before he got kicked out of high school in September, Jamie Gordon was the guys' sad sack. Small, plain, and unathletic, Jamie's only distinction was the way he flipped people the finger, so the guys hung the nickname Flipper on him. When Flipper came back from North Dakota in May before their graduation, he acted real depressed about missing his senior year.

The guys asked Pete Dwyer what he thought they should do to cheer Flipper up. Since Pete's parents were divorced, the guys felt Pete was more mature than any of them because his father was never around, and so Pete always acted as their counselor. And Pete also read books, wrote most of their term papers, and had a knack for looking at things from the outside.

Pete suggested that they each chip in twenty-five dollars and buy Dave's 1936 Dodge and give it to Flipper as a welcome-home present. Pete, Rob, Hubie and Ray felt a little guilty because, even though they all had skipped school together in September, none of them had been kicked out with Flipper.

Flipper got the ax mainly because his father was a minister and he was considered a failure of Lutheran upbringing, smoking and hanging around O'Rourke's house with the gang. It didn't help, either, that he was only a third-string linebacker and the other three guys were first stringers on what appeared to be a possible championship team, so Flipper was made into an example for the rest of the school, and his father exiled him to North Dakota, where he graduated in mid-May.

Even before being banished, he always moped about things the guys used to do, and Pete said that driving the Dodge would remind Flipper of their runs out on the res, and maybe he'd stop moaning about what he missed.

One day Flipper picked up Rob, Hubie, Ray, and Pete after school and told them that they were going to blaze a new trail in the boonies with the Dodge. "Like the old days," Flipper said, "out in back of the rubber tree." The rubber tree was a dead gray pine that stood at the entrance to Lovers' Lane. Hung in its branches were the used rubbers of departed lovers.

The guys all said sure, why not, but Rob O'Rourke kidded Flipper: "Did Little Flipperdipper miss the rubber tree when he was in North Dakota?"

At Lovers' Lane, Flipper raced the Dodge around a few gravel roads, and then he swerved off into the Scotch broom and immediately hung the car up on a stump. The guys all piled out to take a look. One tire was on the ground, and the other tire was up with a stump planted underneath the axle. They tried different ways to get the Dodge off the stump. First they jacked up the lowest tire, revved the engine, and then kicked the jack out from under the spinning wheel. The hoped that the Dodge would lurch off the stump when the tire hit the ground, but it did not do that. The only thing it did was put the smell of burning clutch plate in the air.

That excited Rob O'Rourke. Rob was the leader of the guys, and they hung out at his house, because his mother Merla had made a pile of money on real estate speculation, bought her darling son a new blue Pontiac, and filled their new brick house full of playthings for Rob's friends — a pool table, a trampoline — and also because his father, Big Rob, and Rob himself were loony-tune Irish and both were physically fearless. Their family life was one long bout of arguments, often conducted for the sheer joy of talking loud, the ones between Merla and Big Rob often ending with broken windows and squealing tires. Big Rob was their hero, because nothing bothered him, even when one evening he found a railroad-crossing sign leaning in his garage. "Well," he'd say, dragging off his Camel, "what are you little bastards up to today?" All the guys found the O'Rourke house the best show in town and camped there as often as they could.

Red-haired, with freckles all over his pug nose, Rob strutted around the Dodge, saying, "You know, guys, we ought to roll her on the res."

Another reason why Rob was their leader was that he could say things like that perfectly: "Roll her on the res." As a remark, it ranked right up there with his idea that one day they should cut a hole in the runway fence, take his new four-speed 325 horsepower Pontiac out, and race an F-86 fighter to takeoff, "just to see what would happen."

"Rob's right," Hubie agreed. "No lie, that Dodge is about shot anyway."

"Yeah, let's roll her on the res. Pete, Ray, you guys aren't backing off, are you?" Rob challenged them.

"Boooolshit," Flipper said. "The guys do not back off."

"First, we have to get it off the stump," Pete pointed out.

ROB HITCHHIKED HOME, drove Big Rob's Jeep back to Lovers' Lane, and winched the Dodge off the stump. Rob also took his father's new camera out of his Jeep so that if they did roll the Dodge, they would have a record.

On the drive out to the res, Pete spotted a Coca-Cola truck in back of the Piggly Wiggly and sent Hubie and Ray in the store to distract the driver while they stole a case of Coke off it. That success jacked everyone up a little bit more. Rob couldn't stop giggling, Hubie talked real fast, and Flipper flipped everyone the finger, no matter what they said. What no one was talking about was, *how do you roll a car?*

They had all seen cars rolled in the movies, but no one had even been in a car when it went up on two wheels, let alone roll it.

Once they got to the res, they put the case of Coke and the camera under a tree, and then Rob drove around the prairie, flattening Scotch broom and clipping limbs off pine trees, swerving this way and that. But he couldn't get the Dodge up on two wheels. In the back seat Pete Dwyer and Ray Steen only laughed. They both had predicted that nothing was going to happen.

Flipper challenged them. "Why don't you guys try? We'll watch."

"Screw you," Pete said. "It ain't going over, and you're happy it ain't, you little chickenshit."

Then Rob remembered how the Dodge had almost tipped over once when Hubie had run it off a low ridge over by the woods. They loaded up the camera and the Coke again and drove the Dodge over there. The ridge turned out to be almost three feet high.

"That ain't no ridge," Flipper said. "That's a ledge. Naw, that's not even a ledge. Why, in North Dakota that's just a long bump."

"Aw, screw North Dakota," Rob said. "We're taking the Dodge off it."

"Go ahead," Pete said. "We'll watch. You take Flipper, since he knows so much."

They unloaded the camera and the case of Coke under a pine tree by the ledge, and Ray stood by with the camera ready, in case the Dodge did roll. Flipper was forced to ride shotgun with Rob. To get the Dodge up to max speed, Rob made a circling run through the Scotch broom and then sent the Dodge flying off the ledge. It landed with a loud crash and roared off. It hadn't even tilted.

"Maybe if all of us got in and *leaned*," Hubie suggested.

The Dodge came back, dragging several Scotch broom bushes under it. When Rob and Flipper got out, Hubie repeated his leaning idea to Rob. It seemed reasonable enough, so all five got in the Dodge. Rob backed it up for a straight run off the ledge. Pete was sure that all the extra weight would only make it harder to roll the Dodge, but he didn't say anything.

"This is gonna work, no boolshit," Flipper predicted. "We'll all lean to the right." He grabbed onto the hand strap by the door.

"Hey, that's mine," Pete said. "Guys in the back seat get the hand straps."

As the Dodge raced up toward the ledge, Pete argued with Flipper, and they fought over the strap, slapping each other's hands away.

"Hey, shut up, you guys. Hey, maybe when we go off, I'll cramp the wheels to the right, too!" Rob yelled.

"Sure!" Pete yelled. He got a hold on the strap above Flipper's hand. "Over we go!"

"That's it, guys. As we go off, let's all yell, 'Over we go!'" Rob shouted back.

"Sure!" they all screamed.

Rob headed the Dodge off the ledge. As the car flew off into the air, they all yelled, "Over we go!" and Rob cramped the wheels.

When the Dodge hit the ground, everyone leaned right, and the Dodge went up on two wheels. Pete felt Ray and Hubie's weight hit his left side, the door next to him swung open, and then Pete watched the rocky prairie flying up at him.

The next thing Pete knew, he was hitting his head on the roof, the sky turned around outside the windshield, and then they were leaning on him while the door flew open again, but this time the Dodge didn't go all the way over but tipped back, the door shut, and then the Dodge was quivering underneath them. With his left hand still clawing the front seat upholstery and his right hand in a death grip around the strap, Pete stared at the door thinking, *That door was never open. It was always closed.*

Rob turned to them, his nose bleeding. "So, that's what it's like."

All five climbed out of the Dodge to see how it had survived. Only the right side of the roof was dented. Other than that, nothing looked different.

"You know"—Hubie's voice was squeaky—"I vote for getting a rope and tying the back doors shut before we do that again."

"Jesus, I coulda broke a leg," Ray said. "I'd been out of the state track meet this month."

"I almost fell out," Pete said.

"I ain't getting back in that car." Flipper had tears in his eyes.

"Heyyyy, what's the matter, Flipperdipper? Did little Flipperdipper piss his pants?" Rob pinched Flipper's ear. Blood was still running out of Rob's nose and dripping down his chin. "Aw, Christ, guys, we made it. And look, this old Dodge is still running!" Rob got back in and gunned the engine a few times. "Nothing to it: *over we go!*" He laughed and turned the wheels, showing how it was done. Then Rob wiped his bloody nose with his hand and made a big show of smearing the blood on the front seat.

None of the four others wanted to get back in, so they followed

the Dodge on foot, walking in single file, while Rob drove back to
the case of Coke. Rob jumped out and picked up the camera,
pretending to take their picture as they trooped up to the Dodge.

"No one will believe it," he yelled. "We gotta show Dad."

"No lie, Big Rob's got to see this," Hubie agreed.

As Rob snapped the pictures, they opened some Cokes and
toasted him. They all imagined what Big Rob would say and what
they'd say back to make it sound real casual, no big deal. Then they
stood on the bumper and sprawled over the hood, so they had the
same kind of photographs as they had seen in family albums of
their fathers posing on the wings of their bombers or the sides of
their tanks.

Mary Lou and
The Perfect Husband

MARY LOU LANG was blond and pretty, but she was not part of the school's ruling clique, the Lutheran girls from Parkland. She lived too far out in the boonies, among the chicken farms, meat lockers, and welding shops. Mary Lou was not even planning a college career, so it was a surprise to everyone when she was allowed in their junior literature class.

In 1960 the better students were separated from everyone else because the Russians had beaten the Americans by launching the first satellite, Sputnik. Putting the cheerleaders, jocks, and soshes into their own junior literature class was just one way the school did its part for national pride. Everyone assumed that Mary Lou had scheduling difficulties and that was why she was in Mrs. Newton's class.

Mrs. Newton was new to the school, but she was assigned to what she called "the gifted ones." The class called her Fig because she looked like one. With a bottom-heavy figure that sloped up to a gray stem of a head, Fig hobbled around the classroom in a roll-and-jerk motion, leaning to the right because of a bad foot, with her right arm hung low. She had a parrot's beak for a nose and a dim, nearsighted stare. The students were sure that Fig Newton had previously been in retirement, and they joked about her coming from a mothball fleet for old teachers. She treated them as if they were still in junior high school. On the first day she divided the class up into rows of boys and girls. Mary Lou was assigned the last seat at the end of a girls' row. She did not say much in class, but then, no one had a chance to say much. Mrs. Newton did all the talking.

Fig Newton only talked about two things: Edgar Allan Poe and Margaret Mitchell. It did not matter what they were supposed to be reading, those were her two favorite topics, and she returned to "The Tell-Tale Heart" and *Gone with the Wind* again and again. When Fig talked about Edgar Allan Poe, she drew a target on the chalkboard and then put an arrow to one side of it. "A short story is like an arrow hitting the center of the target," she said. "It goes straight to the mark." And then she erased the arrow and drew it with its point in the center of the target. And then Fig would go on and talk about how, besides hitting the center of the target, a short story does not waste any time, either.

When Fig talked about *Gone with the Wind*, her eyes misted over, and she would turn to the girls' side of the room and ask them what they thought about Rhett Butler or Scarlett O'Hara. The class wasn't reading *Gone with the Wind*—it was considered too dirty for classroom use—but Fig assumed that all the girls had read it. The boys did not talk much, anyway.

ONE MONDAY, Pete Dwyer was walking into class when Peter Dawson took him aside. "It worked," Dawson said. He handed the book report to Pete. On the top was a big red B in Fig's handwriting. "See, I told you it would work."

"Christ," Pete said. He couldn't believe that Fig was that dumb.

The Friday before, Pete had been rushing out book reports for all his buddies for a dollar apiece. Dawson had been the last one. By that time Pete had run out of books to use. He searched through the latest *Junior Scholastic* magazine for a book review that he could rewrite, but there wasn't one. So instead, Pete took a movie review and rewrote it as Dawson's book report, putting the Hollywood producer Darryl F. Zanuck as the author. Pete made a deal with Dawson that if Fig caught the fraud, Pete would pay Dawson back the dollar.

"You win, Dwyser babe," Dawson said. "Hey, but you hear about Mary Lou?" He turned away from the doorway so no one in the classroom could hear. "She's knocked up." Dawson laughed. "She's leaving school Friday. This is her last week." He nodded at the classroom. "Look at them in there." He snapped his fingers. "Them broads look like there's a prayer meeting going on in there. No one knows who the guy is. He's out of school, I guess." Dawson gave another little laugh. "I was thinking of taking her out myself. I mean, before this." He rubbed his chin. "Too late now."

Pete walked in and sat down. Sometimes he could not stand Dawson's bullshit. Pretty soon Dawson would be hinting that he was the one. Pete saw that the girls were all at their desks, busy looking down at stuff. In the last seat Mary Lou was staring out the window.

When Fig came in, she babbled away as usual. It was clear that she had not heard about Mary Lou's situation. This confirmed what Pete thought. The other teachers saw Fig was a dummy too and didn't include her in on the gossip. Pete wondered if Fig was the only one in the school who didn't know.

Fig rambled on, writing down the week's assignments on the chalkboard. It took her about ten minutes to get upset because the girls didn't pitch in and feed her lines. So she decided to shake everyone up a little and talk about *Gone with the Wind* again, by leading a discussion on whether or not Rhett was the perfect husband.

"I know it is Monday morning, children, but that is no excuse. Everyone is interested in romance — let's not kid ourselves. So what about it? What makes the perfect husband?"

She was looking to the girls, but all of them were gazing down at their desks except for Mary Lou, who was still staring out the window.

"I'm going to go by row," Fig threatened.

Pete looked around at the guys. Hubie raised his hand. "Mrs. Newton," he said, "I think Peter Dawson would make the perfect husband."

No one but Hubie laughed. "Just kidding," he said.

Fig looked back to the girls. "Come on, class, you people are perfectly comatose. You know what that means. Okay…if that's the way you want it." Fig arched her eyebrows and began to inspect the last seats. One of the girls in front raised her hand, but Fig shook her head. "Mary Lou, you seem to be daydreaming today. How would you define the perfect husband?"

One of the girls raised her hand, but Fig made a brushing motion, shooing her aside. "No, we'll get to you next. Mary Lou, did you hear me? Are you awake or comatose?"

Mary Lou turned in her seat and faced Fig. "The perfect husband," she repeated.

"Honestly, you people *are* comatose. Come on!" Fig dropped her chalk on her desk with a loud clink. "Well, speak!"

While the other girls stared down at their desk tops, Mary Lou cleared her throat once and said, "I think that the perfect husband would be someone you could talk to, no matter what was on your mind." Mary Lou paused, addressing the alphabet above the chalkboard. "He would be someone you could trust. You could trust him with what you were thinking."

Fig looked sharply at the boys. They were too quiet for her. She was sure they were up to something. "Yes," Fig said, "come along, don't dawdle. Other people want to talk."

Another girl had raised her hand. Then all the girls raised their hands at once. Fig shook her head at them. "And?" she said. "Is that all?"

Mary Lou turned to the side and looked out the window again. "He would be someone that trusted you and could tell you what he felt. You should be able to tell him the things that you can't tell anyone else. And he would understand. He would be around when...you needed someone to trust." Mary Lou looked around the room at everyone. No one met her eye. "And there would be truth between you and him. So she can say the things that are true to her, say them to him...and he could do the same with her." Mary Lou paused, then regarded her desk for a second. "And that's what I think a perfect husband would be like."

"No...no...no," Fig said, picking up her chalk. "Let's make a list. We wanted to make a list. Now." She chalked a number one on the board. "What color hair should he have? Do you want a living doll or what?"

As Fig wrote the numbers two and three on the board, Mary Lou went back to staring out the window. Pete looked that way too, suddenly wanting to see what she saw. Pete wondered if she saw the same things that he did. But then, as far as Pete knew, there were only two things outside the school to see.

First, there was a train track, and sometimes a freight train came past. Every now and then a class would try to count the freight cars without the teacher catching them. One person per car, the whisper would go around the room:...*Ten...eleven...twelve....* Sometimes there was a hobo in an open freight car. He would wave at the school, and then the game was to wave back, but not so the teacher saw you waving.

The second thing to see was the old folks' home. A white farmhouse stood at the edge of the bus parking lot. Every now and then one shell-shocked veteran would sneak away from his nurse and go walking out on the lawn. Sometimes he peed in the ditch. There was a great game then, to get everyone but the teacher to watch him pee. Those were the two things that Pete remembered when he looked out the window.

"Two, what color eyes?" Fig said. "Come *on*, class." She threw her chalk on her desk again. "I don't know what it *is* about you today," Fig said. "I try to spice up the class, and this is all the thanks I get. Maybe you all ought to do a few homework assignments. Maybe that's what you all should do. Everyone is interested in love, but if you want a few assignments, I can certainly give you that instead."

Rick's First Visit to
The A & W

RICK KREBS LIVED on the cheaper side of Parkland, out by the air force base. There the houses did not have any lawns. Most were parked on scraped prairie with a lot of smooth round rocks for grass. Rick didn't even live in a house but in a corner store with his father.

Krebs' Grocery operated out of the converted office of an old tire shop, on what used to be the main road going out to McCord Air Force Base. Most of the military personnel were housed elsewhere and commuted on the freeway. Enough families still lived nearby to shop there. Rick and his father roomed in an apartment over the store and rented out the garage to a welding outfit.

Rick was a short guy with an upturned nose. Squat and tough, he never made many friends in school. He started late and flunked one grade, so he was almost two years older than his classmates. In the tenth grade Rick dropped out and enlisted in the Army Special Forces, the first one in the class of 1962 to join up. Rick did not have much of a future in school, and in Parkland the boys without much of a future joined the armed services. People seemed to think that the Army made you tough and being tough made life easier—if a boy did not have much of a future. Once Rick was gone, no one talked about him.

During that fall, the big rage was going to the new A&W drive-in on Pacific Avenue. After football practice the guys would stand around in the parking lot with the funnel-shaped paper cartons of A&W root beer.

At the end of the next summer, right before their senior year, Rick came back to Parkland, on leave. The guys felt that they should show Rick around. Hubie volunteered because his dad was a twenty-year man in the Army and he'd been around military guys all his life. That was how they took Rick for his first visit to the A&W. Actually, the guys were not going there much any more. The fad had died out. But since they were showing Rick what he had missed by going into the Marines, they took him there first. To them it made sense to begin his first day home by showing him how they had started the school year.

Rick sat with Pete in the back seat of Hubie's car. Flipper and Hubie rode in front, pretending they were chauffeuring Rick around, giving him a deluxe tour. Hubie also wanted to show off the black and white 1954 Ford that his father had bought him when he had turned sixteen. Rick acted like everyone back from the service — withdrawn, as if maybe his tough guy routine got sawed-off a bit. And, like a lot of guys, he didn't seem sure about how he was going to fit back in with the old gang. Krebs had good reason to be worried, because he never really fitted in before, but the guys were ready to overlook that and pretend Rick was an old buddy so they could talk about themselves.

After they gave their orders to the A&W carhop, each choosing a different item on the menu, they filled Rick in on all the crazy stuff the guys had been doing. Lately they'd been going out at night in Rob O'Rourke's two ton truck with a big bull chain hooked to the bumper and two guys sitting in back, holding it up. One night, Rob had whipped the two-ton around a corner in Midland with the chain trailing behind the truck. The chain wrapped around a railroad crossing sign — not a big one — just one with a four-by-four post — and jerked the whole thing clean out of the ground.

"No lie, nobody saw us do it," Hubie laughed. "But they sure heard it."

"And that's nothing," Flipper yelled. "You should have seen old Hube here when we did an eat-and-run on the In & Out. You know that drive-in, down Pacific Avenue out by Spanaway Lake?"

"Oh man, you gotta hear this one," Pete put in.

"Hubie here, why, he can't run for shit," Flipper went on. "We got guys who run faster, but we have Hubie do it because he has the best way of saying 'Thanks, man.' That's why we have him do the pickup when we're eating and running. Say it for him, Hubie."

Hubie smiled and waved a short little wave. "Thanks, man."

"That's what he always says when he's got the stuff and the guy's at the counter expecting him to pay. Thanks, man."

Hubie laughed at Flipper's version, and Pete joined in. "That's what I say," Hubie said.

"So old Hubie here, he goes up and orders five burgers and five French fries, and when the cook gives him the packages, he says he forgot to ask for some milk shakes, see."

"That's a diversion," Pete said to Rick. "Gotta have a diversion planned so you get away clean."

"Hey, Flipper, you forgot to talk about the fry cook, man," Hubie said. "He was a vet, see, and he had this hook for one arm, so I say, 'Thanks man,' and I grab the sacks and take off. And, no lie, out the window comes the fry cook."

"Get this, man," Flipper said, "we were in the car looking back, and here comes Hubie, running to beat all hell, and behind him there's this one-armed fry cook coming after him and waving that hook at him." Flipper broke up. Hubie began laughing too.

"You should have seen it, Rick. You should have seen it."

Pete looked at Rick, and he was bent over his frosty root-beer mug. For a minute Pete thought that Rick was laughing so hard he was crying. Then he saw Rick really was only crying.

Hubie and Flipper glanced back at Rick, who was bent over his root beer, his shoulders drawn in tight, his head down. Then they looked at Pete. Pete could only shrug.

"Hey, uh, something wrong?" Hubie said.

Rick stopped crying. He brought his head up and stared out the window at the A&W drive-in, and then he started crying again, this time without lowering his head, big tears coming down his face.

"Hey," Pete said, and he touched Rick's arm, but Rick stayed doubled up, holding his root beer mug close to his chest, crying harder than ever.

"Rick, hey, come on." Hubie waved at Pete and Flipper, signaling them to look away. "Let me handle this. What's bugging you, man. I seen guys come back a lot. It's okay. Boot camp?"

Hubie leaned over the front seat and touched Rick on the shoulder, and Rick knocked his hand away.

None of them could believe this. Krebs, the toughest kid in school, *a Commando Ranger*, bawling in the back seat. They were all so embarrassed they checked the other cars, but no one they knew was there. Most of their high school buddies had stopped coming there. So all three watched Rick blubber and sniff.

"Hey," Hubie said, "why doncha tell us what's the matter, Rick? Hey, we're your buddies."

Clearing his throat, Rick brought his head up, sniffed once and then he said, slow and deliberate, "I don't feel human any more. I just don't feel human."

Then Rick hunched over again, taking big deep breaths until he stopped crying. He rocked back and forth, as he began to talk into his root-beer mug about killing people. He said that he shot people from helicopters, machine-gunned water buffaloes and villages. He hosed down anything that moved or looked like it might hide someone. He talked about what the bullets looked like when they hit.

Hubie and Pete and Flipper didn't know what to think. They were sure that Rick must have gone crazy. There wasn't any place to do that. They weren't at war.

Finally Hubie asked, "Uh, Rick, where...was that?"

"Vietnam." Rick looked up at Hubie. "I was in Vietnam."

Hubie shook his head at Flipper, like he didn't know how that could have gone on.

"How'd you get over there?" Flipper asked.

Rick was still sniffling as Flipper said that. He jerked once, as if he'd been smacked up alongside the head, and he stared at Flipper for so long that the tears dried on his face. Then he looked away.

In the front seat, Flipper wilted. Later he said that he thought that Rick was about to come over the top of the seat after him.

Hubie put his mug back on the tray, and Pete passed his stuff over the seat to Hubie. Then Flipper gave Hubie his empty carton. The only mug left was in Rick's hand.

"Hey, he was just asking," Hubie said. "I mean, my old man's in the Army, and they sure as hell aren't in Vietnam."

Rick sat with his mug in his hand, not drinking any but only swallowing hard every now and then.

The carhop came up to their window and took the tray away. Hubie fiddled with his keys. Then he said, "No lie, I heard there were military advisers, or something, but you're a first-year grunt, right? What would you advise them about?"

When Rick didn't answer, Hubie started the Ford. "Keep the mug," he told Rick. "They don't care. They do, but hey, you know." He gave a little laugh and waited for Rick to say something, but all

Rick did was sit there, sniffing and swallowing hard and staring out the window.

Hubie backed out of the A&W and turned onto Pacific Avenue. "Rick?" he said. Hubie looked around the car, and he waited for someone else to say something, but nobody knew what to say.

Hubie let Krebs out in front of his father's grocery store. He still had the A&W mug in his hand. Nobody knew what to say, so nobody even said see you later. Hubie put the Ford in drive and pulled away, leaving Rick in the gravel by the front of the grocery store.

None of them heard anything more about Krebs. The last time his name came up was when his father died. His father killed himself while he was standing behind the counter of his store. Krebs' Grocery wasn't doing very well. A lot of neighborhood base personnel were clearing out, shipped overseas, but no one knew why his father would shoot himself. He didn't leave a note. A customer had come in and found Rick's father dead behind the cash register.

Spanish Castle

SPANISH CASTLE was a roadhouse, built in the 1930s on Highway 99 between Tacoma and Seattle. Surrounded by marshland, blackberry brambles, and swamp alder, its name came from the false front of notched parapets and a square tower. On top of that tower sat a smaller tower with a flagpole. Originally a club for swing bands, Spanish Castle changed briefly into a roller rink, then evolved into a country-and-western beer joint, before it was ruined enough to finish its days as a rock-and-roll dance hall. Once rock-and-roll dances moved in, a cyclone fence was built from the northeast corner out to the highway embankment to cut off any hot-rod traffic and prevent drive-by bottle throwing or any other hoodlum routines.

Over the front entrance, the marquee sported a neon sign with *Spanish Castle* written in loopy flowing green letters underlined by two yellow bars. Sections of the neon tubes were burnt. A skeleton frame for a canvas canopy stood over the sidewalk leading into the foyer. A few frayed pieces of black and white canvas hung down from the top of the frame's spine. In front a dirty strip of canvas remained, with the words *New Man gemen* in red, the letters *a* and *t* hidden under triangular strips of ripped canvas.

Spanish Castle's last paint job had been pink, but this had weathered so much that the white of a previous painting showed through on its cracked and peeling walls. At one time the two front windows had art deco eyebrows of red tile over them, but only a few tiles remained. The windows were barred with heavy grilles, backed up by thick wire mesh.

Along the south side, most of the windows were painted over. On the north side, those that weren't painted had graying sheets of plywood nailed over them. For use as a second fire exit, a door had been cut in the north side and a short entranceway built out into the parking lot. Sets of doors at either end of this provided double checkpoints for quick frisks on incoming patrons and for crowd control during exits for intermissions.

The north parking lot was where the gangs usually parked, staking out their turf and drinking on the sly. Behind it, hundreds of empty brown and green bottles were suspended in the thick sea of blackberry vines. Scattered around the top layer of vines were new red and white Rainier, gold and white Olympia, and black and red Carling Black Label beer cartons. Farther into the vines, the cardboard slipped into various states of decay, down to those lost at the bottom of the jungle, bleached white clots of paper pulp bleeding mushy colors. Gray spars of dead alders angled out of the brambles, slowly sagging from the weight of the vines growing over their limbs and dragging them into the marsh. The ditch lining the edge of the parking lot was filled with worn tires and more empties. Floating on its scummy water were rainbows of oil slick and mossy green rotting cardboard. On the northeast corner of the parking lot, a ditch fed into the culvert along Highway 99. The embankment's hard clay was studded with gravel and shards of broken glass that glittered under the streetlights.

Below Spanish Castle's fake parapet hung a cheap electric billboard. On it letters of various colors and sizes spelled two words, *Checkers* and *Wailers*. Four holes had been knocked out of the white plastic backing, and ragged beams of the fluorescent lighting shot out at odd angles into the misty spring night.

DEAN HAGENBARTH eased the stickpin through his left collar, under his tie, and through his right collar. Holding the collar down with his finger, so the stickpin remained in place, he threaded on the little gold square. Then he looked at himself in the mirror. The Windsor knot on his shiny emerald green tie was humping up just right over the gold pin, a big tight bulge.

Dean stepped back from the mirror, tilted his head one way and then another, checking out the look. He sure enough looked tough. Watching his profile in the mirror, he pulled open his closet door. Then he took his eyes off himself, eased his rust brown blazer off a clothes hanger, and put it on. His blazer was made of a spongy material that Dean really liked. With no lapels it looked so cool because the Windsor knot appeared to poke out even farther. Looking down, he inserted his fingers into the two watch-fob style pockets and held them open, admiring their satin white lining.

In his emerald green tie and gold stick pin and white shirt and rust blazer, Dean had to admit that he looked real sharp. Not just sharp, but *real* sharp.

He laughed, thinking about how sharp he looked.

Taking out his wallet, he checked the four crisp fives, before he stuck the tip of his finger in the side pocket, feeling the smooth plastic package of the Trojan rubber. Dean looked in the mirror again. That angle on himself looking up, like he was in a mood, thinking about something—he liked that. Putting his wallet away, he felt a sudden rush of sharp saliva in his mouth and excitement coming over his scalp in a long hair-prickling wave. He was ready to roll.

Rock and roll.

A hot date *and* Spanish Castle.

But the best thing was *nobody knew.*

FRANCI TEPPING STOOD in the hallway between her bedroom and her mother's bedroom, looking at herself in the hall mirror. Franci had on a black angora sweater. With both hands Franci held her short black skirt at the sides and pulled it first one way and then another. She kicked out one leg and looked at her new sheer black stockings. White quarter notes ran down the side to a single treble clef above her ankle.

"Because, that's why," she said to her mother's bedroom door.

"Franci, you can tell me. Is it a big date?" her mother called out from the bedroom. "You haven't been out on one in two months."

"And you'll find some way to say that to him, won't you?"

"No I won't."

"Mother, it's just a date."

"Then you can tell *me*, your own mother, who it is, can't you?"

"No."

"Why not, honey?"

"Because then you'll act weird when he comes."

"No I won't." A sniff. "Really I won't."

Franci adjusted the V-neck of her sweater, hiking up her bra a little. She turned sideways and checked her profile.

"I won't. Really I won't."

"*Mother! Please!*"

Franci turned her head to the side, putting her hands under her hair and fluffing it out.

"Frances honey, I really won't. Who is he?"

THE GARAGE STOOD about thirty yards off Kitts Corner Road. Built of unpainted wood on a foundation of busted concrete, the garage slumped at the end of a rutted gravel road, its sagging doors propped open. The nose of a gleaming dark green 1950 Mercury faced out. Leaning against the smooth bulbous hood were two boys dressed identically in tight gray pegged pants, white shirts without ties, and shiny black sport coats. On the left side lounged Bouger Bowder, short and chunky with a greased red-haired flattop cut. On the right side Ron Loustalot stared down at his reflection, checking the look of his dark hair, its swept-back sides topped by a Gene Vincent sloppy roll. Both Ron and Bouger were smoking Pall Malls and watching the traffic on Kitts Corner Road.

In back of the garage stood a chalky green clapboard house. The front porch slanted to the left, the foundation settling into the marshy ground. One of the pillars had torn free from the porch roof, and its exposed twisted nails were sticking up, spiky and rusted. The screen door was grimy, and the screen was torn on the bottom. One window showed a light behind its white curtain.

Ron turned and smiled and held open the right side of his sport coat so Bouger could see. In the inside pocket the top of a long black switchblade knife poked up, shiny polished metal against the coat's red lining. Bouger opened his coat and flashed his inside pocket at Ron: a slim flat piece of steel stuck up from his. Then Bouger reached under his arm. In his hand appeared homemade brass knuckles.

"IT'S ALMOST ten to eight, he's going to be here in twenty minutes."

"I can't find it, Franci," her mother said. She was still down on her hands and knees in the closet doorway, pawing through the purses and shoes on the floor.

"It's *got* to be there, mother, I saw you *sling* it in there," Franci said. She looked at her wristwatch. It was five past eight. "You lost it, didn't you? That's why I don't bring guys over here. They'd see things like this, your big butt sticking out of the closet as you try to find one more thing you lost."

Franci's mother sat back on her heels, a hurt look on her face. "When you brought Pencil by, you never said things like that to me," she said. "Whatever happened to Pencil?"

Franci leaned out of the bedroom doorway and looked through the front window blinds, checking for headlights in the street. "Mom, I told you. Pencil's working in Walla Walla." Franci let out a long exasperated sigh. "I *told* you that, remember?"

"You can bring your dates over here. I never said I didn't want you to."

"It's what you say, mother, and it's what you *do*."

"I don't do anything anyone else—"

"Oh for god's sake we've *had* this conversation a *hundred* times, and I told you I have stopped bringing anyone by, mother. It's easier that way for both of us. Can't you understand that?"

"I don't do *any*thing *any*one—"

"You already said that. Now let's not argue. Could you *please* find my purse."

"I don't think I had your purse." Her mother lifted up a box of tangled underwear from the closet floor and looked under it. "I'd forgotten about this. Here's some jewelry. I wonder how it got here." She pawed through the box. "You shouldn't be ashamed of your mother. I bought you the clothes you wanted, didn't I?"

Her mother still was wearing her morning housedress and her old pink slippers with the rabbit faces on the front. On her left slipper, a rabbit's bead eye was dangling by a thread. "Sure, that's because you're always borrowing *my* things, trying to look like my *older* sister."

"Pencil said I looked like your older sister."

Franci peeked out the door again, checking the front of the house. "Pencil's *gone*, mother, for good."

Going through the underwear, her mother strung bra after bra on her arm, until she noticed how many she had collected. Holding her arm out straight, she viewed the lineup of bras. "Is he a nice young man?"

"Who, *Pencil?*" Franci laughed. "God," she said. "Yes, mother. My date tonight's been elected the senior class president. He's a big step up." Under her breath: "For a change."

DEAN'S MOTHER DROPPED him off at his older brother Jake's apartment by the College of Puget Sound. Jake was having a poker game and beer bust with his football buddies, so he loaned Dean his customized blue and white 1957 Olds for the night. After warning him not to be hot-rodding around with his car, Jake gave the keys to Dean, and Dean left the apartment. In the Olds on the ride over to Midland, Dean got so happy that he felt like dancing while he drove. He cranked up the radio — "Runaway" by Del Shannon — and he let out a few howls, to show himself that he was ready.

I'm sneaking, he kept thinking, *but I bet I get away with it. Wow!*

Dean was pleased that he had thought of Spanish Castle. No one from the high school would see them together there. He was sure that word would never get back to Joyce Habersom, his steady date.

Dean had only been there once, with his older brother a year ago. Spanish Castle was always a little rough, but Dean felt safe with Jake and his teammates. No one was going to mess with those guys. Some of them were animals. Of course, Dean was older now, and he'd heard Spanish Castle had quieted down. A few months ago the cops busted some hoods. Most of the gangs had been banished and the fights stopped, but still no one from Dean's crowd ever went there.

That weekend the Checkers and the Wailers were playing, so there was sure to be good wipe-out rock-and-roll. Even though he'd never seen her dance, Dean had a feeling that Franci never faked anything and he was going to have himself a time. He had been playing it straight for too long.

FRANCI HEARD the Olds before she saw the headlights. She partially opened the bedroom door and leaned her head in. "Mother, will you get back in the closet and find my purse, please?"

Her mother nodded. Distracted by all the bras on her left arm, she pushed the box to one side and started to crawl forward. When her mother was halfway in the closet, Franci closed the bedroom door. The last thing she saw was her mother's butt up in the air, her left arm trailing a clot of brassieres across the floor.

Franci heard the car door slam, and she hurried down the hallway. In the living room Franci lifted up the couch cushion, took out her black clasp purse, and found her house key. Franci pulled the cord on the lamp beside the couch, plunging that end of the room into darkness. Only the porch light and the kitchen light were left on.

"Honey, are you sure your purse is in here?"

Franci waited for the knock on the front door. As a soft *rap-rap-rap* sounded, she closed the hallway door, cutting off the end of her mother's whine. Perfect.

Franci hustled across the living room, opened the door, and smiled. She waved her house key at him. "Let me turn off the kitchen light, and we can go."

THE BRIGHT BLUE 1950 Studebaker rumbled off Kitts Corner Road and turned into the driveway in front of Ron and Bouger. A primer-gray 1947 Chevy pulled off behind the Studebaker but stayed parallel to the road. No one got out of either car for a long time.

A tall guy wearing the same outfit as Bouger and Ron got out of the blue Studebaker. He pulled on his cuffs, and a black piece of rebar fell into his right hand. He smiled at Ron and Bouger.

They both smiled back.

Out on Kitts Corner Road, the Chevy honked once. Three guys inside pounded on the windows of the car three times, chanting "Rebar, rebar, rebar." The guy with the rebar carefully slid it back up his sleeve.

A purple 1951 Ford with four guys inside pulled up and parked behind the Chevy. A single chrome strip from a 1955 Chevy had been added to its side.

Ron and Bouger looked at each other over the gleaming green hood of the Mercury. They nodded once, then stepped back into the garage and got in the car. The Studebaker backed out of the driveway, and the Mercury rumbled forward and took its place at

the head of the cars. Slowly all four drove down Kitts Corner Road
toward the old Highway 99.

DEAN CAUGHT a glimpse of the corner of a worn couch. Then
Franci walked out, shutting and locking the door behind her.
Franci was looking so boss, with that black skirt and sweater and
those tough black stockings. Dean opened the car door for her and
watched her sit down and swing her legs in. Then he got in on the
other side.

"I'm so mad," she said.

"What's wrong?"

"Oh, my mother is giving me a hard time." Franci smiled up at
Dean. "I sure am glad to be going out. I couldn't stand another
night at home."

"Hey, we're going to Spanish Castle," Dean said. "Rock-and-roll'll
help that." Dean laughed, but Franci didn't join in. He looked over
at Franci. "What's wrong? Don't you want to go there?"

"Uh, no. That's fine."

"You seem a little shocked," Dean said. "You don't want to go
there?"

"Well, I didn't know you went there."

"Oh yeah, been there a couple times. I heard the cops cleaned
up the kids' act since then, though. It's pretty tame now, but when
I was there, it was rumble city," Dean said casually, looking down.
"Hey, what are those called? Those musical notes. They got a
name?"

"Well, they're called clocks."

"Clocks?"

Franci laughed at the expression on Dean's face. "I'm not putting you on." She turned her leg sideways so he could see better.
"These are quarter notes, and that's a treble," Franci said, pointing
down at her ankle.

"I like the quarter notes better." Dean reached over, lightly
touching one at the side of her knee with his fingertip.

"Well, no matter what they are, things like that on stockings are
called clocks."

"Clocks, flocks—I like em," Dean said. Franci smiled shyly, looking away. "They look really cool. Hey, you feeling good tonight? I'm
feeling good." Dean liked it that Franci didn't say anything about

the Olds. She accepted how tough the car was. That was cool. As she slid across the seat a little closer to him, he caught a glimpse of her skirt climbing up her thigh, showing more of those sheer black stockings.

Dean turned the key over, letting the ignition catch. He hit the gas hard, the burst of power rocking the car from side to side. He backed off the gas fast, the Smitty mufflers barking out exhaust. Reaching down over Franci's knee, he put the floor shift hydromatic in drive and let the Olds rumble out onto the street.

As he turned onto Portland Avenue, he looked to the right and caught a glimpse of Franci caressing the rolled and pleated seats. *Oh, yeah*, he thought, turning his face away so he could smile, *oh, yeah, going to Spanish Castle.*

THE WIGWAM DRIVE-IN at Milton was a single-story building made of concrete blocks with a stucco wigwam erected on the top. The Wigwam's sides were a muddy brown with a few arrows and wavy stripes painted on in red, but they were now faded. A crack from the earthquake in the early 1950s ran up the front of the wigwam and disappeared around the left side. A repair job had since decayed, and the plaster flaking off left a long white scar around the Wigwam's cone. Since the Interstate 5 had gone through east of Highway 99, the Wigwam Drive-in had seen its last paint job years ago.

The four cars rumbled into the Wigwam Drive-in and circled it once before parking in the back row of the lot, facing Highway 99. For a half hour, the cars remained in the back row.

Then the doors of the Mercury opened, and Ron Loustalot and Bouger got out. They walked across the parking lot to the front of the Wigwam. Opposite the front door of the restaurant, a blue 1955 two-door Chevy was parked, its back to the highway. No one was in it. On the front bumper was a gray steel plaque, with Renton Rats engraved above a drawing of a huge rat in a tiny hot rod, shades on, tongue hanging out, and his right hand on a stick shift rising up behind the windshield.

Bouger sat down on the hood of the Chevy, and behind him Ron knelt by the left front fender. Slowly the Chevy's front end drooped and tilted to one side. Bouger waved his hand at the other cars, imitating a parade queen on a float.

The back fender started to drop too, slowly sighing down as air left the tire. Ron Loustalot jabbed the knife into the fender, leaving a sharp nick in the blue paint as the knife blade was shoved back into its handle.

Ron brushed back his sport coat and put the switchblade in his pants pocket. Bouger smiled back at Ron, and Ron nodded, and they slowly walked across the parking lot, their eyes on the front door of the Wigwam, hoping that someone would come out and try to mess with them, but no one did.

Ron started the Mercury's engine, and all four cars drove slowly past the lopsided Chevy. As each car crossed between the drive-in and the Chevy, they stopped to rev up and let out one snort of exhaust before rumbling on.

DEAN PARKED THE OLDS in the narrow strip in front of Spanish Castle closest to Highway 99. There were only about twenty slots there, but that was where traditionally the toughest cars sat, and Dean was careful to back under a streetlight so the Olds really took on a shine. For a while Dean and Franci stayed in the Olds, checking out the other cars pulling into the southside parking lot. For a second Dean panicked when he realized that none of the cars looked like someone's parents' car, but then he remembered, *What the hell, I'm not driving some station wagon myself.*

Dean kept his hand on the hydromatic floor shift, his wrist resting on top of Franci's knee. "Lot of kids coming tonight."

"If things get a little rowdy and we get split up, let's meet back here, okay?"

"Sure, but things would have to get pretty wild. I heard those new owners keep a tight lid on things." Dean laughed. "Why? You think there'll be some excitement tonight?"

Franci looked over at the cars streaming into the parking lot, feeling the hard part of Dean's palm resting on her knee. "Oh, you never know."

WALKING TOWARD SPANISH CASTLE, Franci thought it was so neat that Dean had taken the trouble to get that tough Olds. Earlier that night at home, she'd imagined herself sitting in some station wagon at a crummy drive-in movie. She smiled, remembering what Dean had said about her new stockings—"Clocks, flocks." That made her laugh—him talking a little rowdy, getting loose. Maybe this was going to be okay.

While Dean paid at the box office, Franci eyed the bouncer taking tickets at the big double doors. He was one huge dude with a black beard and a logger's shirt. He looked *very* rough. He had to be hired by the new owners. Then she saw the poster for the dance.

GRUDGE MATCH of the Year!

the

CHECKERS

vs.

the WAILERS

Losing band to have heads shaved on stage!

• YOU ARE ONE OF THE JUDGES •
• LONG AWAITED *GRUDGE MATCH* •
EXTRA GUARDS HIRED TO KEEP BANDS APART
• DOOR PRIZES •
*******Excitement*******

"Dean, did you know this was going to be a battle of the bands?" Franci asked when he came back with the tickets.

"Huh?" Then Dean saw the poster. "I heard something about that. Should be wild, huh?"

"Well, the Wailers aren't going to lose," Franci said. "Those guys are going to be crazy."

"Heyyy, I don't mind if they're crazy. That's okay," Dean said. "I'm a dancing fooooool."

Once inside, Franci looked past the side exit at the dining area, and she noticed that the chairs weren't there any more. And the little round tables were now bolted to the floor by their heavy steel stands. The mahogany railing separating the dance floor from the dining area, now had a long iron pipe strapped across the top. A new wire-mesh cage stood to the right side of the bandstand. Inside were white wire chairs and wooden chairs, and there was a big shiny padlock on the cage's steel door. Directly behind the stacks of good chairs were broken chairs, their splintered legs sticking out at strange angles. Beneath them were stacked some of the plaster decorations that used to hang on the walls.

The Checkers were on the bandstand setting up their instruments: two guitars, a bass, electric organ, and drums. The five guys wore identical red blazers with white shirts and black pants. Slanted red and black checkered bow ties conformed perfectly to the sharp cut of their collars. Above them was a steel box bolted to the wall, with a metal screen welded across its front. A rectangular hole cut in the screen revealed the face of an instrument with the words APPLAUSE METER under it in black. To the left of the bandstand, new thick black mesh covered the windows. The booths, there when Spanish Castle used to be a beer bar, had been ripped out.

"Boy, they really gutted this place, didn't they?" Franci said.

"Oh yeah, I guess during the rumbles—about a month ago, before the new owners bought it—guys knew that the place was sold, so they were tearing stuff off the walls and hitting people. Look." On the balcony, only the outlines of the plaster decorations were left.

"This used to look kinda like a night club," Franci said. "Those booths were neat. I mean, whatta you supposed to do now, *stand* around and drink a coke? Geez."

Dean nodded at the side exit. "The new owners got bouncers. The poster said they'd have extra guards."

At the side exit doors leading out to the northside parking lot, Franci saw two bouncers checking names on a clipboard. Franci guessed that they were letting in guys with passes, probably from the bands.

"Oh wow, that's not going to do any good," Franci said.

"What isn't?" Dean glanced at the side exit.

"Well, these bands, hey, they run with the gangs and car clubs, too. For a grudge match, I bet the bands handed out passes right and left," Franci said. "Those new owners are dumb. They shouldn't let anybody come in from the parking lot. Geez, that just gives them their own private entrance."

THE GREEN 1950 Mercury drove in first, followed by the 1947 Chevy, the 1950 Studebaker, and the 1951 Ford. They circled around Spanish Castle and backed into the corner of the last row. Across the parking lot were cars with the steel plaques of the Renton Rats on their bumpers.

Inside Spanish Castle the organ started playing. Under the big light covered with wire screen at the side entrance, the people pressed toward the music. The light shining through the wire covered the crowd in a pattern of bright squares. The music began to get louder, "Green Onions," the organ vamping harder and harder. Then the drum began to hit the beat, and after two bars the bass joined in. Then the guitars chorded behind the rhythm section. Guys at the door began complaining, asking why the right-hand door wasn't opened too. But the bouncers kept the door closed as the first guitar solo chugged out over the organ and rhythm guitar and bass.

In the last row, the Mercury turned off its headlights, and the three other cars' lights blinked out too. But no one got out.

The night air began to get heavier, more misty. The fogs from the swamp had already drifted out of the blackberries over the parked cars, and the beams from the side-entrance light slowly turned a wet yellow. Over the doors the light fixture began to tremble, making the shadows of the wire screen quiver like a huge net over the people in line, as the rock-and-roll grew furious and began to shake the place.

WHEN THE CHECKERS went straight from "Hully Gully" into "Let's Go, Let's Go, Let's Go," a circle of dancers formed around

Dean and Franci. Dean was having a ball, going crazy with Franci, who was a great dancer.

When the song powered to its end, Dean looked up at the singer-rhythm guitarist and he saw how the whole crowd was going nuts. Dean gave him a rolling motion with his hand, yelling to let it roll. The singer turned around and signaled the drummer at the end of "Let's Go, Let's Go, Let's Go" to keep going with the beat, but he put his hand palm down for the drummer to slow down. The rest of the band cut out, letting the drummer's back beat ride, and then the singer whirled around and stepped out front. He pointed down at Dean and Franci, put out his hands like he was holding someone's hips, gave those imaginary hips a shimmy shake, and yelled out, "I couldn't sleep at ALL last night!"

And everybody let out a roar, and the band jumped in on the opening chord of "Tossin' and Turnin'," and the whole place felt as if it was about to shake to pieces.

When the song ended, the Checkers' set was over, and Dean took Franci by the arm and steered her off the floor. The people had gathered around while Franci and Dean had danced, and now they congratulated them. Dean was sweating like crazy and yelling back at them, and it seemed like the whole joint was cranked up and going nuts.

Dean noticed a bunch of guys in red and white car-club jackets over by the refreshment stand, and he realized that some gangs had come in while everyone was dancing. But Dean needed a Coke bad, and he started back toward the old dining area. People were crowding into the hallway to the side exit, trying to get out for intermission, and Dean tried to guide Franci through them. Halfway there, Franci's arm stiffened in the crook of his arm, and she gave him a tug, and that's when Dean saw another gang in dark sport coats standing off by the side door. Franci didn't say anything but started to pull Dean back into the crowd.

Dean balked. Franci was staring off at the other end of the floor and keeping pressure on his arm. "Franci!" Dean said, and she mumbled something about going back by the bandstand. Dean gave her arm a little jerk, about to say that he *really* needed a Coke, when he felt a hand on his chest.

FRANCI WAS TOO SHORT, so she didn't see Loustalot and Bouger Bowder until the crowd parted and she saw the gang moving toward them. Ron spotted her and he grinned. She tried to veer toward the other end of the dance floor, using the people ahead as a shield. But the people were splitting off, heading for the refreshment bar or the side exit, and Ron knifed through and pulled up in front of Dean. Putting out his hand, Ron stopped him.

"Heyyyyyy, High School," Ron said to Dean.

Immediately the rest of Ron's gang moved into positions around them, with Bouger at Ron's left, shading Dean so he could slip in a sucker punch if he had the chance.

Franci felt Dean's body stiffen as he rocked to a stop against Ron's hand. He glanced down at Franci, but she looked away, over Bouger's left shoulder at the side exit, hoping a bouncer would come out, but the bouncers were stamping people's hands for the intermission.

"Hey, what is this?" Ron turned to Franci, ignoring Dean. "What are you trying to do, *dancing* to those shitkickers? Getting everyone riled about the Checkers. The Wailers are gonna kick ass tonight."

Bouger laughed at Ron's comment, and Ron put one finger up and reached over to tap Bouger on the chest. "Bouger here knows. The Checkers are gonna have their heads shaved up there, not *our* band, not the Wailers, 'cause this is our turf and the new owners are gonna find that out tonight." Ron paused. "This pisses me off. Frenchy T. here should know the Checkers are not for *dancing*. Especially not with High School here."

Ron paused to look up at Dean, and Bouger snickered. Ron nodded, pretending that something was just dawning on him. He tapped his forehead as if realizing it. "Oh heyyyyyy, High School doesn't know who we're talking about here, does he, Bouger?"

"Naaaaw." Bouger rolled his eyes and snickered. "Naw, he don't know."

"Well, then I'd like to introduce you to your date." Ron kept his eyes on Dean for a second, then let his gaze roll down to Dean's hands, waiting for Dean to swing at him. He pointed at Franci. "High School, this is Frenchy T. Did you know this was . . . Frenchy T.?"

Dean cleared his throat. "Nu-no."

"Well. Hey, what'd you think she was called?"

Dean gulped once, and cleared his throat. "Franci Tepping."

"Naw," Ron looked to the side, and Bouger laughed on cue. "Naw, naw, naw. You're wrong. That's not her name. Frenchy T.'s her name. Know why we called her that?"

Franci moved up a little in front of Dean and glared at Ron.

Ron paused and tilted his head to the side, regarding her for a second. "'Cause she can French you to a T."

Ron and Bouger shifted a little, Bouger cocking back his arm, as Dean leaned to his right. Franci glanced down and saw the flat steel sliding out from Bouger's coat sleeve. *Please, not here.* She pulled Dean's right arm behind her, trapping it.

Ron and Bouger watched Dean closely. "Ah, yeah," Ron said finally, as if he had just confirmed something disgusting about Dean. "High School, you play basketball?"

"Yeah." Dean tried to shake Franci's arm loose and step out ahead of her again, but Franci held on hard.

"I don't like basketball players."

There wasn't a sound from all the guys around them, and Franci kept her eye on Bouger's right hand hanging by his side, palm in, hiding the flat steel rod.

Ron nodded, still watching Dean closely. "So I'm going to take your date here outside for the intermission. Got to talk to her. You don't mind, do you?"

Dean did not move, and Franci glanced up at him. He slowly swallowed once.

Ron acted as if he didn't have to wait for an answer. "Bouger here will stick by you until we get back, so nothing will happen to *you* while we take Frenchy outside."

Ron looked down at Franci's arm hooked in Dean's. "So let's go, I mean, unless you want us to take High School here outside with us."

Franci let go of Dean's arm and stepped in front of him, turning her back to Ron and Bouger. "Five minutes, be at the car," she said under her breath, as she walked away. Stepping between Ron and Bouger, she faced Bouger so he had to back up a few steps, moving away from Dean. Franci turned her head slightly to the side and shrugged at Ron impatiently.

"Oh, geez. Didn't know you were in a hurry for this. Ladies first," Ron said, turning away from Dean and gesturing with his arm. Then he laughed out loud. "Chickenshit," he said to Dean.

THROUGH THE SIDE door Dean watched Franci walking across the parking lot. Dean noticed that each corner of the hall had been taken by a different gang. Fanned out in front of the refreshment stand was the biggest gang, all wearing red and white jackets with *Renton Rats* on their backs. And Dean saw that gang hard-asses had begun to hassle people.

The bouncers were busy stamping people's hands for readmission after the break. During intermission at Spanish Castle before, the bouncers constantly roved, breaking up fights before they got started. Now Dean could imagine how the brawls would start — first, incidents in all four corners, and then, if the fights weren't stopped, they'd spread as the gangs spilled across the dance floor.

Out the side doors Dean watched the shadow shapes of the gang members in a half circle around the hood of a 1950 Mercury. Dean thought he saw Franci break away from the gang, walking across the parking lot, but then a bouncer closed one of the double doors. Dean headed straight for the Renton Rats.

"Hey! High School! Where you think you're going?" Bouger said, trying to cut him off.

"Get something to drink." Dean used a passing couple as a shield and got a step ahead of Bouger. Walking fast, Dean aimed for the right edge of the Renton Rats.

RON LOUSTALOT and his friends surrounded Franci as they walked across the parking lot. One of the guys nudged Ron and nodded toward the Renton Rats. Two guys were doing guard duty in front of the cars.

"I bet they found out about the Chevy at the Wigwam by now." Ron laughed, and the rest of the guys joined in. "Spiked a Rat Chevy tonight," Ron said to Franci.

"Big deal."

When they got to Ron's 1950 Mercury, Ron opened the door on the driver's side and sat down behind the steering wheel. "Get in," he said, nodding toward the other side.

Franci stayed beside the Mercury, looking down at Ron. Then she turned and regarded each of the other guys. Behind her, three of the gang remained close. A little shiver started down her right leg. Franci pressed her foot hard into the asphalt, trying to stop the shaking.

Ron was primping in the rear-view mirror, checking his hair. Then he tilted his head to one side, put his right hand up on the steering wheel, and stared at the parking lot as if he were thinking hard. "So, you heard from Pencil in the state pen?"

She nodded.

"He don't write us," Ron said. He let his head fall to one side and looked up at the night sky. "I wonder why?" The guys around Franci laughed at the joke. "Maybe because we're out and he's in," Ron said, playing to his audience. They sniggered.

Franci took a deep breath, and she shrugged, acting bored with Ron's routine.

Ron waited until she was looking at him, and he gestured at the passenger side. "You don't wanna get in? Hey guys, she doesn't wanna get in a Kitts Corner mob car. Well, you were the queen when Pencil was around. But even with Pencil in the joint, the Kitts Corner mob sticks together. Right, Frenchy?"

Franci could feel her hands getting sweaty. She knew that she had to stay out of the car.

"Am I right, guys?"

Around Franci the guys agreed that Ron was right, but a couple of guys shifted around a little, nervous at Franci's silence.

"So, you been the Queen, and so you don't leave the Kitts Corner mob. Pencil may do time, but Pencil, you, all these guys — they don't leave. No one leaves. Once you're in, you're in."

Franci smiled. "Since when have you been a *mob*?"

"You didn't read the papers? When Pencil got popped, we were a mob. Judge said 'cause we're a mob, a lot of us guys pulled probation." Ron appealed to the gang. "Right, guys?"

Two of the guys behind her eased closer, trying to edge her toward the Mercury. She glanced once behind her. "Keep talking, Ron," she said. "One of these days, why, it may come true."

Ron flushed. His right hand began to clench and unclench around the steering wheel. He opened his mouth and rolled his tongue around his lips. "Hey, why doncha tell us how you first got your nickname?"

"Sure." Giving Ron a big smile, Franci broke her pose and sauntered over to the Merc. Ron, startled by her sudden change of attitude, almost shrank away from her. She stopped short of the car door and looked over at the two guys on the hood of the car. "Just for you, though." They backed off a little. "And I'll tell you something else, too," Franci said, putting both hands on the Merc's door and slowly shutting it on Ron. The two guys behind her stepped away as Franci leaned against the car, so they couldn't overhear.

"You wanna hear it, Ron?"

Ron smiled. "Yeah. I wanna hear it." He leaned his head toward Franci. "Put it in my ear."

Franci bent over the door, and then, cupping her hands to her mouth, she whispered into Ron's ear. "Pencil's brother is out of Folsom. If I have any trouble, Pencil said he'd handle it for me."

Franci paused and then whispered the next words real slow. "I think I'll call you trouble, Ron."

Ron jerked his head away. "Oooooooweee!" he howled, making a big show of rubbing his ear. Around the car the guys burst out laughing. Then Ron wet one finger and stuck it in his left ear, quivering as he turned the finger around and around, darting his tongue in and out of his mouth, miming what had been done to him.

Franci stepped back from the Mercury, staring at Ron. Then she looked around at the guys laughing, and she laughed at them.

"Gwan! Get outta here!" Ron yelled, waving Franci off. "Frenchy Teeeeeee!" he yowled. "Oooooooooowee!"

Brushing past the two guys by the hood, Franci sauntered off, trying hard not to show fear, but her legs felt so rubbery that she was afraid they would crumple under her if she turned for the side door. All she could do was keep walking straight across the parking lot. Halfway across, the shakes started, and she slowed down. In the opposite corner two Renton Rats guys shifted their pose when they saw that she was heading straight for them. Taking a deep breath, she forced herself to turn, her knees so weak she almost fell, but she kept walking, light-headed and giddy. She prayed that Dean would be in the car. That jerk Loustalot was mad, and if poor Dean was in the dance hall, Ron would stomp him.

ONCE FRANCI was gone, Ron opened the door and got out of the Merc. Ron sniffed loudly and took out his comb, bent at the knees so he could see his hair in the side mirror, and swept up once on each side, letting the hair curl in the middle and down over his forehead.

"What about High School in there? Should we tell Bouger to let him go?"

Ron put away his comb, then checked his cuffs. He stretched his neck, adjusting his tight shirt collar. "Naw," he said. One of the gang started to titter. Then a couple of other guys laughed, getting what Ron had said. Ron looked surprised. "So, what do I care about High School? We gotta go in there and get Spanish Castle back. That's what we're here for tonight. Let these new owners know that this is our joint. Fuck High School. Tell Bouger to waste him."

Then they heard an uproar from inside Spanish Castle. Ron yelled, "That's it. Let's roll!"

COMING ACROSS the dance floor, Dean could feel Bouger right behind him, crowding close. Dean glanced back and saw that Bouger was watching the Renton Rats more than he was watching him. And the Renton Rats were eyeing them, too.

As Dean approached the Rats, he slowed and turned, slipping his left arm behind his back, allowing two couples to crowd in ahead of him.

"Well, if it isn't Bouger Bowder," one of the Rats said. "I hear he likes slit tires."

"That your date tonight, Bouger?" one of the other Rats said, nodding at Dean.

"Real cute," another one said.

Turning to answer, Bouger bumped into Dean, and his hand touched Dean's left arm, trying to stop him from walking on. Dean dipped, exactly as he'd been taught in rebounding practice, and got Bouger up on his hip. At the same time Dean jabbed his left elbow just under Bouger's ribs and swung his right arm around, hand out, and shoved him offbalance into the Rats.

As a roar went up, Dean dove between people's legs. Scrambling to his feet, he glanced back and saw Bouger being shoved and slugged by the Rats. Bouger staggered, and a slim flat piece of steel suddenly appeared in his hand. He took a swing, to clear a space for himself, and someone in the Rats howled as he got clipped. The crowd fell back. Bouger jabbed and whirled around again, swinging wildly.

As Bouger backed up toward the refreshment stand, Dean saw a Rat step out of the crowd behind him, his red and white arm swinging. A shiny chrome dog chain came flying out of his sleeve. The chain wrapped around and then jerked off of Bouger's forehead, the links leaving a neat row of red cuts spurting blood.

Bouger screamed, blood streaming into his eyes. He clawed at his shredded forehead with his left hand, blindly swinging out with his steel.

Dean shoved through the people stampeding for the front door. Two bouncers were running toward them, waving big black sticks. At the door the crowd surged in to see what was going on. Only one of the double doors was open, but Dean managed to squeeze through. He saw Franci on the edge of the crowd over by the cyclone fence. He tried to cut across, but he got tossed to one side by the crush of people.

Jumping up on the fender of a car, he saw Franci lose her balance and go down. He jumped from bumper to bumper until he was clear of the crowd rushing toward the front doors. At the edge of the crowd, Franci was sitting on the ground, holding her left ankle.

"Franci, c'mon, c'mon!" He helped her up. When she tried to stand, it hurt too much, so Dean held her up, and they hobbled across the parking lot to the Olds.

"Goddamn it, I hope I didn't mess up my stockings." Franci tried a few steps. She put her weight on her right foot and twisted her ankle in the air, inspecting the stocking.

"Screw your stockings!" Dean hissed, unlocking the door. "Get in! A bad rumble. Bouger got cut with a chain." He hurried to the other side of the Olds. "Well, come on!"

Spanish Castle's double doors swung open, and people spilled back out, screaming. The bouncers were driving them back with long black sticks. Bouger was pushed out, and he raised his bloody forehead and spotted Dean just before people were shoved in front of him. The canopy's skeleton frame tottered and went down. The aluminum frame rode on top of the people until the furious mob tore it apart and threw pieces at the bouncers. Enraged, the bouncers charged back, their black sticks rising and falling.

Suddenly Dean saw that Franci was still in front of the Olds, staring at the fighting. Franci shrugged, looked back at Dean and waved to him, before she hobbled back toward the mob.

For a moment it seemed like a nightmare, and Dean stood paralyzed, watching Franci totter toward the riot. Dean rushed out and grabbed her by the shoulders.

"It's okay," Franci said in a calm voice.

"No, it's *not* okay!" Dean yelled at her. "I started that! Let's get the hell out of here!"

Dean picked up Franci and carried her back to the Olds. Setting her down, he opened the door, pushed her in, and ran around to the driver's side. He got in and started the engine, while Franci continued to stare out the open door. Franci leaned forward as if she were going to climb out again, and Dean reached across her and slammed the door shut. Dean jammed the Olds into drive and pulled out between the cars. In the rear-view mirror every blurred face he saw in the thrashing crowd looked like Bouger's.

BY THE TIME Bouger circled back to the Mercury, the Pierce County Sheriffs were making arrests. Bouger saw Ron Loustalot pushed into a Sheriff's squad car. Bouger pulled the bill of his baseball cap down a little lower, shielding his face. Stuffed up inside the front of the cap was a wad of Kleenex, soaking up the blood steadily draining from the cuts in his forehead.

Bouger eased the Mercury out of its parking space and drove behind Spanish Castle, keeping his face turned away from the cops. Bouger touched the shredded knees of his best slacks. Crawling out from under the mob had totaled his pants. He crossed Highway 99, heading for Interstate 5. He was sure he had seen that high school kid's Oldsmobile going in that direction. Bouger vowed to stop at every drive-in clear to South Tacoma and find that high schooler if it took all night. Bouger took out his brass knuckles and put them on his right hand. He might have lost his steel bar, but he hadn't lost his knucks. As he turned onto Interstate 5 and drove south, he kept his hand up on top of the steering wheel, letting the streetlights shine off the polished brass.

THE HIGHWAY PATROL weigh station was closed for the night, so Dean parked on the scale beside the station shack facing the three truck inspection stalls. Turning off the car lights, he leaned back, closed his eyes, and let his head roll back and forth, as he told

Franci how he'd shoved Bouger into the Renton Rats and sparked off the riot.

"If it wasn't for me, you wouldn't have been in the middle of that."

"Oh bull, Franci. Anyone there was in the middle of it. Had nothing to do with you. Besides, you were out there with those jerks. I didn't know if you were coming back."

"I *said* I was coming back." Franci picked at a quarter note on her stocking, trying to ignore the memory of Dean picking her up and carrying her back to the car. The thought that she had wanted to return to the riot scared her. Franci had been so sure that she'd left all that gang crap behind her. *Queen.* "Why'd you think I wouldn't come back?"

"Geez, Franci, you were walking back. What was I going to do, leave you there?"

Franci laughed when she heard Dean say that. *Plenty had.* Putting her hand on his chest, she leaned her head forward and listened. "I can still hear your heart pounding away." Franci laughed and gave Dean a hug. "You're kind of crazy. Here you've got that creep Bouger after you, and you take time to waltz me around the parking lot."

Dean laughed with her. "Yeah," he said, "I'm still all wound up." Dean pushed his feet hard into the floorboards, his body went completely rigid under the steering wheel, and he rolled his head back and forth, yelling. "Ooooooooweee!"

Franci laughed, leaning away as he bounced up and down a few times. "You're really nuts, you know? Calm down," she said, putting her hand on his leg. "Don't go spaz on me."

AFTER TALKING about the riot for a while, Dean had to go to the bathroom, so he walked over to the portable toilets next to the weigh-station shack. Dean was stepping out of the john when he saw a 1950 Mercury slowing to a stop on the highway shoulder. Franci rolled down the window of the Olds. "Dean! That's him! Bouger!"

Dean ran for the Olds as the Mercury weaved in reverse back down the gravel, skidding to a stop. While it roared into the weigh-station entrance Dean jumped into the Olds. Dean floored the gas, but the Mercury caught up with the Olds between the weigh station and the truck stalls. The surge of the Olds broke its back tires loose, and its rear end fishtailed. The Mercury pulled ahead, blocked the exit lane, and slowed.

Dean yanked the hydromatic into reverse and hit the gas, swerving back toward the truck stalls. The Mercury came flying backward. Dean braked again, stopping short of the truck stalls. The Mercury screeched to a halt alongside the Olds.

From a standing start, the Mercury was no match for the Olds. Burning rubber for fifty feet, the Olds roared ahead onto Highway 5, and Dean cursed because there were no cars coming to slow the Mercury down. He stood on the accelerator as the big engine wound out past seventy-five.

At the Fife off-ramp, Bouger wasn't far enough behind to chance an exit, so Dean jacked the Olds up to ninety-five, praying over and over, *Please let me get out of this, please let me get out of this.* Franci's face was pinched white. Her left hand clutched Dean's leg, and her right hand was pressed against the dash. "This Olds will do a hundred and ten easy," Dean yelled, but he didn't want to do that, not at all.

On the curve past the Tacoma exit Dean saw the Mercury's headlights fade away, trapped behind two cars. Dean sent the Olds into the banked turn at ninety. Cutting across two lanes to get in front of a semi-trailer, the rear end broke loose again. Franci howled, and Dean screamed, "No, no, no," fighting the wheel until the Olds straightened. As he swerved over in front of the semi, behind them the Mercury's headlights were pulling out into the passing lane.

Dean decided to ditch him on the Fifty-Sixth Street exit. He turned off his lights and aimed the Olds for the off-ramp, hoping that the Mercury would lose sight of them. The Olds screamed around the exit turn, and Dean saw the stop sign. *No time to stop.* Dean panicked, hit the brakes hard, and the Olds whipped from side to side while Dean wailed, "Ohhhhhhhhhhhhh shiiiit!" Franci's fingers clawed into his leg.

The Olds drifted in a slow dreamy slide into the side street. As Dean spun the wheel, the car's back tire hit the curb. The Olds snapped around, barely missing a telephone pole, then stalled and died. "Hope that fucker piles up on that curve!" Dean screamed. He pumped on the gas and started the Olds again.

There was no traffic on the Fifty-Sixth Street overpass, so Dean ran the stop sign and turned right, switching his lights back on. As he turned right on Wapato Street, Dean glanced back and saw the Mercury coming after them. "Goddamnit!"

Remembering the dogleg around a nearby park, he turned left, but the Olds went into a slide leaving a black trail of rubber. Dean cursed. *Might as well leave a goddamn trail for that Bouger to follow.*

Whipping through the dogleg around the park, Dean headed down the straight road alongside the old Tacoma Cemetery. There were no roads coming out of the cemetery. Dean punched the Olds up to forty, driving in the left-hand lane so he'd miss any cars pulling out on his right. As the Olds passed over a slight rise, Dean checked his rearview mirror and saw the headlights of the Mercury making the turn three blocks back. He swung the Olds right on South Tacoma Way. "I've shook him! I've shook the bastard!" Dean yelled.

He hung a quick left through the sparse oncoming traffic, drove one block more, then slowed. The Smitty mufflers that he had always admired for their loud rumble now seemed stupid. Dean was sure that he had lost the Mercury. Bouger would have seen him turn right, and he'd follow, probably thinking he was heading north for Busch's Drive-in.

Turning left on Washington, Dean drove south, parallel to South Tacoma Way, cautiously checking all the side streets until he came to a feed-mill parking lot half a block ahead of Fifty-Sixth Street. There he pulled in behind two bulk feed trucks, leaving himself an escape and also a view up Fifty-Sixth and down Washington.

Then Dean noticed Franci's hand kneading his right leg. He hugged her, and they shivered together, wave after wave of fear sending them limp in each other's arms.

BOUGER CRUISED BUSCH'S first, and then he drove over to Puyallup Avenue to Cass's Triple X and the Dairy Queen and the Doors Drive-in, before he started up Pacific Avenue, stopping at each drive-in along the way where high school kids hung out. White Rose, Dart's Y-Not, King's, the A&W, the Pacific Avenue Dairy Queen, Parkland Triple X, the Wagon Wheel, the In & Out, the College Drive-in—all the way to the Hand Out, and then he gassed up the Mercury at Denny's Do-All, turned around and started back.

The bloody cuts on his forehead had dried and the Kleenex tissue jammed under his cap was stuck to his skin. When Bouger found the Olds, first he was going to beat that kid into a bloody pulp with his brass knucks, then maybe take a tire iron to the windows if he had the time.

WHEN FRANCI CAME out of the john of the Standard gas station on Seventy-Fourth Street, Dean was circling the Olds. Dean went slowly around the car four times, bending down to check the fenders and hubcaps for dents. Franci watched him feel along the back bumper for any scrapes. As he peered along the fender, she came up to his side and took his left arm. Still staring at the Olds, Franci felt him relax, leaning into her for a second.

"If anything happens to his car," Dean snuffled. "God, I hope nothing's wrong with it. My brother Jake would murder me if I munged up his Olds."

Franci put her right arm around his waist, almost holding him up, as he fought back his tears. Dean sighed, and under her hand his back muscles trembled. Leaning her thigh into his, she pressed her palm against the fluttering until it stopped.

When they were across the freeway overpass, heading east on Seventy-Second, Franci asked where they were going. "You can't take me home to my house. He probably knows where I live," Franci said, catching Dean's eye. "Two months ago I used to go out with a friend of his, so he might know." Then she looked away. "I never went out with *him*, that's for sure. But he knows. And we better not go to a drive-in, either," Franci said. "He's probably cruising every one in town." She giggled. "I bet he's *pissed*." .

"Well, where do you want to go? It's too late for a movie."

"Someplace, any place," Franci said. "I don't want to go home."

AT KING'S DRIVE-IN, the first word was filtering in about the riot. Some car-club guys from Wapato were talking about it. Over the radio the newscasters were calling it "the rumble at Spanish Castle." Bouger liked the sound of that. He didn't stick around too long at King's Drive-in but kept moving up and down Pacific Avenue.

Bouger had a hunch that the tall kid was going to make one big mistake that night, and all Bouger wanted was to be right there when he made it.

INSIDE THE OLDS the windows were fogged up. Outside, the dim outlines of high-tension towers loomed above the moonlit tree line, and through the misty night air came the low hum of the power lines above the car.

Franci stretched out across Dean. As she eased back from their kiss, his hand pulled on the steering wheel, trying to scoot back into a sitting position. Dean slid out from under her, and Franci felt her loose skirt slide down around her knees, her skin prickling up with goose pimples as the cold white Naugahyde touched her bare thigh. She lunged back across Dean, pressing him down and feeling him hard under her belly, and she pulled his head down for a kiss. "I don't want to get pregnant," she whispered.

"No, no, it's okay," Dean gasped, struggling to sit up again. "I got..."

As he heaved himself up, trying to get at his wallet, Franci raised off him and with her right hand pushed him back against the door. His hair swiped a clear patch on the wet window. The ribs of the floor mat wobbled under her knees as she let her weight down. With her left hand she pressed the front of his pants, and the zipper, already partly opened, split completely. Jerking her sweater above her right breast, her bra in a tangle around her waist, she touched his left hand, guiding it down to her chest. She arched up over him, her hard nipple pushing into the base of his palm. And as her breast filled his hand, she filled herself with him.

IN FIFE at the Pick Quick Drive-In, Bouger listened to news reports about Spanish Castle. Eight Kitts Corner guys were in jail, which pretty much wiped the gang out. There was no point trying bail: most were still on probation from Pencil's bust.

Bouger was hungry, but he didn't want to go in the Pick Quick. He'd have to take off his cap and start bleeding again. So he started up the Mercury and drove back toward Tacoma, thinking he'd hit the A&W on Pacific Avenue one more time. They had carhops, and he wouldn't have to get out to order food. His forehead was aching from the cuts, and on his back he could feel a sore spot where someone had kneed him when he got trampled outside, and all of this made him feel meaner and meaner until he was ready to smack someone around, anyone, just to do a little smacking.

OUTSIDE HIS BROTHER'S apartment, Dean knelt on the pavement beside the open car door, feeling around on the floor. The overhead light was on, but he couldn't see under the seat. Fishing around with his left hand, he finally found the torn foil wrapper. He stood up and added it to the wadded Kleenex in his right hand that held the used rubber. He dropped the Kleenex and the foil wrapper in a garbage can under the apartment stairs.

When he opened the apartment door, the front room was dark, except for the lighted kitchen doorway and what Dean thought were some floor lamps beside it. As his eyes adjusted to the darkness, he saw that the round lights weren't lamps, but two holes in the wall. A third hole held only a dim halo because the huge right hand of Goslovich was jammed in it up to the wrist. Goslovich himself was passed out, slumped on the couch, his square head resting on his extended right arm, using it as a pillow, while his fist was stuck in the wall. Goslovich, a mammoth sophomore tackle on Jake's college team, was notorious for unpredictable and sometimes loony behavior. Among his teammates there was a betting pool on how long he'd last at the college. Tiptoeing past the snoring giant, Dean studied the scene and decided that Goslovich must have given the wall a right-left combination, keeled over on the couch, and got that last punch in before passing out with his hand still in the wall.

In the kitchen his brother and his roommate, Ken Everton, were playing blackjack. Ken was dealing, his back to Dean. Around them on the floor were ripped open half-cases of Rainier beer, empty bottles, and ravaged packages of potato chips. The kitchen counter was littered with more beer bottles and piles of dirty paper plates with the crusts of pizzas on them. In the sink, surrounded by smashed beer bottles, sat a blackened wastebasket filled with water. Burnt cardboard from a pizza carton floated on top.

Jake glanced up at his brother and then checked his wristwatch. "Little late, aren't you? What is it? After three o'clock in the fucking morning?" He tapped the table, signaling to Ken that he wanted another card. Peeking at it, he glanced back at Dean. "Oh, Jesus," he said.

Ken turned and looked at Dean's crotch and started laughing. "Hot date, huh?"

"What?" Dean looked down and to his horror saw that he had a huge stain all over the left pocket of his pants.

"You're lucky you didn't go home with that," Jake said. "So, are you no longer a virgin, or was it just a hand job."

"Oh, screw off." Dean hurried into Jake's bedroom.

"Look at him. He's in love," Ken said without looking at him. He flipped his cards over. "Pay twenty. I bet she's a nice girl, too."

"Nice and easy," Jake said, flipping over his hole card. "Twenty."

"Sheeeit!"

In the bedroom closet Dean found Jake's bathrobe. Stripping off his pants, his shirt, and his shorts, he put it on and lay down on the bed. "What happened to Goslovich?"

"Goslovich lost. So first the animal tried to burn the place down. Then he took on the wall," Jake shouted. "The wall won. He passed out when he got his fist stuck. We're playing for his money now. You wanna go to Seattle, get some breakfast?"

"When?"

"In about ten minutes, as soon as I whip this phony's ass. We're taking Goslovich. He's throwing the shot tomorrow at the invitational track meet, and me and Ken got hot dates, waterskiing way the hell out at Mercer Island. You wanna go?"

On the wall opposite Jake's bed hung *Playboy* pinups, Miss April and Miss May, in scrolled gold frames. Dean stared at them, trying to remember what he thought about when he saw them before. Whatever it was, it was gone now. "I'm tired."

"I'd be tired too, man, if I was carrying my cherry that long," Ken said. "Dean! Don't fall asleep on us, goddamn it. We're gonna need some help rolling Goslovich up in a blanket and getting his big ass in the back seat."

PULLING THE FRONT DOOR open, Franci listened for sounds from the dark windows of her mother's bedroom. Except for the bathroom, the lights were off. Franci let the door shut slowly, pushing in the catch with her finger and then letting it nudge out on the door frame, so it didn't make the usual loud click when it locked.

In the bathroom Franci stripped off her panties and skirt and put them both in the dirty wash. She took her sweater off, checked it, and slung it over the towel rack. From her purse she took her black stockings and her garter belt. She dropped the stockings in the wash and hung the garter belt over the towel rack with her sweater and her bra. She took her robe off the hook on the door and put it on. Then she washed her face and brushed her teeth. Crossing the hallway, she saw the door to her bedroom was open a crack, and Franci softly shut it behind her before she turned on the light. Sprawled across her bed was a woman dressed in her red sweater and skirt.

Franci almost let out a shriek, and then she recognized that it was her mother. Franci's breath came fast, and she stared down at the Christmas decorations spilled across the bedroom floor from closet to bed. Around her mother's head was a garland of golden tinsel. A strand of Franci's fake pearls was thrown up over her face. Black pumps were on her feet, and below them a clear vodka bottle poked halfway out from under Franci's bed. Backing up, Franci turned off the light. She tried to calm herself so she could hear if her mother was breathing. Finally her own breathing slowed, and she heard a low shallow rattle of breath.

OVER COMMENCEMENT BAY, only a few columns of smoke were rising from the plywood mills in the mud flats. Bouger drove the Mercury out of the Pick Quick Drive-in in Fife. He'd run into a buddy who needed to ditch the leftover Country Club malt-liquor eight-ouncers that he'd liberated from a party. His buddy was too plowed to drive home with booze in his car, so Bouger drank the last six pack in the parking lot. The six Clubs had given him a little buzz and numbed the pain in his forehead. Bouger had given up expecting to find the kid, but he cruised the Poodle Dog restaurant anyway, a twenty-four-hour truck stop and the last joint on his way home, and that's when he saw the Olds in an unlighted spot in the back parking lot.

He checked for any Highway Patrol or Pierce County cops in front, before he turned left off the highway and pulled in behind the Poodle Dog. The Olds was backed up to a cyclone fence, so Bouger parked across its front end, blocking it with the Mercury.

No one was in the car. Bouger took his time fitting the brass knuckles over his right hand. Getting out of the Mercury, he strolled over to the Olds and patted the front fender, listening to the sound the brass knucks made. Bouger faced the Poodle Dog and stared at the windows. With the Country Club working on him, he was sure that the kid was sitting right there, scared shitless.

"I know you're in there, you prick! And I know you're in there watching me." He laughed, thinking High School was finally going to pay. Bouger made a fist and ran the brass knuckles down the fender hard, paint curling up with a high thin screech.

Looking up, he gave a casual wave to the Poodle Dog's side windows. "And you're gonna have to come out sometime, bumfuck," he gloated, "or else your hot rod's gonna be nothing but scrap fuckin' metal." Bouger rocked the fender. "You're not coming out, huh? Well, maybe *this'll* get you out," Bouger laughed. Raising his hand up in a salute, he stepped in front of the Olds and with a swift backward chop shattered the left headlight, glass showering down on the gravel. Bouger leaned against the Olds, striking the pose of a man about town, casual, as the lights were turned off in the side windows of the Poodle Dog. Bouger knew instantly that the section had just been closed to customers, and no one had watched his little show.

"Sheeeit, I guess I gotta go in there and drag High School outta there," Bouger complained, giving the headlight another chop and knocking out some leftover shards of glass. And then Bouger felt the Olds rock under his hand. He turned around, leaning his left hand on the fender. "Aha," he said, making a fist with his brass knuckles, "someone's in there."

He watched a blanket humping up in the back seat. The driver's side of the front seat was pushed forward, and the door opened. Bouger's smile froze as a huge square head poked out of the door, followed by a monstrous leg, the blanket slowly falling off Goslovich as he climbed out.

Bouger's mouth dropped open, staring up at the nasty, squinty-eyed face looming over him, as Goslovich trapped Bouger's left hand on the fender. Bouger swung with his right as hard as he could. The brass knuckles connected with the side of Goslovich's neck, and a foul *Huh!* blew down over Bouger's face. Still trying to wrench his left hand free, Bouger pulled back for another punch, and he felt his fist, brass knuckles and all, enveloped in Goslovich's left hand. There was a moment when Bouger's hand bent back, the brass knuckles cutting into his fingers, and then he let out a scream as his fingers broke, his wrist cracked, and he collapsed.

Goslovich grunted and then dragged Bouger by his collar across the gravel. Bouger's cap fell off in the struggle, but the wad of Kleenex stayed on his forehead, glued there by the dried blood.

"Buss our fuckin' lights, will ya." Goslovich hauled Bouger in front of the Mercury and turned him around facing the Mercury. Goslovich laid a big hand on the back of Bouger's head. Bouger started to scream but that was cut off when Goslovich smacked the top of his head into the Mercury's left headlight, knocking him out and leaving the wad of bloody Kleenex stuck in the shattered glass.

Hanging onto Bouger's collar, Goslovich dragged him to the Mercury. Goslovich stood Bouger up and heaved him into the front seat face first, jamming his legs up so there was room to shut the door.

Then Goslovich noticed that the Mercury was blocking the Olds way out. He opened the door and shifted the Mercury into neutral. Then he shut the door, grabbed the door handle, and began to push. For a moment the car resisted, but then it started to roll. Ten yards away there was a slight incline leading out to a side street. When the Mercury reached the incline, Goslovich gave it a shove and walked back to the Olds. Behind him the Mercury rolled out into the side street, crossed it, continued through an open gate into a lot filled with stacks of wooden pallets, and disappeared in the dark between two stacks.

Goslovich crawled into the back seat of the Olds. Wrapping himself up in the blanket, he stopped and sniffed a few times. He looked down at the blanket and brought it to his nose. Then he sat up and, hanging his big head over the front seat, sniffed again. "Smells like pussy in here," he muttered, and then he fell back into a drunken sleep.

DEAN SAT on his brother's red satin bed cover. He'd taken the two framed *Playboy* Playmates of the Month off the walls and laid one on each side of him. Dean stared at his face in a mirror propped up on his lap, then at the two Playmates. He tried to remember

why they looked so different when he was a virgin. He thought
about what words he'd use to tell his buddies that he'd lost his
cherry. *Laid at the Castle. Broke my virge at the Castle.*

None of them sounded quite tough enough.

Lost it at the Castle.

That sounded tough, but the problem with saying it was that no
one ever called it *the* Spanish Castle. It was always Spanish Castle,
just like Spanish fly was always Spanish fly. No one ever said *the*.
So he was going to have to say it some other way. And besides it
wasn't true: they'd been under the high voltage lines in Puyallup.

He wasn't going to tell the guys it was Franci. Rob or Hubie
would all badger him until he told, especially Rob. He made up a
couple of stories, so they wouldn't know, but he gave up on that.
Maybe he wouldn't tell anyone.

Dean and Franci had talked about what they could do next, but
none of them were school things. At first it'd been awkward, because whenever Dean referred to something at high school, Franci
didn't seem to know about it. She didn't really care. She was even
thinking about skipping her senior year, because with all her extra
secretarial courses she had enough credits to graduate. That had
amazed Dean. None of his friends would ever dream of dumping
their senior year.

He didn't know where he was going to take Franci on their next
date. He sure as hell wasn't going to go back to Spanish Castle.

Dean let the mirror drop on his lap, and he considered what was
going to happen. No one in his crowd would accept Franci. She
was too Midland, living out by those old houses with tar-paper
roofs and junked cars in the yards. Thinking about how she'd be
sure to be rejected made Dean mad, because it wasn't fair. But
then he didn't know how he could change what people thought.
He knew that if he started dating Franci steady, no one would invite him to their private bashes. He'd have to go to the school
dances because he was president, but then they could split. Other
guys had told the soshes and those types to kiss off. But Dean didn't
know if he could do it. He told himself he could, but he didn't know
if he could stand it. The best way was to take her out maybe two
or three more times.

Dean flipped the mirror up and stared at his face. That was what
he'd do. Play it cool. Maybe call her on Sunday. Maybe slip out for
three or four more dates.

STACKED UP NEXT to the couch were the four drawers from Franci's bedroom dresser. On the couch beside Franci was an open suitcase filled with her clothes. At her feet a brown leather bag with shoulder straps was full of clothes, too. Franci checked her makeup kit. In the mirror her eyes looked red, and she turned the lamp away so she didn't look so bad. She zipped the leather bag shut and checked the kitchen clock. It was six-thirty. The sun rising over Mount Rainier was flooding the kitchen with pale pink light. Franci dialed the operator for a collect call to California.

Her father accepted the call. "Why, hello, honey. Kind of early, isn't it?"

"I wanted to get you before work."

"What's the problem?"

"Mom's drinking again."

There was a silence, and then her father cleared his throat. "Bad?"

"I can't help. I'm only making things worse. I can't bring anyone home. She's been putting on my clothes, after I go out on dates, like she's my sister, and then she drinks and waits up for me."

Her father was silent. Then a lighter snapped open. A cigarette pack rustled. There was a click, as a cigarette was lit. He took a long slow drag. "So," he said, exhaling. Then he coughed once. "So. Tell me what I can do."

"I want to leave. If I go to her sister in Seattle, she'll come get me. Then it'll start all over again."

The clink of a cup. "You're not in trouble, are you, daughter?"

"No, nothing like that."

Another silence. "So. You want to come down here?"

"If it's okay."

"Oh hell, I've always said you could." Trying to sound cheerful. "And say, come to think of it, I may even have a job for you. I'm driving truck for these clothing-store guys in Sunnyvale. They need a new secretary, a receptionist type. Last summer you did that with that kitchen-cabinet outfit, didn't ya, daughter?"

"Still do temp work there. Dad, I just want to go."

"Don't blame your mother."

"Will you call her around noon? I don't want her calling the cops. She'll wake up in a panic if you don't call and explain."

"Can't you leave her a note?"

Franci looked down at her fingernails. "No. I won't."

A long slow exhale. "Okay. But I'll say it's only for the summer. I'll take care of things from my end, okey-dokey?" He drew deeply on his cigarette again and sighed the smoke out. "So, if you're sure you're not in trouble, or nothing."

Franci didn't say anything.

"Okay. So. As far as I'm concerned, everything's copacetic. Now, you got enough money, don't ya?"

After Franci hung up, she looked through her dresser drawers again. The whole time she'd been sneaking them out of her bedroom, she was afraid that her mom would wake up. Except for her new stockings, Franci left all of her school and party clothes, taking only the stuff she needed to go job hunting in San Jose. Her teenage clothes were her goodbye note for her mother, something for her to think about. Sometimes Franci thought of herself as never having been a teenager. She closed the suitcase and the leather bag and carried them to the front door. Then she checked the new Larchmont D bus schedule. Last summer she'd taken it into Tacoma to her job at the cabinet shop, but she wanted to make sure nothing had changed.

The bus-stop bench was wet with dew, so Franci stood, leaning her hand on the back of the bench, favoring her ankle. She thought of the night before, in Spanish Castle's parking lot, and tears came to her eyes. She had to leave now, or she'd go back, so far back that she might end up like her mother. That had been the worst. When Franci had flipped on her bedroom light, for an awful moment she thought she was looking at herself, sprawled on some bed in the future.

On the bus ride into Tacoma, Franci began to make a list of things she would have to do once she arrived in California. She decided not to write the list down, so she could keep her mind on what she was doing, not on what had happened before. First thing was to write school, request an incomplete in psychology, and ask for a makeup test to be mailed to her. All the rest were business-ed classes — no finals for those. In California she'd need a night U.S. history class for her last graduation requirement. Write to Kitcheneers and say she couldn't work this summer. Drop a note to her best friend, Millie MacDonald. Get Dean's address out of the phone book at the Greyhound terminal. Maybe she would write him. Franci couldn't think of what she would say, so she left it just one of the items on her list, *Get Dean's address*. The night before seemed like years ago. Starting over—she'd been stupid to think she could start her life anew on a date. Dates were just dates. Franci thought about Dean's world of sports and Friday dances, and she knew she had only been kidding herself. That dream was over for her—had been for some time.

In her purse Franci found a Kleenex and dried her eyes. No matter what she thought, she was not going to stay. She would not turn around. Franci started to go over her list while she stared out at Commencement Bay.

As the bus started down the Pacific Avenue hill into downtown Tacoma, the pink morning light turned the smelter smokestack a dull red. From its mouth a tall purple spume of smoke flowered straight up against the leaden sky. The edges of the smoke peeled off, and little red streamers arced out over the bay. Down in the mud flats the plywood mills were pumping out clouds of steam and smoke. With no wind stirring, the bay water gleamed a flat pewter color, and under the raw morning light the town slowly was being buried in a thick gray haze.

A Little Surprise

CHERI EVERS and Pete Dwyer had lockers together, so when they got to school, they could see each other. One Monday morning in the fall, Cheri was waiting for him. "You'll never guess what I've got for you," she told him.

Pete was busy putting his stuff in the locker and taking out some books. "What?" he said.

"You'll need the car Friday night."

Pete did not know what she was talking about. "Okay, I'll ask my mom for it. What do we need it for?"

"I've got a little surprise for you." Cheri was smiling at Pete. But it wasn't just *any* smile.

"What surprise?" Pete felt a space growing large and empty in his chest.

"Oh, you'll like it," Cheri said. And she laughed. "You look so funny. Just get the car on Friday. You'll see."

Pete watched her walk off for her first class. He felt as if he had been ambushed. "Hey." He ran after her and caught up. "What are you talking about?"

"You don't know what I'm talking about?" Cheri smiled at him again. She walked into her class. "You'll like it," she said over her shoulder.

AT LUNCH ONCE they were away from everyone else, Cheri turned to him and smiled that smile again. "Well, are you getting excited?"

"Cheri, what are you doing?"

Cheri laughed at him. "Oh," she said, "you're worried."

"No."

"You're blushing."

"Chereeee!" Pete said, taking her by the arm. "What's going on?"

"I hope I don't have to show you." Cheri laughed, and then she hugged his arm. "Just get the car for Friday."

By TUESDAY MORNING Pete was mad. He knew Cheri was only joking with him. "Look," he said to her in front of their lockers, "I don't like you joking with me this way."

"You're really getting nervous, aren't you?"

"Stop laughing at me."

"Pete, just get the car," Cheri said. "Did you ask?"

Pete had forgotten to ask. He had been too wound up. "Uh," he said.

"You didn't? Oo-la-la, you *were* nervous."

"I GOT THE CAR for Friday," Pete told Cheri on Wednesday morning. He didn't say any more than that. He'd decided to let her do the talking.

She nodded. "Good," she said. "Come over at eight and pick me up, okay?" She paused. "You look awfully nervous, and it's only Wednesday."

"Chereeee," Pete wailed, "don't do this to me. Are you serious? Look at me? Are you? Because if you're lying...."

Cheri smiled, and it was that smile again. Pete felt his chest begin to float away.

"Oh, god," Cheri said, "you're going to be a wreck by Friday."

FRIDAY MORNING when Cheri came up to him, Pete was kicking the books on the bottom of his locker. He couldn't even look over at her. "My mom needs the car tonight. She told me late last night. I would have called you but...." Pete shrugged.

Cheri shrugged and took her books out of the locker. "That's okay," she said. "I'll get my dad's car. I'll pick you up at eight, okay?"

Cheri looked over at Pete. He had stopped kicking his books and was staring into his locker.

"Oh, god, what am I getting myself into? Stop looking that way!" Cheri jerked him along down the hall.

Pete felt weak in the knees.

"Stop acting so dumb!" Cheri hissed. "And stop smiling!"

She turned off into her classroom and left Pete standing there in the hallway. He was grinning at his reflection in the window. He couldn't help himself. *Friday, today is still Friday. A little surprise.*

AT FOOTBALL PRACTICE that afternoon, Peter Dawson and Ripolla were waiting for a timing drill with Pete. "Hey, Dwyse, baby, you want to go get a buzz on?" Peter said.

"I'm getting a case tonight, man," Ripolla said. "Dawson is buying."

Pete shook his head.

"Come *onnnn*, Dwyer," Ripolla said.

Pete stepped into the next drill and got down in his stance. The halfback came through, and Pete flattened him.

"Hey! Dwyer! No contact!" the coach yelled. "Save that for the game Saturday."

"Sorry, coach." Pete walked to the end of the line, and Ripolla slipped to the back with Pete when the coach looked the other way.

"Can't wait for the game, eh, Dwyse. Listen, me and Dawson got something better than the game."

Pete shook his head. *And everything will be different on Saturday.* "No, I gotta get my brother's car tonight." Pete couldn't believe how easy the lie came. "Sorry, guys."

THAT NIGHT CHERI'S father drove a 1952 Lincoln home from his car lot for Cheri to use. When Pete saw Cheri pull up to his house in that long black car, he felt as if he were going to a funeral.

Pete admired himself in the hallway mirror. His new London Fog trench coat looked very adult. When he walked outside to the Lincoln, Cheri moved over to let him drive. She was wearing her soft gray sweater, just as Pete had imagined she would.

"Where shall we go?" Pete said. "Over by your place?" That was where they usually parked.

"Ummmmmm, I dunno." Cheri burrowed her head into his shoulder.

Pete looked down over the wide shoulders of his London Fog trench coat at her, and somehow it didn't seem right to park in their regular parking spot. He drove out the old highway toward Mount Rainier. He felt lightheaded, dizzy. The big Lincoln steering wheel moved slow and clumsy in his hands. At every turnoff, Pete looked but then rejected each side road. He didn't know what would be right, but as long as he kept driving, he wouldn't have to make any other decisions. What he really wanted to do was drive the Lincoln right into Mount Rainier, now a soft pink snowcap.

FINALLY PETE DROVE down what looked like a long driveway going off into the trees. He stopped the Lincoln in a small dip in the road next to a barbed wire fence. Turning off the engine, he switched on the radio. A sweat broke out on his hands. He put his arm around Cheri, and they kissed, very long and slow.

"Well," Cheri said, "shall we get in the back seat?"

Pete panicked. "Uh," he said. "I'm a.... Uh." And then he didn't know what he was.

Cheri gave him a nudge with her hip. "Get out. I'm not going to climb over this front seat. It's too high."

Pete opened the door and stepped out. He had never been in the back seat with Cheri. This was going to be another first. As Pete opened the back door of the Lincoln, he joked, "Is this where you're keeping that little surprise?"

"That's where you're going to get it." Cheri hiked up her short gray skirt and stepped up into the Lincoln.

Pete looked down at his London Fog trench coat, undecided whether to take it off now or later. He stroked a sleeve. Then he slowly took the trench coat off and folded it over his arm, before stepping into the long black car.

TWO HOURS LATER Pete was naked, leaning over the back of the front seat. His London Fog trench coat was folded up on the front seat, and he looked down at it fondly. Cheri's bare breasts touched his back and her chin rested on his spine, as she traced his vertebrae with a finger.

"One, two, three, four, five," she said. "You know, I never could figure out that five-minute business."

"What five minutes?"

"You know, when they say at school that you shouldn't throw it away for a five-minute thrill."

"Is that what they tell the girls?" Pete felt uncomfortable. The first time, he had been a little too excited.

"I was just thinking that when they say that, that tells us more about *their* sex life than it does ours." Cheri snuggled into his back. "Five minutes?"

Pete laughed and stared out at the night. All of a sudden it seemed to be darker outside. How could it be darker? The light on the radio dial was barely on, and the radio was playing softly, when he hadn't turned it down.

"Oh, Jesus." He twisted free of Cheri's arms and climbed up over the front seat.

"What's wrong?"

"Gimme the keys," he croaked. "They're in my pants." He turned off the radio, and Cheri handed him the keys. "The battery," Pete said.

"The radio was on," Cheri said. "There's nothing wrong with the battery."

Pete turned the key over in the ignition. There was a flurry of dry clicks and then nothing, no sound at all.

PETE CLIMBED BACK into the car, opened his Boy Scout knife to the biggest blade and pushed it toward Cheri.

She was bundled up in the car blanket, trying to keep warm, and her hand came out of the folds and took the knife. "What am I going to do with this?"

"Just stay in the car, lock the doors, and everything will be okay."

"You mean you can't push the car out of here?"

"I tried. I'm too goddamn weak." Pete opened the door and got out in a hurry.

"Oh, god, Pete," Cheri whispered, "you're not leaving me here alone, are you?" She looked down at the open Boy Scout knife in her hand. "With this?"

Pete leaned back in and kissed her cheek. "Cheri, I love you," he said. "Just lock the car. You'll be safer here than out there with me.

I'll be right back." Without looking in at her, Pete shut the door and started walking back toward the highway.

WHEN PETE GOT to the old Highway, it was fogged in. He couldn't see twenty feet in front of him. He pulled the belt of his London Fog trench coat tighter and put the collar up. He wished that he wasn't in training, so he could smoke a cigarette. He would look perfect then.

Putting out his thumb, he tried different hitchhiking poses. He was so pleased with the way he looked, the first car was past him before he started waving for it to stop.

By its headlights, though, he saw a mailbox ahead. As he trudged past a line of trees, a dim yellow porch light glowed fifty feet back from the highway. Pete imagined how it would all happen: a kindly old logger with a big truck, Pete standing beside the Lincoln, a borrowed Pall Mall hanging out of his mouth, Cheri proudly looking on in gratitude.

The house was a tar-papered shack with two blocks of wood for steps under the front door. Pete knocked, hearing a television inside. Someone had to be home. Pete began to imagine that he was blond and looked like Richard Widmark. He wished that he had a cigarette for that nonchalant effect: *Had a spot of car trouble down the road*—taking a drag—*could you help a guy out?*

Someone came up to the door but didn't open it. "Yes?" A woman's voice.

"My car stalled down the road," Pete said out of the side of his mouth. "I need to call a tow." Pete looked at the door, expecting it to open.

"Go away," the voice said. "Now."

"I need to use the phone." Pete tried to make his voice sound young. "Really, I gotta call someone for a tow."

To his left, a head peeked out at him from behind the window curtain, then ducked back. Pete wished that he didn't have his London Fog trench coat on. Putting down the collar, he tried again. "I *gotta* call," Pete yelled at the door. "It's my dad's car," he lied. "He'll murder me if I don't get it back tonight." Pete wished that he hadn't used the word *murder*. "Really," he added.

"No," the voice said. "Go away."

"Look, here's my driver's license," Pete said. He poked it under

the door. "I'm only sixteen." That was another lie. Pete was seven-
teen, but he figured whoever was inside would not notice. The
license was slid out from under the door.

"I'm just a kid," Pete added. "Honest."

CHERI WAS KNEELING on the floor of the Lincoln, her face buried
in the car blanket and sobbing, while holding the open blade of the
Boy Scout knife up over her head.

"What are you doing?" Pete said, getting in and closing the door.

"Get them away!" Cheri screamed.

"Huh?" Pete locked the door and looked around the car. He
hadn't seen anyone near the Lincoln. "Who?"

"They're *out* there!" Cheri cried, and she threw herself into
Pete's arms.

"There's no one out there," Pete said. He brought out his driver's
license from his pocket. "Look, I've got a great story for you, Cheri,
see?" He held it over her head and pointed to the white smudges
on his license. "My driver's license has got flour all over it."

Slowly Cheri raised her head and looked up at Pete's license.

"She stuck it in a can of flour, in case I murdered her or
something."

Bewildered, Cheri stared at the license.

"It's a great story. See, I had my collar up like this, and the
woman thought I was a murderer like Richard Widmark. I must
have looked like a crazy guy to her, talking out of the side of my
mouth like this, and so she hid in the other room while I made a
phone call to Ripolla."

"Ripolla!" Cheri sat straight up and threw the Boy Scout knife
down on the floor. "Not Ripolla!" she wailed.

"Wait, wait, wait. It's a great story," Pete said. "So, anyway, this
woman was scared."

"I don't care about any great story! You've got *Ripolla* coming?
My reputation will be *ruined!*"

"Chereeee, I love you. Listen. It's a great story." Pete shook the
license at her. "Did you see the flour here on my license? This
woman hid my license in the flour while I made the phone call, so
when the police came after I murdered her, they would find my
license in the flour bin. She must have seen that on some TV show."

Cheri froze, and then she jabbed Pete in the ribs. "Oh, my god.

There," she said, pointing out the window. "Do you hear it? There?"

Pete listened, and he heard something. Reaching down, he grabbed his Boy Scout knife off the rug.

"That's them," Cheri cried. "They were all around the car."

"Lock the door!" Pete ordered.

"It *is* locked!" Cheri screamed, and she almost tackled Pete as she dove face first into his lap.

Pete turned and stared out the back window. The fog was drifting past, and all he could hear was breathing. Heavy, low breathing.

Pete felt faint. His Boy Scout knife slipped and almost dropped out of his hand. He stared and stared out the side window, and there were thumps and rubs and more breathing. Then, between two pine tree trunks he saw the muzzle of a cow poke through. "Oh shit," Pete said. "Get up. It's a cow, Cheri."

CHERI WAS HYSTERICAL about Ripolla, the foulest big mouth and dirtiest mind in school, coming to their rescue. She threatened to start walking, until Pete calmed her down. The Lincoln had to get back to her father, and she had to be in it when it arrived. Besides, no one would believe anything Ripolla said anyway, he was such a liar.

Finally Pete told her he was going to miss Ripolla if he didn't get back, and he left Cheri with his Boy Scout knife and walked up to the old highway. What he didn't tell her was that the Ripper sounded dead drunk on the phone.

Pete heard Ripolla's 1953 Studebaker in the fog long before he saw it. After Ripolla had taken off both mufflers on that big Studey V-8, it sounded like a B-29 taking off. Pete began waving his arms as the roar came closer. Two headlights barreled out of the fog, and Pete leaped to one side, still waving, as the Studebaker flashed by him. Pete screamed, but the Studebaker's two taillights disappeared in the fog.

Feeling a sudden flow of cold air, Pete looked down. He had ripped out both armpits of his London Fog trench coat.

PETE RAN down the side road to the Lincoln ahead of the Studebaker and pounded on the window. "Cheri," he whispered, "lay in back. Don't say anything, don't get up. I told Rip this was my brother's car. He doesn't know you're here."

Throwing the car blanket in the back seat, Cheri hiked up her skirt and rolled over the top of the front seat. She ducked down, dragging the blanket over her.

Up the road, the Studebaker's taillights came over the top of the rise as Ripolla backed his car down. When the Studebaker was up to the Lincoln's front bumper, Pete yelled for Rip to stop. Ripolla climbed out of his car with a Rainier beer in his hand. "I'll get the chains out....Dwyer! Want a beer? Come here! You're going to have a beer with the Ripper. Here!"

Pete took the beer and watched as Ripolla staggered around to the front of the Studebaker and stood there, mystified. Then he laughed, remembering that he had backed in, so the trunk of the car was the other way.

"Heyyyyyyy Petey! Dwyse, baby, you gotta have a beery beer with the old Rip." Ripolla draped his arm around Pete's shoulder and began shaking him.

"I've already got a beer, Rip," Pete protested.

"You're not getting away from the Rip this time." He began to wrestle Pete around the middle of the road. "You're getting drunk, right now, with the Rip. C'mon."

"Sure, sure, but first let's tow the car outta here." Pete waltzed Ripolla over to the Studebaker's trunk. "Open the trunk."

Ripolla found his car keys and opened the trunk.

"Where are the chains?" Pete said, peering in. There were only half-cases of Rainier beer in the trunk.

"Chains?" Ripolla said. "Chains, we got chains. Chainychains, beery beer, unchain my heaaaaaart, baby set me free." Ripolla fell into the trunk headfirst, and he passed out.

Pete wrapped his arms around Ripolla's waist and pulled him out. "Rip," Pete yelled in his ear. "You brought chains, didn't you?"

"Suuuuure, I did," Rip said, and he suddenly stood up in Pete's embrace, chains clanking in his hands. As he held the chains out over the red taillights of the Studebaker, Pete saw that they were snow chains.

"You said you were up by Mount Rainier, stuck, so I brought snow chains! Where's the snow?" Ripolla tried to drape the snow chains over Pete's head, but Pete ducked away. Ripolla laughed. "Where's the snow? Huh? Fuck the snow. These'll work. Fuck the snow. Huh? You got a beer? Hey! Dwyer, you got a beer?" Rip fell sideways into the trunk. "Where the fuck are we? Hey, I want snow!"

After lifting him out of the trunk, Pete carried Rip back and put him into the driver's seat. Then he tried to use the snow chains for a tow. By doubling the chains over the Studebaker's trailer hitch and then winding the chains around the bumper guards of the Lincoln, Pete managed to make a web and tie the Lincoln to the Studebaker.

But the first three times the Studebaker started forward, the snow chains broke. Pete kept yelling at Ripolla to go easy on the gas, but he was too drunk. Finally, on the fourth try, the chains held, and the Lincoln was towed out to the old highway. When the Studebaker stopped, Pete jumped out of the Lincoln, disconnected the chains, and told Ripolla to give them a push.

"Say, what the hell, I didn't know your brother lived out here," Ripolla said.

"Just get behind the Lincoln and push-start us." Pete threw the chains into the back seat of the Studebaker and closed the door on Ripolla.

When Ripolla drove behind the Lincoln, Pete looked over his shoulder at Cheri huddled in the back. "He'll never even remember this," he hissed to Cheri. "But stay down."

The Studebaker began to come forward for the push. Out the window Pete motioned with his arm for Ripolla to keep coming forward, guiding him up to the Lincoln's bumper. There was a jolt, as their bumpers hit and the Lincoln was bounced forward a few feet. Then Pete heard the roar of the Studebaker engine behind them.

"Nooooooo! We're not together, slow down!" Pete screamed. The Studebaker collided with the Lincoln's back bumper and Pete was thrown forward against the steering wheel, knocking the wind out of him. The back bumper began to grind and screech, as the Studebaker's front bumper raked back and forth across the chrome, and then the Lincoln lurched onto the road with the Studebaker in full throttle, spinning gravel behind it.

Pete fought with the wheel, trying to steer as the Lincoln swerved back and forth across the road.

"Slow down, you asshole!" Pete yelled out the window.

Cheri started screaming as the Lincoln careened into the fog. "He's going to kill us," Cheri moaned. "He'll kill us!"

The battery was so low, the headlights were still out as the Lincoln hurtled through the fog. Pete could see that the speedometer needle was up to thirty, so he popped the clutch. Nothing happened. The car was still in neutral. Panicking, he put the clutch in and shifted into second gear at thirty-five and popped the clutch again. The engine started, the headlights went on, and Pete floored it, pulling ahead and then swerving to the right as the Studebaker went roaring past, making a speed shift into high gear.

Pete watched Ripolla's taillights disappear down the road. His hands were wet with sweat and his chest hurt from hitting the steering wheel. Pete slowed down. "You can get up now."

Cheri looked up over the seat, her hair a mess, her face streaked with tears. "He almost killed us," she wailed.

Seeing her, Pete couldn't help it. He started laughing.

"Stop laughing. This isn't funny!" Cheri began beating on the back of his neck with her fists. "He almost killed us!"

THE NEXT MONDAY MORNING, when Cheri walked up and put her books in her locker, Pete tried to think of what he should say. Everything he thought of saying seemed stupid. Cheri bent down and took out books for her first class. Pete opened a book and looked in it. He was going to wait until she said something first. She was not looking at him.

His heart felt tight. Was that *it*? He could see them never getting together again. One Friday. That was it. Pete stood beside her, feeling more and more miserable. He looked down at his feet. He should have said something to her when she first came up. Hi, maybe. He should have telephoned on Saturday or Sunday. It was all his fault. He never should have called Ripolla, even though he'd checked on Saturday, and Ripolla never remembered a thing. Cheri would never have anything more to do with him, ever. He just knew it.

Cheri shut the locker door and then bumped him with her hip. "Doing anything after school today?"

"No. I mean, after practice. Yes. No, I mean."

She burst out laughing. "Don't get that look on your face," she said.

They both laughed.

"We got away with it," Pete whispered. "No one knows."

"Shhhh," she said.

"Why Friday?" Pete whispered. "Why that Friday?"

Cheri looked up at him. She shrugged. "It was a surprise."

"A surprise," Pete repeated.

"I like surprises."

"Just on Friday?"

"No," Cheri said. "See you this afternoon? After practice?" She looked over her shoulder at him. "Don't just stand there," she giggled. "Anybody could tell by looking at you. Go away."

"Monday," Pete said. "Mondays too."

A Can of Smoked Oysters

AFTER SCHOOL, Hubie and Pete drove over in Hubie's car to get Orin Sloat. Orin's family lived in the old housing tract near McCord Air Force Base, where both his mother and father worked as cooks. Most of the homes had new paint jobs. Here and there newly seeded lawns fronted the houses. Some had lawn decorations, little wishing wells or borders of red bricks, but Orin's didn't. Orin's home looked exactly like a cheap tract house, twenty years later: faded pink stucco, a warped green garage door, and a lawn dotted with dandelions and bald spots. A thick blot of oil glistened in the middle of the front drive. On the strip of lawn to its side was one worn brake shoe next to a sagging cardboard box filled with water.

Hubie and Pete didn't bother to knock. They walked right in.

The front-room blinds were drawn. The TV was turned to a game show. The air smelled stale, the floor was bare, and the brown couch opposite the window was faded from sunlight. A woman's slip was draped over one end. Above the couch hung a rattan mat with the word *Manila* woven in red.

Sitting in the middle of the room was a green leather chair with wide flat arms. The top of the right arm, toward the front, was spotted with two black cigarette burns. On the other arm of the chair was a can of smoked oysters, a toothpick sticking up out of the last oyster.

Hubie and Pete stood there looking at the TV. Hubie shrugged and nodded toward the bedroom door, but Pete shook his head slow: *no*. Hubie grinned and pointed at the slip. Just then Orin came out of the bathroom, clearing his throat and pulling on his belt buckle. Orin's moon face pushed above his white shirt and a thin green silk tie. Under his tight Windsor knot was a gold stickpin. He was wearing his good sport coat, plus his best black slacks, tightly pegged at the ankles. No shoes on, only white cotton socks.

"Hey, now," Orin said.

"Dressed for the job," Hubie said. "Good man." Pete and Hubie were both in jeans and T-shirts. Hubie also had on an old Clover Park High School Band sweater.

Orin settled down into his easy chair, leaned back and picked up the toothpick and stuck the remaining oyster in his mouth. He sucked the oyster off the toothpick, and then pointed with it at Hubie's band sweater. "Camouflage," he said. "You're a real pro. They'll never guess you're from Franklin Pierce High School."

"No lie," Hubie said. "Got it out of my older sister's closet."

"Where you sure nuff get your other dress-up clothes, too, huh?" Orin said. Both Orin and Hubie laughed, Orin a little longer than Hubie.

"You ready?" Pete said.

"No," Orin said.

On the floor to the other side of his chair were three unopened cans: PX stick potatoes, PX sardines, and Hormel's Vienna sausage. Orin bent over and picked up the cans one by one, opening each and putting them on the arm of the chair. First the Vienna sausages and the PX stick potatoes and then the PX sardines. He stuck the keys with their tin strips wrapped around them into the empty oyster tin. Orin went into the kitchen and came out with a dish towel tucked in under his chin. Then he sat down in the green chair and started to eat.

"Jesus," Pete said. "I don't like watching this."

"Then go outside," Orin suggested.

"Your sister here?" Hubie nodded toward the bedroom door and grinned. "We could pass the time."

"Not with you." Orin laid a sardine on three potato sticks and eased it into his mouth.

"What do you call *that*?" Pete said.

Orin chewed for a moment, then shifted the load into his cheek and spoke around it. "Sardine boat."

HUBIE AND PETE went back outside and sat in Hubie's black and white Tudor Ford coupe. They looked down the rows of houses stretching out to the end of the street, where the cyclone fence for the McCord Air Force Base cut it off. A hard rain started to fall.

"I can't stand to watch Sloat eat the stuff out of cans."

"Army cans, too," Hubie said. "You remember he told us that when he got a house of his own, he wanted a refrigerator in the floor? So all he had to do was roll over and eat?"

"Well, who else we going to get to do this?" Pete stared out the window. Muddy rivulets were draining off the newer lawns into the street. "It's goddamn June, and look at it. Flooding."

Hubie imitated the cracked voice of some old western-movie sidekick. "Say, you suppose that Orin is really screwing his sister?"

"I wonder if that's how he got so good with his hands, peeling open those cans all the time," Pete said.

"All I'd like to know is, is he getting into his sister?" Hubie said. "No lie, man, I'm a service brat myself. I been around them. These goddamn white trash like Orin are deeeegenerates."

AFTER FIFTEEN MINUTES, Orin came out the front door. Pete noticed that he had on a new London Fog overcoat and even his shoes were shined. Orin inspected himself in the reflection on the Ford's wet hood as he walked around the car. Pete opened the door and leaned forward so Orin could get in the back seat.

"Uh-uh, I ain't going to fuck up *my* threads, man, getting in back. You get in back."

Pete got out and climbed in back. Orin flipped the seat upright and climbed in the front.

"Where's your sister?"

"Home."

"She busy tonight?"

"*Forget* it."

Hubie laughed. "You don't let her out much, do you?" Hubie looked over the seat back at Pete. "Look at that grin on his face, Pete. No lie, when God handed out pervert pills, Orin was at the head of the line."

Orin regarded Hubie for a moment. Then he looked out the side window and wiped his mouth. Pete noticed there was a line of salt crystals on his index finger. Orin turned and glanced back at Pete. "Got the place picked out?"

"Yeah. It's a cinch. I'll go in first. Hubie will come in, you come in, and then Hubie will do the stumble."

"Where is it?"

"Federal Way shopping mall."

"Great. You sure get around."

"A friend's sister works near there. Last Sunday, while the family was visiting, I went over. I hope there's only one clerk. Otherwise we'll have to work a little of the old yo-yo on them."

Orin laughed. "What are you worried about? Relax. You got the hands with you, man."

THE FEDERAL WAY sporting goods shop was set between a shoe store and an optometrist. As Pete went in, he saw that there was a new shipment of water skis leaning next to the door. He had to grin. That was the edge they needed. They could use those. Only one clerk, too.

Pete started the clerk talking about basketballs. The clerk was a slick-looking guy with a Kennedy haircut and a Pendleton shirt. He seemed to think he was really cool. Pete kept feeding him questions—which basketballs were best for gym or cement. Pete made out like he was thinking of buying two. The guy showed him the Wilsons, then the Voits, one for playgrounds and one for wooden floors.

When Hubie came in, Pete asked to see scuba gear. After the scuba gear was dragged out, Hubie got the clerk over and started talking up the new water skis, so Pete knew that Hubie had noticed them coming in the front door. *Good old Hubie, a real pro talker.* Then Orin breezed in and walked right to the glass case with the stopwatches and underwater watches.

Pete crossed over in front of Orin, between him and the clerk. He set down two scuba face masks on the glass case. Pete started to ask the clerk something, and then turned to Orin. "Maybe you better help this guy first," Pete said. "I can wait." He picked up some brochures and began to thumb through them.

Orin asked to see three of the stopwatches, and the clerk moved back behind the counter. Orin bullshitted for a moment, talking about how he was going to an awards banquet for Evergreen High

School. He needed to price the stopwatches for his uncle, who was an assistant coach there. The clerk asked him if he went to school there, and Orin said yes, he did, but he had graduated. He was only shopping for a birthday present. "My uncle's birthday is coming up later that week. Thought I'd give it to him at the banquet, as a surprise."

Pete asked to see a scuba knife and an underwater watch, "as long as you're at it." Both items were in the glass case. He chatted the clerk up, scattering the brochures on the glass case right over the other stopwatches. The clerk had left the little sliding door open.

At that moment, Hubie had some trouble getting the water skis stacked right. They fell over, and Hubie let out a whoop. The clerk hustled over to help him.

Pete watched the clerk and Hubie, waiting until they were both bending over, and then he leaned against the case, blocking the clerk's view. Behind him he could feel Orin's weight on the case as he leaned over for a second or two. When the weight shifted back, Pete said thanks to the clerk, leaving the knife and underwater watch on the counter, and walked out.

As the door closed behind him, he heard a couple of water skis smack down on the floor. "I'll get em," Hubie vowed. "Two out of three falls." The clerk laughed. *Good old Hube.*

Pete walked around the corner of the shopping mall where the Ford was parked. Hubie had left the keys on the floor of the car, as always. Pete got in the driver's side and started the engine.

Orin came around the corner, walking slowly. He opened the side door, tipped the seat forward and climbed in the back. "Don't matter now if they get creased," he said. "The show's over." He belched.

Pete could smell oysters and sardines on his breath.

Orin smiled at him. "Damn good, too, the second time."

"I wish you hadn't mentioned this was for a sports banquet. The guy might remember that. And with Hubie wearing that Clover Park sweater, too. I'd hate to get caught on the backside of something as clean as this."

"Look, mastermind, I *said* it was for my uncle. Stop worrying. Besides there's one banquet for every high school next week. Can't check all of them." Orin sniffed. "Besides, that dope probably won't

even notice the good one is gone. Nice setup, Pete. You got an eye
for the easy touches."

Hubie turned the corner, loped over to the car, jerked open the
door, and hopped in. "Let's hit it."

"Like a rabbit," Orin said.

"Outta habit, bappity-bap!"

Pete pulled forward into the exit lane of the parking lot, real
slow. As they passed the sporting goods shop, Orin looked sideways
at the front door, sinking back so his face was partly hidden.

"Did you tip over the whole stack of skis?" Pete asked.

"Naw, but I dropped two over as I left. Did you hear me? Man,
'Two out of three falls.' I was hot, wasn't I?" Hubie was still nervous
from being the last guy out of the store. "No lie, that jerk-off clerk
thinks I'm a spaz. He's getting back to the case about now. C'mon,
c'mon, let's make tracks."

Pete gunned the Ford and pulled out into a side street. He
turned right, then left, and then they were on a long residential
street, one that Pete knew ended facing the highway entrance. All
he had to do was to stop and look both ways for cops, and then they
were on the freeway back to Tacoma, free and clear.

Hubie took out a paper sack from his sweater pocket and pulled
open the glove compartment, leaving the door down. Inside the
sack were folded dollar bills.

"Shit, Hubie, did you take *that* in the store with you?"

"Couldn't leave it in this heap, man. Someone might steal it. You
can't trust people around these shopping malls."

"What if you'd got busted? We'd be out the cash, too."

"Ehhh," Hubie said, waving him off. He started to stack the one-
dollar bills on the open door. He divided the cash into three piles,
putting an extra dollar on the third pile each time he came to it.
"If the other guys on the track team could only see where half their
cash collection was going. Orin Sloat."

Orin belched again. He slipped the stopwatch, still in its red and
black box, out of his sport-coat pocket and handed it over the seat
to Hubie.

"Nice going, Sloat, the coach'll love this. Hey man, no lie now.
Orin? You ever get it on with your sister?"

"Jesus, Hubie, calm down. It's over, man. He's still all jacked up
from the job," Pete said glancing back at Orin.

"Hey, this Sloat guy's a thief *and* a sex pervert."

"Hey, now, Hubieeeee. Hey, we're all perfect in our own way." Orin nodded. "And if you dig that, hey, no struggle."

"Oh, yeah? Well, what about that time I came in and there you two were, about naked, Orin the boring here in his skivvies and her in her goddamn slip."

"It was a hot day."

"And it smelled, man, stink-finger city."

Orin bent forward and held up his hands over the front seat. "You know, Hubie, the Philippines is a great place to get shit. Your dad ever stationed there? No? Me, I picked up a lot there." He leaned his elbows on the back of the front seat and showed his hands to Hubie, first the palms, then the backs.

Hubie continued to count the collection money.

Orin put his left hand over the back of his right hand, and then snapped his fingers. A spring knife appeared in his right hand and the blade shot straight out, stopping about an inch from Hubie's temple.

"But I still got the touch, don't I?" Orin said. "Haven't lost that, have I?"

Hubie stared down at the piles of bills, one dollar held in his hand. He cleared his throat. "Naw," he said. "You were eating oysters that day."

"Was that it?"

Hubie swallowed once. "No lie." He was still holding the money in his hand.

Orin leaned back in the seat. He pushed the point of the spring knife against the window glass behind Hubie's head. There was a heavy click as the blade slid into its handle.

"Probably was," Orin said. "I sure do like oysters. Gotta have me those *smoky* ones."

Tell the Truth

You know you can make me do
What you want me to.

Tell The Truth
lyrics by Lowman Pauling
sung by Ray Charles.

MR. CUPAT SLIPPED the short piece of chalk in his green sweater vest pocket and rested his right thumb in the pocket. Then he looked up at the ceiling and smiled, giving the class a perfect profile of his round, fat, cleft chin.

"Think about it," he said. He picked the long red cigarette holder up off the window sill and walked back toward the chalkboard, holding the empty cigarette holder at the same angle as his upraised chin.

"You're not children. You're seniors. You have a mind of your own." Using the empty cigarette holder as a pointer, he tapped its tip on the word *Canadian* scrawled across the top of the chalkboard.

"Just remember to tell your parents that these are Canadian communists that we are going to hear. Not American. Our going has been cleared by the school board. The communists have been invited to lecture at the university. Get that clear. They are *Canadian* communists, and they are talking at the university. Not here in our school."

In the front row, Jim Glustich, the student-body president, a tall kid with a wheat-colored crew cut, raised his right hand. Mr. Cupat nodded at him. Before speaking, Jim glanced over at Lorraine Onderdonk, sitting next to him. She raised her eyes from her *Time* magazine. "How can the university invite subversives to...you know. Invite them to subvert on their campus?"

Mr. Cupat leaned back against the chalkboard tray and appeared thoughtful. "Because it's a free country, Jim."

"Yeah, but..."

"No *yeah buts*, Jim. This is *free* speech. They can say their piece."

"But if they talk subversion, hey, you know."

"We don't *know* that they're going to talk subversion, Jim. How do we know that before we hear them? Do you know that they are? Be honest. Think about it."

For emphasis, he pointed his cigarette holder at the class and nodded toward Lorraine. She changed her bland expression to one of interest by tilting her head to one side.

Jim was outraged. "Well, what's the difference between a communist and a subversive?"

Mr. Cupat shrugged, tilting his head back and bringing the cigarette holder up at a jaunty angle. "None."

"Is that why we don't have a communist party here?"

"Oh, but we do."

"In Washington state? Where?"

"Not around here, I'll tell you that. In the whole country, yes. But back east, there, well, to tell the truth, there's a lot of immigrants. Why they would come to our country, from commie countries, and still be communists is beyond me. But they do, Glustich. They really do. It's a free country."

Jim Glustich thought about this for a moment, suspicious that he was being led into a trap. "So why does Canada have them and we don't? Washington state doesn't have a communist party."

"Oh, we could. And maybe we do. You would have to check with the voting registrar and see if they are a registered party. That's what I'm saying. But they can't do anything here. We watch them too close. They can't get away with it here. Back east, New York, New Hampshire, it's crowded, busy. People can't keep tabs on their neighbors. Cities. People can get away with anything. And up there, in Canada, they have all these political parties." Mr. Cupat nodded toward the north wall. "It's a donnybrook. And they have a parliament, so they can have lots of political parties and even communists get one or two seats."

Mr. Cupat put down his cigarette holder, leaned on the desk, and smiled past Jim at the rest of the class. "And *that's* why I've been talking about parliamentary procedure these last few weeks, and *that's* why I asked you to pay par*ticular* attention to your *Time* magazines this week. I didn't have you subscribe to *Time* just to read the sports or look at pictures of our handsome President Kennedy and his fashionable wife, you know. And, people, I got a lot of flak, believe me, for requiring *Time* in this class. But my motto is, If you can't take the heat, get out of the kitchen. I know some of your parents might have objected. *Time* probably leans a little to the liberal side, a side you might not get in the *Tacoma News Tribune*. Be that as it may, let's talk about this parliamentary procedure. Open your *Time* to page fifty-three."

In the back row Shone Dunnigan tugged at the crotch of his pants and sniffed contemptuously. With dark slick hair and conventional good looks, he sported a Pendleton shirt worn over a white shirt with a button-down collar, tight brown pants, all in current fashion, but because of his large flat feet, he wore 1950s Wedgies—thick crepe-soled black leather shoes with round tips. "Straight Arrow Glustich falls into another Cupat trap," he sighed across the aisle to Pete Dwyer. "When's Q-Tip going to learn a new trick?"

Pete shook his head. "Glustich falls for it every time—why should he?" He found the right page in *Time* and opened it on the corner of his desk so Shone could read along with him.

Shone pointed at an ad of a woman modeling a swimsuit. "That looks just like Lorraine." Shone raised himself in his seat and stroked the front of his slacks. "Oh," he exhaled, pressing both palms against the crotch of his pants and staring down the row. "Lorraine," he whispered softly.

Mr. Cupat walked up and down the aisles, handing out parent-permission forms for the field trip to hear the communists.

"But, Mr. Cupat," Lorraine Onderdonk said, "how are we going to talk to our parents about this? They're just going to get worried."

"Well, Lorraine, for Mrs. Glaubinger's class you went to see the Greek Orthodoxes, didn't you?"

Lorraine nodded. "Well, yes, but that was religion, not politics."

"Freedom of religion, freedom of speech." With his cigarette holder Mr. Cupat pointed toward a bulletin-board poster of the Four Freedoms. In the middle was a portrait of Franklin Delano Roosevelt smiling with a cigarette holder clamped between his teeth. "Those are part of the Four Freedoms. Franklin Delano Roosevelt—you remember when we studied him." Mr. Cupat smiled at Lorraine, pointing his cigarette holder. "But you're not children any more. You can make up your own minds."

"Yeah, sure," Shone called. "But then why do we got to take these forms home so we can see if it's okay with our parents if we can make up our own minds?"

Mr. Cupat wheeled around and faced the back of the room. "Dunnigan, I'm not sure everyone would rush to agree that you have a mind."

"Well. I'm going to go," Shone said, looking around the room. "I've never seen any communists. Everybody says they're the bogeymen, but no one here has ever seen a real one, I bet."

"That's how you know they're *around*, Shone." Jim Glustich twisted around in his seat and glanced up at Mr. Cupat for confirmation. "Because you don't *see* them. How could they be subversives if you can see them anytime you want? I would get *more* nervous if I wasn't seeing any subversives than if they were talking on a soapbox down in front of the Parkland tennis courts every day."

"Why would the communists be down at the tennis courts, Glustich?"

"That's where everyone hangs out. They could, you know, proselytize everyone there."

"Maybe that's where *you* hang out," Shone shot back.

"Children, children," Mr. Cupat said. "Remember, no form signed by parents, no trip. Anyone not going will be assigned to a study hall. Just because I'm gone, this won't be a Chinese fire drill with you guys having a blast. So you better make up your minds."

HUBIE COOPER'S ROOM was on the north side of his parents' house, top floor. Because the side stairs gave access from the parking strip alongside the house, Hubie's was one of the guys' hangouts, since they could come and go without bothering Hubie's parents. As soon as Hubie joined the Marines after graduation, his folks planned to rent it. When Pete and Hubie returned from taking their girlfriends, Cheri and Pia, home in Hubie's 1954 Ford, Shone was waiting for them in Hubie's room. He got up as soon as they entered and shuffled off toward the bathroom. Pete followed Shone up to the bathroom door, imitating his flatfoot walk. Hubie asked Shone how the afternoon ride home with Lorraine had gone.

"Hubie, don't start talking about Lorraine. Don't encourage him. Look at him, going in there to whack off again."

"I'm not whacking off," Shone said, closing the door on Pete. Then, through the door: "I'm in love."

"Sure, with yourself," Pete slumped down on the couch beside Hubie and laughed. "Hubie, isn't it something how a girl can change her haircut and suddenly everybody thinks she's *so neat*."

"Lorraine started looking pretty good lately, lost some weight," Hubie said. "It's scary sometimes. She gets a different cut, and wow, no lie, everybody's eyeing her."

Hubie got up off the couch and stepped over to the stereo. He held up the album cover for *Green Onions*, by Booker T. and the MGs.

"Put on some Brother Ray," Pete said. "Every time I see that *Do the Twist with Ray Charles* album I get sick. Man, that's so phony. Just because the twist is the big dance, they put out a Ray Charles twist album."

"Brother Ray don't do no twist," Hubie said. "But it's got that great '*Tell the Truth*' on it." Hubie and Pete sang along to the song. "*You know you can make me do what you want me to.*"

Hubie addressed the bathroom door. "And speaking of the truth, hey, Dunnigan, how *are* you doing with Lorraine?" There was only the sound of water running in the bathroom. "Did you make your move?"

"Naw, you guys don't know nothing about women's psychology."

"Why are you bothering with her?" Hubie said. "Her parents won't let her go out until senior prom night. That'll be her first date. You know, Sara was talking about you, Shone," Hubie continued. "She still thinks you're going to take her to the senior prom, man."

Shone came out of the bathroom, his dark hair wet, his eyes red. He was sniffing. He walked in a flatfooted shuffle, scuffing the rug as he crossed the room to the window.

"Maybe he wasn't jerking off—he was crying. Look at those eyes," Pete said. "Oh, Lorraine."

"It's my allergies." Shone turned away from the picture window and took a tissue from the Kleenex box on the table. "I gotta get alone with Lorraine. My allergies always get worse when I go without sex."

"Jesus, you are the most neurotic bastard I know," Hubie said. "Pete, look at him, he likes to be called neurotic. No wonder why he reads all his sister's college psych books—he's reading about *himself*. No lie, you got a girl, you could go out with Sara, and what do you do? You start chasing some religious nut, whose parents don't even let her date."

"I'm working on that," Shone said. "I take her home every day that I can, and I go talk to the mother. Now, Pete, you got it set up for Cheri's swim party Friday?"

"Yeah, yeah, yeah, I got the key to the guesthouse. I made a copy and returned the original. I'll give it to you the day of the party. But, Shone, I don't know how you got this key, okay? That's going to be my version. Cheri would skin me if she found out."

"Lorraine will go to Cheri's party, and we'll slip away." Shone took a few swipes at his hair with his comb, viewing the results in the reflection of the window. "Look, guys, seriously. You got to help me with this. Now, when we go to see the communists, I'm going to count on you guys to distract old Q-Tip."

"Sure, we'll hit Cupat in his sweater-vest pocket and send up a smoke screen of chalk dust," Pete said.

"You ever think how much chalk dust there is in that moldy old green sweater?" Hubie wondered. "He never has it cleaned."

Shone glanced down at his Wedgies. Plucking another Kleenex out of the box, he knelt on the rug, touched the Kleenex to his tongue, and began to polish the fat tip of his right shoe. He smiled at his shoe tip, seeing his reflection. "Now, if I get my chance, I'm going to make my move at the university. There'll be a spare room around somewhere. That's all I'll need. And if I can't make it *then*, I'll do the groundwork for the swim party at Cheri's that night. See, you gotta think sequentially. You guys don't know how to think sequentially." Shone sniffed again. He stood up and dabbed at his eyes with the clean edge of the used Kleenex. "I got to get rid of these allergies, and there's only one way."

IN THE FRONT ROOM of the Onderdonk house, Lorraine watched her mother start to read the field-trip form. "It's just a field trip, Mom, to the university for Mr. Cupat's class." She handed her mother a pen. "I was thinking that I would like to see the university anyway," she said. "I hear they have a good dental assistant's program, and maybe I could stop by and get some brochures."

"Who is going with you?" Mrs. Onderdonk signed the form. "I hope it's not just Mr. Cupat."

"Oh, Mrs. Glaubinger's going." Lorraine carefully folded the paper in half. "She'll be chaperone."

"Is your friend Shone going?"

"He's in the class. I don't think he will be going. He's not interested in politics. He's more interested in religion." Lorraine turned away from her mother. "Besides, this will happen Friday, and he'll need to be working on the graduation address."

"Oh, he's giving an address at graduation," Mrs. Onderdonk said.

"Yes, they are breaking up the speeches into categories. Jim Glustich's talk will be called Governmentally, and then someone will be doing one called Scientifically, and Shone will be giving one on Socially. He's awfully interested in psychology," Lorraine said.

"Oh, dear, I didn't know *that* about him."

"There's nothing wrong with knowing about the *mind*, mother," Lorraine said. "That's not a sin, you know. The Bible is all about how people think, too."

"Is that what they've been telling you at Young Life?"

"Oh, Mother! You are so old-fashioned sometimes."

MR. CUPAT LOOKED out the window and sighed. "Okay, we're going to have to waste a day on this. I know this is as boring as you think it is, since we have already gone over this, but the school board wants us to review this, because *someone's parents complained.* But, be that as it may, we will go over it *again.*"

He turned to the classroom. "The way the communist cells work," he sighed. Hooking his thumbs in his sweater vest pockets, Mr. Cupat cocked his head to one side and regarded the acoustic tiles in the ceiling. Someone had thrown a pencil up and stuck it into one of the tiles. He followed the probable path of the pencil's flight, and his gaze rested on Shone Dunnigan, who was sitting with both hands under the desk top.

"They never let the right hand know what the left is doing. It's a technique for sealing off the various members of the cell from one another. As a technique it is invaluable." Mr. Cupat picked up his cigarette holder from his desk top and regarded its round empty mouth.

"Now, the way it works is this way. Say someone asks you if they can use your office. They never say what for. You know the person, perhaps they know a friend, and you say sure. Then they get some-one else to go there, not the friend who asked for the office but someone else entirely. So if the F.B.I. asks you and you say X asked to use the office, X will say, 'I never went there that night, I don't know who could have used the office.' And the people who come there—they don't know the person who really owns the office. They are all sealed off from each other."

"That's cool."

Mr. Cupat looked toward the back of the room. "What, Dunnigan?"

"That's good psychology," Shone said. "No one feels guilty, right? They're just doing favors for each other, but they don't know what for."

"Well, they can *say* that. Actually, everyone knows what is going on. They can claim as many alibis as they want," Mr. Cupat sniffed. "We know better. They have signals too. Say one guy is wearing a hat. That means the meeting has been held. Doesn't mean any-thing to anyone else. They have these *signals* and they stand for whole plots. People, you've got to understand that those people think differently than we do. The communists are involved in a web of deceit. Constant conspiracy."

Mr. Cupat nodded, thinking over his words. "We have a democracy, so we don't have to think that way. So, I won't bother going into the interrogation techniques—how they corner you, and one person poses as your friend while the other browbeats you. Or how you are denied access to colleges if you don't toe the party line. They call you in, one by one, and beat down your resistance with accusations, innuendoes—does everyone know what they are? Sooner or later, everyone joins the Party, they have to— absolutely no choice. Now, we have a choice. We take into account human nature. That's why the capitalist system works for all of us. We have human nature on our side."

MRS. GLAUBINGER was a tall horsy woman with a large hooked nose. She loomed above the front rows of her classes, her hands on the back of her broad hips. In her classes no one sat in the front seats, because she always jammed her legs against them and leaned over as she talked, shoving the chairs back. And with her nose she sniffed out immorality and deviations from social norms. She finished her lecture: "And tomorrow I'll be coming along on the field trip to the university."

"Oh! Mrs. Glaubinger."

She smiled. "Yes, Lorraine."

"I think you forgot you have to be at the prom committee."

"I do?"

"They said you would be there." Cheri added. "They are planning the chaperones for the night cruise."

Mrs. Glaubinger straightened up and walked back to her desk. She flipped her desk calendar over one page. "The next day is missing," she said. "I know I wrote that down. That's funny. I remember I checked this when Mr. Cupat asked me to chaperone and saw that my day was free. I must have been looking at the wrong day, Saturday. Well, I'll have to go to the cruise meeting. I'm sure Mr. Cupat is more than adequate for the task of chaperoning you seniors to the university."

FRIDAY MORNING, Mrs. Onderdonk saw Lorraine going out of her room with a big paper bag in her arms. "What's that?" she asked.

"Oh, just some laundry, for P.E. class." Lorraine picked a white sweatshirt off the top and waved it at her mother as she walked by.

Mrs. Onderdonk regarded her daughter's outfit: the long wool skirt and white blouse and brown jacket. "You're wearing nylons today?" she said, eyeing Lorraine's smooth girdled waist with approval.

"Yes, we're going on that field trip for current events class. To the university? You remember that? Anyway, I was going to check into the dental assistant's program there and see what they have. I gotta run. Bye."

Mrs. Onderdonk held out her arms. Lorraine paused at the door, returned to her mother, and gave her a little hug, scooting the paper bag up into the crook of her left arm. Mrs. Onderdonk bussed her left ear and peered down into the mouth of the sack. Under the sweatshirt on top was a layer of white sweat socks.

"G'bye, Mom. I'll be going to Cheri Evers' swim party after school," she said. "I'll be home about ten. Cheri said she would drive me home." Lorraine went out and got into the car waiting at the curb, throwing the paper bag in the back seat.

Mrs. Onderdonk watched as Lorraine's friend, Millie Mac-Donald, drove away. Suddenly Mrs. Onderdonk remembered that it was the end of the school year and Lorraine wouldn't have any more P.E. classes. She went back into her sewing room thinking about that.

Across the sewing table was Lorraine's senior-prom dress. Mrs. Onderdonk looked at the dress and noticed that it had been moved. She checked and saw that the light green thread was no longer on the machine. Instead, there was a spool of brown thread. Mrs. Onderdonk frowned. Then she saw the note.

> *Mom, had to repair skirt hem.*
> *Sorry, no time to replace.*

Mrs. Onderdonk smiled. Such a thoughtful girl. Sometimes she didn't know why she was worried about her daughter.

In shone's red Sunbeam convertible, Hubie and Pete watched as Shone and Lorraine came out of the shadow of the school breezeway into the parking lot. Hubie had loaned Shone his mother's 1961 Rambler station wagon so he could drive some of the class to the university, and Shone had given Hubie his Sunbeam. The real reason they had traded was that the Nash's seats folded down into a bed. As Lorraine got into the Nash, Pete and Hubie talked about the switch she'd pulled after school, changing from a long skirt with a girdle to a short skirt. They watched Shone bend over the Nash door, chatting with Lorraine and looking at her bare legs.

"I can't believe it," Pete said. "Earlier today I thought, No way is Shone gonna peel that girdle off Onderdonk."

Hubie agreed. "Look at Lorraine give Shone another look at her legs."

"And Glaubinger couldn't come along, so that means on the drive back from the university, Shone'll drop everyone off first, and she'll be *unchaperoned*," Pete said. "Look at him staring, how can he be so obvious?"

"She doesn't look like she minds," Hubie laughed. "I bet more than Shone's nose is running."

"Allergies, my ass," Pete said. "The only sinus condition Dunnigan's got is below his navel."

THE LECTURE was held in a large library room at the university. The seniors hushed as Mr. Cupat ushered them in. All around the polished wood molding were leering gargoyle heads, their faces shining in the light from the windows above. Eight rows of wooden folding chairs were divided by a center aisle. In the front of the hall an oak library table had three chairs behind it and a microphone on top with a stack of paper. Mr. Cupat went up to the table and returned with some handout sheets. On them were brief biographies of the two Canadian communists, followed by the name of the moderator, a professor at the university.

On the ride to Seattle, Shone had been quiet, letting Glustich do the talking. Glustich was riding in the front seat, and he wouldn't shut up the whole trip. In back, Pete guessed that his leg against Lorraine's newly bared leg was the reason for that outpouring. At the university, Shone had neatly divided himself and Lorraine from the rest, disappearing down the hall as Mr. Cupat herded the other seniors into their seats.

The moderator came in, a short man in a dark brown suit with a tie that was so badly knotted that it looked as if it was strangling him. He looked thoroughly uncomfortable, fussing with his papers in front of the room, adjusting the microphone and tapping on it, before he nodded at the two communists coming down the side aisle. The first one was short and the second quite tall. The taller man was lame in the left foot. He dragged it a little with every step. The shorter communist was plump with a wild mane of shaggy black hair. There was only one thing they had in common. Both communists were wearing green sweater vests under their sport coats.

The moderator plicked the mike once with his finger and went into his introduction. Then the short one stood up and started to talk, idly fingering the right-hand pocket in his sweater vest, beginning what turned out to be a long analysis of capitalism.

When shone brought the Rambler back at two o'clock, Pete and Hubie cornered him up in Hubie's room. Locking the bathroom so Shone couldn't hide in there, Hubie hassled him to tell what had happened but Shone refused. Only after Pete gave him the key to Cheri's guesthouse, for the Senior girls' swim party that afternoon, did Shone start talking.

"So you snuck out of the lecture, and you and Lorraine were in the room alone," Pete prompted.

"Yeah, and I locked the door. There were a lot of books at the other end, see, and two easy chairs there, stuffed ones. You know. So we drifted over there and, uh, I sat down."

"He sat down!" Hubie howled. "No lie, I would have made my move."

"No, see, that's your style. That's not my style. So, I sat down. And she stood there, and I reached over and touched her skirt, the hem, and said something about how nice looking it was." Shone tilted his head to one side and looked out the window. He sighed, put his hand under his sweater and rubbed his belly. "So she sat down in my lap, and we made out for a while."

"Naw! One compliment on her new skirt and she fell in your lap and started to make out?" Hubie exploded. "Lorraine No-Go Onderdonk?"

"You don't know women, man. She knew what I was saying." Shone sniffed and took out a Kleenex.

"He didn't get diddley, Pete. Look at him—his nose is still running," Hubie said.

"So is that *all*?" Pete prompted.

"No, that's all I'm saying. Wait until after tonight. Then I'll file a whole report."

"Aw, you prick teaser," Hubie complained. "I was getting *hot*, man. Come on, let's get him, Pete."

Pete and Hubie grabbed Shone and threw him down on the couch, and Hubie mussed up his hair a bit. Pete handed Hubie a pillow and Hubie began to smother him. Shone struggled until he complained about his asthma. Pete told Shone they would let him up if he told them everything, one detail at a time. From under the pillow, Shone said okay, so they got off him.

"Don't muss up the hair." Shone checked his reflection in the window, sniffed and tossed the Kleenex at the light fixture in the ceiling. He shrugged. "So, you know, we made out a little, and then I lobbed it out."

"*What!*"

"*No!*"

"*Lorraine?*" Hubie was outraged.

"How could you do that, you weasel?" Pete yelled at Shone.

"I love her," Shone said. "And who *else* are you gonna lob it out for, if you don't lob it out for the one you love?"

Hubie and Pete slowly collapsed on the couch in fake shock. Hubie shook his head wearily. "Well, you gotta admit, Pete, he's got a point there," Hubie sighed. "But, geez, what an awful way to say it."

Shone held up one of his big feet. "Do you really think I'll get out of the draft because of my flat feet?" he said, eyeing his long black Wedgies. "They're not that flat, are they?"

"Wait a minute, I can't *believe* that," Pete said. "You didn't go any farther?"

"No."

"Why not?" Hubie yelled.

Shone shook his head. "Got to give her some time to think about it. Tonight at the swim party. You guys get to messing around as a distraction, and Lorraine and me'll slip off. She'll be ready tonight." Shone took out his comb and began to rearrange his hair.

CHERI EVERS' FATHER was living with Beryl Mains. She owned a ranch house by Clover Creek. White with green trim, the house was fronted by a big well-tended lawn encircled by a white slat fence. The asphalt driveway ended in a two-story garage, and to its side was a duplex guesthouse with a peaked roof. Between the guesthouse and the garage was a concrete path meandering across a large grassy back yard to a bridge over Clover Creek. In back of the creek was a rectangular swimming pool with patios at either end.

When Pete and Hubie drove up in Shone's Sunbeam, the Nash Rambler was parked in front. As they walked around the corner of the garage, they saw at the north end of the pool two tables with lawn chairs grouped around the diving board. Some senior girls in swimsuits were watching one another dive off the board, yelling out scores as if they were judges at a diving event.

"Pete, I told you Shone wasn't going to go home. He came straight here, the horny mother." Hubie pointed at the guesthouse. "I bet he's in there with Lorraine."

Pia Swift, Hubie's girlfriend, saw them first. She was wearing a maroon one-piece bathing suit that showed off her long brown legs. She headed for them. Behind her Pete saw Cheri with a clipboard in her hand, writing down the scores. Millie MacDonald dove off the board and landed in a huge splash of water.

All the other girls laughed. "Give Millie a three!" There was a roar of approval.

"Three then," Cheri said. "Next!"

Pia came up to Hubie and Pete. "Well, what brings you boys around?"

Hubie looked Pia up and down and then sighed. "Ohhhhh, you know," he said, and he pretended to eyeball the other senior girls.

Pia jabbed him in the ribs. "Keep your eyes to yourself," she teased.

"Where's that weasel Shone?"

Pia put her fingertip up to her lips. She nodded toward the house. "Lorraine and Shone went in the house. All the other girls think they're gone to the store." Pia took Hubie by the arm and began to lead him toward the pool. "No one can stay the night except me," she said. "Everyone else has stuff to do on Saturday. So it'll just be me and Cheri here."

"Well, we'll keep you company tonight," Pete said.

"You better," Pia said. "It gets dark out here quick."

"Hey, hey," Hubie said, disengaging his arm. "Where you taking us?"

Pia laughed and bumped Hubie with her hip. "What's the matter? Scared?"

"I ain't going over there with all those women."

"Hey, bring the guys over!" Cheri yelled at them. "We need some good help!" Cheri handed the clipboard to another girl and came down the path. "I'll bring them back, girls," she shouted. "Then you *all* can have them."

The other girls laughed and whooped. "Bring them over here!" they yelled.

"Hey, what is going on here?" Hubie joked. "This is a conspiracy, Pete. We better make a run for it."

"Oh, no." Pia grabbed Hubie's arm. "We *need* you."

"Hi, there," Cheri said, hooking Pete's arm. She rubbed up his side with her still damp suit, leaving a long wet streak on his shirt and jeans. "Like that? The girls are bored, come on and give us a hand."

"Or anything else you've got," Pia added.

"You guys can play spin the bottle with us. The winners get to go with you guys into the guesthouse. We're not the jealous types, are we, Pia?"

"Hey, great," Hubie joked. He glanced at Pete.

"If you start, though," Cheri said sweetly, "you have to play with *all* of us. Come on."

"What's got into you girls?" Pete said.

"It's the end of high school. The senior girls all want to have a little fun." Cheri pretended she was going to unbutton Pete's shirt.

"Wait a minute." Pete twisted away from Cheri. "I think we're outnumbered, Hubie."

"Well, you always talk so big," Cheri said, poking Pete in the stomach. "Now here's your chance. I don't mind. Share and share alike, right, Pia?" They both burst out laughing.

"Too bad you guys didn't bring your swimsuits, but that's okay, we'll take off ours too!" Pia and Cheri both laughed again, as Hubie looked uncomfortably back at Pete.

A car pulled into the driveway. Pete turned away from Cheri and peered between the garage and the guesthouse. Behind the Sunbeam and the Rambler he could see the right side of Glustich's green 1955 Plymouth. "Oh, balls, here comes Mr. Student Body," Pete said.

"Pete, send him away," Cheri said.

"I thought you girls were ready for some fun? Gluey's great fun."

"No, I'm serious," Cheri said, turning Pete around. "You've got to get him out of here." Cheri pulled his head down. "Lorraine and Shone are in the house. Get Jim out of here!" She shoved Pete toward the garage.

Pete walked backward, holding his palms out. "Okay, okay. We walked into a regular fast deal," Pete said to Hubie.

When they came around the garage, Glustich was coming down the back steps of the house. "What's going on here? The house is locked."

"Just the girls having a good time without us, James," Pete said.

"You're uninvited. We're leaving too. I just stopped by here with Hubie to drop something off." He touched Jim's sleeve.

Glustich pointed at Shone's Sunbeam convertible. "Where's Shone?" He craned his neck and looked at the pool. "Lorraine around?"

"Shone's not here," Hubie said. "I drove the Sunbeam over here."

"Who's driving the Rambler then?"

"I am," Pete said. "Hubie's taking the Sunbeam back to Shone. Now, Cheri asked me to ask you to leave, Glustich. Her dad said no guys were allowed."

Jim shook Pete's hand off his arm. "What'd you think of the lecture today? You saw what I saw, didn't you?"

"A lot of boring dopes?"

"No, the *sweater signals*." Jim seemed incredulous that Pete hadn't noticed. "You don't think that was just chance, do you? I always thought maybe Mr. Cupat was just a dupe, but I don't know now. To tell the truth, I didn't know it was as widespread as this. Man, I told."

Pete was outraged. "*I told*. What the hell does that mean? I told?"

"Come on, Dwyer, you were there. The sweater signals."

"Are you serious? Q-Tip wears that sweater because he thinks it makes him look like a college professor."

"Oh, sure," Jim said. "That's what he'd *like* you to think."

Pete squared around in front of Glustich and tapped him on his arm. "Glustich, am I going to have to hammer you, or are you going to leave?"

"Hey, you don't have to get shitty. I was leaving." Glustich got in the green Plymouth. He started it and backed the car out of the driveway. "You'll be a dupe, too, Dwyer," he yelled.

"That jack-off," Pete said. "He thinks Mr. Cupat is a communist now. I bet his John Birch father is going to cause trouble."

"No lie, I am sure glad I'm going in the Marines and leaving guys like him. Jack-offs like Gluey wouldn't last a day in the gyrenes."

Hubie turned to go back to the pool. On the patio there was laughter and shrieks from the women. "Hey, those chicks seem a little crazy. Maybe we ought to make sure Gluey really left." Hubie shrugged. "You think Cheri was kidding about that spin the bottle? Hey, I got an idea." Hubie pointed at the house. "Let's ditch Shone here without any wheels." Hubie laughed at the idea. "Let's split on him. Leave him with all these women and see what *he* does."

TUESDAY MORNING, Mr. Cupat came in late to the current events class and went straight to his desk. The class hum dropped to lower and lower, while Mr. Cupat tapped his cigarette holder on the desk top until there was only the *clink-clink*.

"People, or children, be that as it may," he said, "I guess it is time to remind you again what democracy is all about." Walking over to the corner of the room, he tilted his head and regarded the poster of the Four Freedoms with the sunburst portrait of Franklin Delano Roosevelt in the middle of it. "In a democracy we don't have to sneak around, we don't have to plot or inform on each other," he said to the poster. "We have the ballot box and freedom of speech."

Mr. Cupat faced the class. "Now, I knew I was going to get some heat for taking you to that lecture on Friday." He eyed the acoustic tiles on the ceiling. "But I didn't know that an attack was going to be mounted on me personally. But, as I have said before and will say again, if you can't stand the heat, get out of the kitchen." Marching slowly back to his desk, his right index finger massaged the cleft of his fat chin. He stopped and then sniffed once. "It would clear the air if we discussed what was said by these communists. Anyone want to give me a brief description of that lecture?"

Starting with the back, Mr. Cupat viewed the class, row by row. When he got to the front row, he nodded to Jim Glustich. "Jim, you're a student leader, an honor student. You're supposed to know about politics. What did you hear at that lecture?"

"Well, I don't know about the rest of you, but what I heard was a bunch of gobbley-de-gook."

Mr. Cupat regarded the top of Jim's crew cut. "Gobbley-de-gook," he repeated. "You heard gobbley-de-gook. That's an interesting analysis, Jim. What kind of gobbley-de-gook was it?"

"What kind? Why, it was confusing gobbley-de-gook, that's what they always resort to. That's part of the plot. They get you confused, and then they move in on your mind, brainwashing it. In my opinion, you can't even *listen* to that stuff."

"And that's what you learned?"

"I learned you can't trust them. Those commies plot all the time. They're not like us."

Mr. Cupat stepped back. "Well, that's Mr. Glustich's opinion. Does anyone else have any other opinions about the lecture?" He

walked over to the windows and opened one. "No?" he said, turning. "Well, I guess you've let Mr. Glustich here represent your opinion for you. Am I right? If that's so, then I have nothing more to
add." He leaned against the window and looked out. "You can go
back to whatever you were doing before I came in."

AFTER HER DAD and Beryl went to bed that night, Cheri and Pete
watched television in the living room. They both listened for her
father's snore from the bedroom down the hall. When they heard
it, Pete got up, turned down the TV, and closed the hallway door.
He held up two fingers to indicate that he had heard Beryl sleeping
too. He sat down on the big white couch and put his arm around
Cheri, and they kissed long and slow. Pete nudged her, and she
reclined on the corner pillow, and he eased his hip under her right
thigh. The TV flickered in the opposite corner, the sound turned
halfway down, so they could hear if anyone got up in the master
bedroom.

"So what happened?" Pete asked in a low voice.

"Glaubinger didn't call *me* into the counseling office. She threatened the other girls with withdrawing their college recommendations."

"Who ratted on you guys?"

"Probably one of the senior girls I didn't invite. Anyway, Lorraine
wasn't one. Mrs. Glaubinger assumed that she didn't have anything
to hide." Cheri winked at Pete. "Besides, old Globe Banger checked
up, and all the girls here knew that Lorraine was home by ten on
Friday night." Cheri giggled. "We dropped Shone off before Lorraine. Shone was *tired*." She poked Pete in the belly. "Why didn't
you guys come back that night?"

Pete ignored her. "I bet Glustich ratted. He sicced some parents
on Mr. Cupat about the communists. Q-Tip was pissed. Today in
class he made a total fool out of Gluey."

"Oh, who cares? We're all going to graduate in a few weeks, and
then we won't have to see any of them again."

"That's easy for you to say, Cheri. You have a job waiting for you.
You don't have to get a college recommendation from Globe
Banger like some of those girls do."

"It's none of her business what we did at my party. *Nothing* happened. Especially since you and Hubie chickened out." Cheri jabbed Pete. "You never came back. You scared?"

Pete squirmed away from her. "No."

"Noooo," Cheri imitated him. "You guys talk big. But when it comes to performance."

"We thought we'd leave that sex maniac Shone to handle all of you. And how can you say nothing happened, huh? What about Shone and Lorraine? How long were they in the house, anyway?"

Cheri gave Pete her best innocent look. "Why, I think they were in here long enough. It's none of *your* business."

"Well, Hubie and I will get him alone and find out what happened. I expect Shone and Lorraine will be hot prom dates."

"She's not going to the prom with Shone. She's going with Jim."

"Gluey? What the hell was she messing around with Shone for?"

"Oh, you know, experience." Cheri gave out a sigh. "I mean, that's all Shone is good for. All the girls know *that*. She wanted a little experience before any serious dating. She figured she had a lot of catching up to do." Cheri gave Pete a nudge with her thigh.

Pete felt himself getting half-hard in his pants. Cheri laughed as she felt it. "Pete, I wish you could see your face right now."

"Ah, it's not that." Pete was blushing. "Come on."

Cheri pulled away from him. "It's okay if your buddies take out Sigrid for a little fun, right, but if one of us does anything like that, oh no. You men are such hypocrites."

"I can't wait to tell Shone." Pete pulled Cheri back, pushing himself against her. "You set this whole thing up, didn't you?"

"You *bet* we did. We even fixed old Glaubinger's calendar so Lorraine could be alone with Shone on the trip to the university." Cheri giggled at Pete's expression. "You're really shocked, aren't you? Look at you." She picked up a hand mirror off the end table. "You're beet red. Look." She pushed the mirror up toward his face.

"Hey, come on." Pete brushed it away. They struggled and Pete pinned Cheri down on the couch, holding her right arm above the end table. Underneath him, Cheri wiggled, and Pete felt himself getting hot as her skirt rode up.

"Look, look." She pushed the mirror toward him. Seeing how red his face was, Pete blushed even more.

"Look," Cheri said. "You don't want to see, do you?"

SHONE WANDERED BACK into Hubie's bathroom. He tilted his head sideways and looked at the left side of his hair in the mirror. Then he took out a comb and took a few swipes. "Nothing much happened."

"Nothing much happened," Hubie said, giving Pete the elbow. "I know one thing that happened, and Shone doesn't know it."

"Maybe Shone would like to know. Who you taking to the senior prom, Romeo?"

"Ummmmmmm." Shone shuffled out of the bathroom, crossed the room, and stood at the window. "I dunno."

"Well, you're not going with Lorraine," Pete said.

"Yeah, she's going with Gluey," Hubie said.

They watched Shone's face as he turned to them. "Oh, yeah?" he said.

"You know what else? She only went out with you to get a little quick experience," Pete said.

"You were just a quickie for her, Shone, baby," Hubie added.

Shone thought about that for a moment. Then he sighed, stuck his right hand under his shirt, and rubbed his belly. "That's cool. I can understand that."

"Look at that phony, Pete! 'That's cool,' he says. Come on, Shone, where's all the love you were feeling, huh?"

"Well, I can understand that. I mean, she came to the right guy, didn't she? You guys are just jealous, that's all," Shone said. "She didn't come to *you* guys."

"Wellllll," Hubie cleared his throat. "Well, yeah, but, uh, me and Pete are going steady with Pia and Cheri."

MR. CUPAT could tell that his wife was gone when the driveway gravel stopped crunching. Scooting back, he pulled out a small green Coleman ice chest from under his desk and slid the chest top off. He eased an eight ounce Country Club Malt Liquor can out of the cardboard carton of twelve. After he replaced the lid of the ice chest he punched a hole in the Country Club can.

Since Mr. Cupat's study was unheated save for a portable electric heater behind him, the malt liquor was slightly chilled. He took the first few sips and read in his unfinished Ph.D. thesis about a boom logging town. When he got to the page where the manuscript abruptly stopped in midsentence, he drank off the rest of the

can, took his yellow legal pad over to the couch alongside his bookcase, and stretched out. After four notes to himself, he fell asleep
and dreamed of being in an oak-paneled classroom. From the class,
a deep masculine voice kept asking him where his place was, and
he turned the pages of his lecture notes, unable to find where he
was. The pages of notes seemed typed, but each time he looked
closer, the typing changed to student handwriting.

The sound of crunching gravel woke him up. As his wife's car
door slammed shut, he dropped the Country Club can in a wastebasket. Reaching up on the top shelf, he selected a fat pile of
graded American history tests and dropped them on top of the can,
the heavy paper making a loud and satisfying thump. As his wife,
Alicia, came up the steps to his study, Mr. Cupat waited for her
knock.

"Here you go," she said. From the large Safeway paper bag, she
took out a six-pack of Rainier beer and handed it to him. "Dinner
will be in a half hour. Did you get a start?"

"Oh yeah. I've got the engine cranked. I think this is the summer
when I'll get at it good."

"Good." Alicia lifted her head a little to see what page number
his manuscript was open to. "Did you dig up any more on Mrs. G.'s
behind-the-scenes work?"

"Oh, she's the one who caused the trouble. Glustich's dad raised
a ruckus but not much of one. Mrs. G. was still smarting over that
senior girls' swim party, and so she used my field trip for a smoke
screen to cover up what she imagined was her own screw-up."

"That old horse thinks she's in charge of the senior girls' virginity
since she did such a bad job on her own."

"Now, Alicia, you don't know that for sure." He took out the
church key and opened a Rainier. "That was hearsay."

"Horse pucky it was," she said. "There's a reason why she's such
a prude. And I talked to her sister from Iowa once at a church
reception, and I don't even want to repeat what she said about
Mrs. G. She's just a guilty small-town snitch."

Mr. Cupat handed the six-pack back to his wife. "Take this in the
house. I won't need but one of these."

"I just hope you get out of that high school and into the junior
college."

"This will get me out." He patted his manuscript.

"Then I won't have to buy your beer for you any more," Alicia said, stepping back out the door. "I can't believe we have to do this."

"Well, you know how these Lutherans are. Word gets around. But I got this communist bunk squelched. Everyone knows now why Mrs. G. kicked up such a fuss. Those senior girls came to me in tears, and I had to straighten things out with Glaubinger."

"Those poor girls. Threatening them with canceling her college recommendations. The nerve of her. You just have to get *out* of that place, Earl," Alicia said. "You're not a hypocrite like they are." She turned away from him. "It's fried chicken tonight, lots of it, so bring your appetite. You can have it for lunch tomorrow, when you take a break. I'll be at Puyallup all day, so you won't be bothered."

As the door shut, Mr. Cupat stared at the manuscript open on his desk. He took a good pull on the Rainier and flipped the manuscript over to the title page. The typed title had been crossed out. To the side, penciled sample titles were crossed out in a long gray column down the right hand margin. Mr. Cupat took up a pencil from his desk and wrote in the empty left-hand margin.

WIKIUP
Wicked City of the Pacific Northwest
Or a Lost Dream

AFTER SHONE LEFT, Pete and Hubie turned on a Ray Charles record and smoked a few cigarettes. They talked about Lorraine and Shone. "I don't know why we're spending all this time talking about Lorraine," Hubie said. "I mean, like old Q-Tip says, think about it. She's sorta nothing special. I don't envy Shone one bit."

"In a couple weeks we'll probably never see her again."

"Hey, talking about people nosing around. I gotta thank you, Pete. That was swell advice you gave me. You know, the guys, Rob and Shone and Flipper, all bugging me about what was going on between me and Pia. One time I'd tell them we were going at it all the time, and then another time I'd say she was shutting me out cold and ask them what I should do. After a while they stopped asking. You know, when I'd tell them me and Pia were at it all the time, they thought I was bullshitting. And when I said she was shutting me down, then they didn't want to hear that because it reminded them of their girls. No one leaves you alone unless they think they know exactly what you're doing."

"Look at Cheri and me. Remember when we first started dating?" Pete said. "Everyone thought we were perfect, just because both of us have divorced parents. Then everybody expects us to stay together, like we got to redeem our parents."

"Hey, Pete, what kind of safes you buying?"

"Forex."

"Those come in those big blue plastic things—can't put em in your wallet that way, can you?"

"No, but three packs of Trojans makes your wallet look like it's got a newspaper in it. I put Forex in my change pocket of my jeans. That way they won't fall out. Sometimes we get carried away, and I don't want to run out. I don't know why we got them in our wallets, anyway, do you?"

"Started in junior high, remember? You got that blackened ring on the inside of your wallet that lets everyone know you got one, in case a miracle happens." Hubie laughed. "Yeah, Pia's that way, too. The first one's hot and fast, and the second one's a lot slower, but if you sit around and talk, you know, and then, hey," Hubie laughed, "gotta have that third backup."

Hubie looked away from Pete and inspected the front of a Jan and Dean record. "Nothing happened at Cheri's that night. I mean," he said to the album cover, "except for Shone and Lorraine."

"You think they really got it on? I don't."

"Naw, not all the way." Hubie looked up from the records. "You know, Pia says that when Beryl and her dad get married in June and go on their honeymoon, Cheri's gonna invite us both over for a weekend. Right before I go in the gyrenes. I thought her dad and Beryl were already married. Cheri always called Beryl her stepmom."

"Oh, that was to keep people from talking. Cheri said something about a weekend to me, too."

"How we gonna keep that from the other guys?"

"Hey, we'll be out of school by then. We won't be seeing everyone every day."

"You feeling the way I'm feeling? You know, it'll be the first time me and Pia haven't had to sneak."

"I know. You get used to sneaking around."

"No lie. It's kinda exciting to sneak, actually. I don't know if I'd like it as much if it wasn't sneaky. Sometimes I think about what married life must be like—going home to the same old stuff," Hubie said. "I guess it's not so much that, cause I mean she's seeing the same old stuff *coming* home too. But you see people together after they're married and no lie, what a change."

"Yeah, it's like they've *said* everything to each other."

"I'd hate to be quiet like that," Hubie said. "Like you're both dead from the neck up. But you don't have to worry, Pete. Your girl's really something else. Wish I was in your shoes. She's got that civil-service job, so she can move down to California when you go to college, right?"

"We're going to wait on that. See how I like the school and playing ball down there."

"Aw, she's got a job, you got a four-year ride. You get hitched to her, nothing bad like that will happen to you guys."

"Cheri says this weekend'll be a going-away present for us both. I don't think they'll do it. They'll chicken out."

"Yeah, but what if they don't?"

"Hey, we'll just have to grin and bear it, huh, Hubie?" Pete said. "Cheri keeps saying it will be different sleeping in a bed together, instead of on the couch or in the car."

"I thought she was living in the guesthouse?"

"I don't know why we don't use that," Pete said. "She always jokes she's saving that for marriage."

"It'll be like being married to go to bed. Doesn't seem all that exciting to me, but then, I guess we'll find out. Waking up with them and all that." Hubie took the Ray Charles *Do The Twist* album out of its black and pink jacket.

"Put on 'Tell the Truth,' " Pete said. "I love it when Ray starts that scream."

"That's cool," Hubie said. He put the record on the turntable. "Ray is trying to find out the truth, and he's *gotta* give out that yell."

"Yeah, gotta—he's gotta howl a little, because it feels good just to be asking for it," Pete said.

"Yeah, no lie, but it hurts good, too, to know," Hubie said, laying the needle in the right groove on the record.

Pete and Hubie sang along. "*You know you can make me do what you want me to.*"

"*Tell the truth*," Ray came in. "*I want to know!*"

"Here he goes," Hubie said, as the song built to its climax. "Tell us the truth, Ray."

"*If I thought it would do any good*," the Raelets sang behind Ray. Ray Charles let out a long falsetto whoop.

"Yeah!" Pete said. "Here he goes."

"*Tell the truth, now, baby, every day, every night, and alllll the time, tell the truth.*"

"Awright!" Hubie shouted. "Here he goes again."

"*Who was that man you were with last night, baby, I want to know!*"

Pete and Hubie leaned their heads back and joined in, as Ray Charles gave out his howl for the truth.

The Ghost of the Senior Banquet

ON THE NIGHT of the senior banquet the tule fog was thick. As Pete stood beside the family 1955 Chevy station wagon, he couldn't see the end of the driveway. Pete started the engine, put the car in reverse, and began backing up. He watched in the rearview mirror until the neighbor's barbed wire fence appeared in the fog. Then he swung the car out onto the road, letting it roll backward a few feet before he put on the brakes. Using the car window for a mirror, Pete checked his haircut. Behind his reflection, a tuft of gray horsehair hung on the fence, as if a piece of the fog had been snagged on one of the barbs.

Pete drove down the road thinking about the pint of vodka his buddy Ripolla would give him at the restaurant. Pete was not excited about drinking vodka but about Cheri agreeing to have a drink with him after the senior banquet.

Cheri did not like drinking. Both her parents drank heavily and divorced because of booze. But since it was a special night, she promised to have one drink with Pete, and then, although she didn't say it, he knew that they would make love in the back of the station wagon.

This excited Pete because he had never made love while drinking. He was sure it would be a whole new experience for him.

The senior banquet itself promised nothing much. As their junior class president, Pete had to make a speech, dragging out old memories. Pete patted his sport-coat pocket to make sure that his three-by-five cards were there.

He had written down lists of events and the names of anyone who had helped with decorating the gym for the senior prom. That made good filler and took up a lot of time. He wished that he could tell the truth about the senior prom. He had run a five-day poker game with the guys, writing passes for them to get out of class. Pete had pocketed a lot of money, too. Whenever anyone came up with the change from buying crepe paper or butcher paper, he took the money back to the game. But he knew that he couldn't tell the truth.

Pete turned on Pipeline Road. The fog was so thick that Pete could only see about eight feet in front of the headlights. He was supposed to pick up two friends, Shone Dunnigan and Dean Hagenbarth. He had been thinking of picking Shone up first, but then he decided to pick up Dean, who lived out in the boonies on Pipeline Road. Pete used the tall grass growing up out of the ditches as a guide for the right side of the road. He knew he was close to Dean's house when he saw the red light on top of the water tower by Yellow Rock.

On the ride over to get Shone, Pacific Avenue had such thick fog blanketing it that Pete felt as if he were constantly driving into a fuzzy gray wall. It was even thicker than on Pipeline Road. At a break in the fog, Pete saw the stoplight at Ninety-Eighth Street. To the right, the Park 'n' Shop sign was a bright green, shining down on the intersection. A little farther down the road, the Lapenski Fuel Oil sign glowed in a red and yellow circle.

The light was red as Pete eased up behind a 1953 Mercury. The Mercury's left turn signal was blinking. The light turned to green, and the Mercury began to ease forward, waiting for an oncoming car to go by so it could turn left.

Pete took his foot off the brake pedal as the Mercury started its turn. The Mercury disappeared into the fog of Ninety-Eighth Street, and a logging truck plowed into Pete's station wagon from behind.

Pete only heard the air brakes behind him. The hiss came over his head, and then a huge suction took all the other sounds away. The next thing Pete knew, he was looking up at the ceiling of the station wagon. The ceiling looked strange.

His right leg felt strained and uncomfortable. Pete stared at the ceiling, unable to look down at his leg, because something about the ceiling was bothering him. Then he saw what it was. There was a huge crease, as if it had been hit from the inside by a giant ax. Then Pete noticed that he was lying on his back.

The seat had broken off from the floor. Pete tipped his body forward, and the seat tipped with him, and he saw why his leg had felt strained. His foot was still pressing down on the brake pedal. Pete grabbed the rearview mirror and pulled himself up into a sitting position.

Out the windshield he could see the telephone pole in front of Lapenski's fuel oil store. The chrome eagle on the hood looked as if it were touching the pole. Pete felt for the door handle, opened the door, and stepped out. It was completely quiet, and he could see the intersection where the grille of a logging truck was poking out of the drifting fog, the reflection of the stoplight changing from red to green in the shining chrome. Pete stepped back and looked at the station wagon. The whole back end was a deep dish of smashed metal, and the roof of the car was crammed up into a giant upside-down V. Long ribbons of blue paint were dangling off the wrinkled creases in the roof.

It didn't seem as if he had been in that wreck. There was only the hiss of air brakes in his memory. Pete stepped a few feet forward and looked at the Chevy's front end again and saw that he had come within an inch of ramming into the telephone pole. Pete vaguely understood that his reflex action of hitting the brake pedal as the seat broke had probably saved the car from ramming the pole. He looked back in the direction of the intersection where there was only fog. He seemed to be the only one around. Then the fog parted again, and Pete could see that the logging truck had no logs on it, only the second set of trailer wheels riding piggyback. *That saved me too*, Pete thought, as if adding up the pluses of the experience.

Then Shone was standing by the logging truck. Pete was startled. He couldn't remember picking up Shone. What was Shone doing here? Where was Dean? Pete looked back inside the station wagon. No one was inside.

Pete remembered that he had only planned to pick up Dean first. He had been thinking so hard about passing Yellow Rock, where he and Cheri would go after the banquet to drink the vodka and make love, that he had imagined the gravel on Pipeline Road and the red light on the tower and Yellow Rock as if they had actually happened. Another possibility occurred to Pete. He could have already been to the senior banquet, and he was only taking Shone home. But where was Cheri then? Pete's head began to hurt as he tried to sort out the possibilities.

Walking back toward the logging truck, Pete wondered if he really saw a driver standing there. Then he was suddenly standing next to the driver. Pete was sure that he had taken only two steps. He looked back, but his wrecked station wagon was covered with fog. Pete checked the truck driver closely. The man was wearing a leather vest, and the tassles on it were shaking as he talked. Pete couldn't hear what the man's mouth was saying, so he watched the tassles closely. The tassles seemed to be trying to tell him something. Pete realized that it wasn't the man talking that was making the tassles shake—it was the man's fright. So that was what the tassles were saying: *fear*.

Pete turned back toward the station wagon again, but there was only fog. He thought about whether or not he had driven the station wagon that night. When he turned to ask the driver if it was a blue 1955 Chevrolet that he had hit, Pete found a highway patrolman alongside the truck driver.

The driver of the logging truck was talking to the patrolman. Pete wondered if the driver could be drunk, because he was still shaking so badly he looked drunk. The highway patrolman only said a few words, even though his mouth looked as if it were making whole sentences. Pete couldn't understand the few words that he heard.

Pete worried that he might not be able to get to the senior banquet that night if this kept up. He imagined the Top of the Ocean restaurant. Down on the Tacoma waterfront, it must be locked in with fog by now too, and then the fog parted, and Pete found himself standing in front of the gangplank leading up to the restaurant.

The Top of the Ocean was an old converted ferry boat, and in the thick fog the giant porthole in the bow of the boat-restaurant was glowing bright yellow. The porthole seemed like a giant yellow eye. Pete walked up the gangplank into the restaurant, pausing to stare up at that giant unblinking eye.

Inside, the tables were covered with bright white tablecloths. People in sport coats and shiny dresses were milling around. Flowers were pinned to the women's straps. A woman in a pink-white gown came up to Pete and took him by the arm.

"He's a little shaky, but I like my men that way," she said. Everyone around them laughed. Pete looked closely at her. He didn't know who she was. She seemed familiar.

Pete let her take him to a long table in the front of the room. She sat him down and then left. Pete noticed that other people were sitting down at the long table too. Some nodded and said things to him, but a lot of words never got to Pete. Some seemed to hit his face but never got inside.

Pete looked down and noticed that there was now a plate of food in front of him. He looked at the food closely. Something didn't seem right. There were mashed potatoes with gravy—that was okay—and little brown rolls on top of a pile of peas—those were all right—but next to them was a Halloween mask. The Halloween mask was brown and scabby. Pete knew that this was a replica of the face of a famous Hollywood horror monster, but he could not remember which monster.

Pete glanced around and saw that the other people were not putting their masks on. They were eating them. Pete shuddered and left his alone, pushing it as far away from him as he could.

Then Shone appeared at a place down the table. A tall woman in a red dress was next to him. The woman had a huge nose. Pete watched the nose closely. The nose wiggled. It flattened and curved. The nose twitched, and the nostrils widened, and then it jiggled on down her face, zipping back up in an instant and starting the motion over again.

A performing nose? Pete was captivated by it. Then he remembered that he had to perform. Reaching into the inside pocket of his sport coat, he took out the three-by-five cards. He thought that he would look around, find a face that he thought went with the written name, and that would be just as good as saying the name. But there were so many more faces than names, the whole business seemed hopeless, and so Pete let the cards drop one by one under the table when no one was looking.

Shone was standing up. "Mrs. Glaubinger," he said to the woman with the performing nose, "a funny thing happened on the way over here."

There was a frightening shout of laughter. Pete saw the woman holding her performing nose, as if she were afraid it was going to do something bad. Pete panicked. He felt something was deeply wrong.

He looked down and saw that the three-by-five cards had all

climbed back up his legs and insinuated themselves back into his hands. He had the notion that Shone needed them. He decided that if he put the cards back into *his* inside pocket, then they would automatically appear in *Shone's* inside pocket.

Pete heard his name and then clapping. Someone jabbed him in the ribs. He stood up and reached into his inside pocket and took out the three-by-five cards. He smiled at the applauding people. He nodded, and then he noticed that he was sitting down again. He started to stand up. The cards were still in his hand.

When Pete stood up again, he was outside of the restaurant. The Top of the Ocean loomed over him, its huge yellow eye shining through the drifting fog. The woman in the pink-white gown was holding onto Pete's arm. A fellow with slick dark hair came up to them. He handed Pete a small flat brown bag with a bottle top sticking out of it.

"See you out at Yellow Rock," he said.

Pete took the bagged bottle, but the woman took it out of his hand.

"He doesn't need that now, Ripolla," the woman said.

Ripolla grinned, and then he laughed. Pete turned to the woman and thought, *Why?* But he looked over her head and saw that everyone from the restaurant was standing in the parking lot with them. They were all covered with the fog. That was when Pete understood that he had died.

He was dead in a car wreck back in front of Lapenski Fuel Oil. He shouldn't be here now. There was some mistake being made. Pete laughed, once he realized how simple it all was. Watching the people, Pete saw that they believed things were real, just as he had believed that Dean was with him before the wreck, when it was really Shone who was in the car.

Pete took a new interest in the people appearing and disappearing in the fog. He heard what they were thinking. All he had to do was look closely at them, and he heard their thoughts. Pete laughed. They were thinking that everyone knew them. They were acting as if everyone would miss them if they died.

Pete laughed until he remembered that none of them had known who he was. Then it seemed sad. They could hardly miss him, if they didn't know each other. Pete was sure that his life had been wonderful up until he died. But he could not remember why he thought that. He knew that he could not ask these people. They wouldn't know. He got angry about this. They would keep thinking about themselves until they died, missing everyone around them and imagining that they all were so particular that everyone would miss them when they were gone.

Pete's anger over this made him dismiss them, and in revenge he imagined them all as dead as he was. Once he had imagined they were dead, he suddenly came back to being Pete. His feet on the asphalt felt cold, and he felt the fog on his face for the first time.

The moment he felt the fog snag on his skin, he knew that he was back inside his Pete face. Then the skin began to ache, and from the ache a pain radiated down. His Pete face looked down and saw the body in a sport coat. Inside that coat was the Pete junior-class president, the Pete vodka drinker, the Pete with Ripolla, the Pete with Cheri, with Shone, with Dean—all the Petes rushed back inside. He could feel them behind his eyes, filling up what had been so empty and pure and clear, *and he wanted back out.* But all those Petes were inside for good.

II

AFTER GRADUATION

The Commercial Break

WHEN PETE was first dating Cheri Evers, they often sat with her mother in the living room and watched television. Mrs. Evers would only talk every twelve minutes during the commercials. Usually she gave advice on sex.

"If you kids want to make out on the couch," she'd say, "go ahead. I've always said I would rather have you do it here. Cheri will tell you that."

One of her mother's favorite comments on sex was, "You wouldn't buy a pair of shoes without trying them on first, would you?"

She said that over and over. "You can ask Cheri. I've always said that, haven't I?"

Cheri could not wait to leave home. "I've got to get out of that house," she told Pete.

Pete thought Mrs. Evers was cool. He laughed when she said some of the things she did. She was always threatening to tell him about "the airplane," but Pete never did find out what the airplane was. Mrs. Evers was the only mother Pete knew who talked about sex.

Cheri did leave her mother during her senior year. She stayed with her father across town. He was living with a woman in a big house with a swimming pool. He gave Cheri the guesthouse to stay in. Her dad left her alone and let her live her own life. Cheri had told her father that she was tired of acting as the go-between for her mother. Whenever her mother had a fight with her part-time lover or Cheri's younger sister, Cheri would step in and settle it.

"Sometimes I feel like I'm the only adult in that house," she complained. And Cheri was tired of her mother always saying those things to Pete during the commercials.

After graduation, Cheri got a good job, so she moved out of her father's place and rented a house just two blocks away from her mother. This was just temporary until she found a good apartment, closer to her work. From the parking strip behind Cheri's house, there was a clear view of her mom's front porch.

One Friday night, Pete returned from his summer job in Seattle, and he ended up staying the night with Cheri. Pete's mother was gone somewhere and he had her car, so he didn't bother to drive home. He left it parked outside of Cheri's house.

About a month later, Pete drove to Mrs. Evers' house one Monday night to pick up Cheri. They stopped going over there after Cheri had her own place, but because Cheri's oven didn't work right, that evening Cheri was baking a chocolate cake at her mother's house for an office party the next day. Afterward Pete and Cheri were going out on a date.

When Cheri let him in, Mrs. Evers was sitting in the living room, and Pete noticed that the television wasn't on. Pete and Cheri went in the kitchen to mix the cake. After they got the cake in the oven, Pete went back to the living room while Cheri cleaned up. He sat in a chair opposite her mother, and he looked over at the television again, thinking it odd that the set wasn't on.

Mrs. Evers sat on the couch, looking at the evening light through the picture window. Pete glanced over his shoulder out the window, but nothing was going on outside. It was only getting dark.

"You know *you* don't have to worry."

"Why's that?" Pete said.

"It's real easy to keep tabs on things from over here," her mother said. "Got a good view from here."

"Then you can keep an eye on Cheri for me while I'm working in Seattle."

"Well, maybe I can," she said. "You'd like that too, huh?"

Pete turned away from her, so he was talking toward the kitchen door. "Sure," Pete joked. "I always like to know what's going on."

"Oh, so you'd like to know what's going on," she said. "I hope you *do* know what's going on."

Her mother had a look in her eye that Pete had never seen before. It was almost crazy. Pete got a little scared, everything happened so fast. One minute her mother was joking, and the next she
was staring like crazy at him.

"Yeah, sure," he said.

"Sure, huh?" her mother said. "That's okay with you, huh?
You're sure, huh? You better be sure."

She waited for him to say something. She wasn't joking any
more. Pete had the feeling that she was about to jump all over him.
He didn't know what to say to her.

Cheri came out of the kitchen then. As she walked in, she looked
down at her mother on the couch, and then she cut between her
and Pete and turned on the television. A commercial was on. Her
mother kept staring at Pete. For a second, she glanced at the commercial but quickly turned back to Pete.

Pete thought that Mrs. Evers was about to cry.

Cheri stood next to the television, but she didn't say anything.
Cheri's mother looked down at the television, and then she
brought her head back up and stared at Cheri.

Cheri put her hand on top of the television set, as if she were
pushing her mother's gaze back down to the screen.

Her mother slowly lowered her head, and then she watched as
a program started.

She didn't look up at Cheri again until Cheri and Pete stopped
at the front door to say goodbye before they left with the chocolate
cake and went on their date.

Blood, Binoculars, And a Blizzard

PELTSTER AND PETE followed the blood spots down the hotel carpet. Past the dirty-linen hamper in the hall, the spots got much bigger, until they stopped at the back door of the hotel. Pete drank from his vodka screwdriver, and Peltster opened the door. Instead of blood spots down the metal steps, there was clean white snow.

Pete stared up into the falling snow, then looked down the steps to the parking lot—all the cars were white humps.

"I'll be goddamned," Peltster said.

"That was fast. It couldn't have been more than fifteen minutes." Pete peered out into the wind. The snow was flying sideways.

"Saved Angstrom's ass." Peltster laughed and let the door shut. They turned around and followed the blood spots back to Peltster's hotel room. Peltster knocked on the door. "It's us." The two of them waited. "Dwyer," Peltster said, "I hope he hasn't passed out on us." Peltster banged hard. "Open up!"

Angstrom opened the door. His right hand was bundled up in a clean white hotel towel. Inside the clean towel, the tip of another towel nestled, soaked with bright red blood. Breathing heavily, Angstrom leaned against the wall and let them pass, holding his right hand up. He was sweating, and with his left hand he kept squeezing his right forearm.

The coffee table in front of the bed was littered with various fifths, glasses, and beer bottles. Pete stepped around it and went to the dresser, which was also covered with bottles. After setting down his empty glass, he picked out his two Smirnoff vodka pints and moved them to the front of the dresser. Beside the pints he placed an empty fifth of Smirnoff vodka. Pushing all the rest of the bottles back, Pete cleared a work space on the dresser top. He wondered if he was drunk. One of the pints was full. He could not remember filling it from his Smirnoff fifth earlier, but he must have done it. So maybe he was drunk. He was making mistakes.

"You got away with this much," Peltster said to Angstrom. "You're dumber than shit, but you got away with it. Snow covered up your tracks back to the hotel."

Angstrom's face was white, and as he leaned against the door, he kept squeezing his forearm and then staring at the white bundle on his hand. He squeezed his arm and then stared at his hand over and over again, as if he were trying to milk his arm of its blood.

"What are we going to do with him?"

"Got to take him somewhere." Pete unscrewed the top of the fifth. He noticed that the other pint, the full one, was not really full. Searching through the bottles on the coffee table, he found a Royal Gate fifth with a little vodka left on the bottom. He topped his almost full pint off with vodka from the Royal Gate. Pete liked to know how much he drank. It was easier to keep track if he drank from pints. Back at the dorms tomorrow, he would have to talk about how much he drank. Pete held up the Royal Gate bottle. There was still a little left, and he drank it. So far, he had drunk a pint of screwdrivers at the party and a corner of someone else's fifth.

Sitting down on the bed, Peltster reached between his legs and hauled out a washtub full of bottles and watery ice. Angstrom watched Peltster open a Rainier beer bottle, using one of the five bottle openers hanging from the bedstead by shoelaces.

Angstrom's mouth moved as Peltster drank. Peltster saw that. "No more for you," Peltster said, wagging a finger at him. "Uh-uh."

Pete kneeled next to the washtub and located a pint of orange juice. Shaking the water off the bottle, he returned to the dresser and poured all the orange juice into the empty Smirnoff fifth.

"We can't take him to the college nurse," Peltster thought out loud, regarding Angstrom. "The police will let them know by now."

As if that were his cue, Angstrom slid down the doorjamb and landed on the floor. Propping his arm up, he stared at the bloody towel, his mouth open.

"There's a blizzard out there. The snow is going sideways. That's the sign of a true blizzard." Pete poured out a pint of vodka into the orange juice. When the fifth was full, there was still some vodka left in the pint, and Pete drank that. A fifth of screwdrivers ready to go. Plus he'd downed one pint of screwdrivers already at the party, along with the corner of someone else's Royal Gate fifth and the corner of his own pint. Pete was keeping track.

"Hey, stupid," Peltster said. "Angstrom! You leave a car somewhere nearby? Near the bar?"

"It won't matter. People are going to be leaving their cars in this blizzard," Pete said.

"A car for us," Peltster said. "I'm not worried about the police finding his car."

Both Pete and Peltster looked down at Angstrom. He didn't say anything. His mouth hung open, and he stared at the bloody bundle around his hand.

"We could get Lance's Impala," Pete said. "But that's a convertible." He stopped shaking the fifth of screwdrivers and wondered why he had just used the word *we*. He *was* getting drunk, he decided.

"Swerrrrrrr, swerrrrrr," Angstrom said.

Peltster squatted down and looked level into Angstrom's eyes. "We were going to get drunk, me and Pete here, after the party was over. After the girls went home. We do it every week with the leftovers from the dormies. And now, instead of getting plowed, I got to drink beer, sober up, and think of some way to get you fixed."

"I got laid right there," Pete said to Angstrom. He walked over to the open door for the adjoining suite and waved at the bed inside. "There's my sweater right there."

Angstrom's head dropped and he stared at his foot. Peltster snorted. He began to pace around the room.

"You're not very good company, Angstrom," Pete said. "You're supposed to be happy that I got laid." Pete waited for Angstrom to say something. "You know what else, Angstrom? You missed a great party. Peltster here got a new Ike and Tina Turner album, and he did his spider dance, too. I love it when Peltster does his spider dance."

Pete sat down on the bed and put his fifth of screwdrivers on the coffee table. Bending over, he reached down between his legs and felt around under the bed. He fished out a pair of bloody binoculars. Pete held them up to his eyes and tried to focus on his two empty pints on the dresser top.

"You fffff-f-f-f…" Angstrom said. "Yourah…yourah…f-f-fucking f-f-fool. Peltsterrrrr, sweerrrr, using you, j-j-just like m-me."

"We'll have to drive him to Mount Hebron and take a chance on the hospital there," Peltster said. "You got some friends down there, don't you, Pete?"

"I get the b-b-boooooze, y-y-you get the…get the f-f-fools."

Pete put the binoculars down, inserting each barrel in a dirty glass on the table, so that two glasses became a binocular stand. Pete looked over at Peltster.

Peltster only smiled. It was true. Peltster was using Pete to bring the dormies so they would pay for their parties, renting out vacant rooms down the hall for seductions and splitting the money with the hotel night clerk.

Pete didn't care.

You, me, booze, we, Pete thought. He examined the binoculars. A drop of blood had run down one of the barrels, falling into the watery whiskey in the glass. The blood floated on top, a red flower.

On Sunday night, a week later, Pete was on his way back to his dorm when he heard that Angstrom had been arrested on Saturday. Angstrom had gone to the school nurse to have his stitches taken out. Both Peltster and Pete had warned him not to do that. The police would have a bulletin out for anyone who was sliced up.

In a panic, Pete called Peltster. He got the hotel night clerk instead, the one who had been making deals with Peltster for the extra rooms. He told Pete never to show up there again. Peltster had split after stealing some money from the till.

Pete called up his friends T.J. and Tony in Mount Hebron. He told them to ditch the stuff in the trunk of their 1947 Plymouth. He'd stashed the loot in there at four o'clock in the morning, while Angstrom was getting sewed up at the hospital.

"What the hell did you do that for?" Tony yelled at Pete. "We haven't even looked in there. You mean T.J. and me have been driving around with hot stuff in our trunk? You come on down and get it yourself!"

So Pete caught the bus to Mount Hebron. He wanted to get away from the campus, anyway, in case Angstrom talked and the police came by his dorm. It turned out that his friends weren't really mad at him. They didn't give a shit about any stolen stuff in the trunk of their car. T.J. and Tony only wanted Pete down for a beer bust out at Bear Lake. That night Pete was thrown out of the party for shaking up a beer bottle and blasting a parakeet in a cage.

It had started snowing again, and he wandered around the resort grounds until he saw the party leave to get a pizza in town. Then he broke into the cabin and found two gallons of tap beer in the refrigerator. He emptied them on the floor, careful not to get his feet wet with the beer, so they couldn't track him in the snow. After that, Pete staggered down to the dock, and he slept under an overturned boat on the beach, wrapped in a bunch of moving pads.

The next morning, Pete called his friends from the Bear Lake resort restaurant. They drove the Plymouth out to pick him up. They couldn't figure out where he had gone the night before. Pete told them that a woman had picked him up hitchhiking, but they didn't believe him. So then he told them the truth. They didn't believe that either.

"Dwyer, you slept underneath a boat?" T.J. said. "It was twenty degrees last night."

Pete made a big show of telling them that he was going straight from now on. To prove it, he took the binoculars and other stuff out of the Plymouth's trunk and marched down to the resort dock. The dock went a long way out into Bear Lake. The boards were icy, old, and shaky. Neither of his friends would go out with him.

"Jesus Christ, the only thing holding that thing up is the ice!" Tony yelled at him.

Pete walked out to the very end of the dock, without making one slip. Once he stopped, though, he noticed it was hard to keep his feet from moving on the slick boards.

Bracing himself against a piling, he took the stuff out of the plastic bag. In the daylight it looked really cheap: rhinestone daggers and fake replica flintlock pistols and costume jewelry. And the bag and everything else was all caked with dry blood. Pete thought that Angstrom was a jerk for stealing this junk. He wondered how much it was worth. Even though his mind was clear, he felt strange at the end of the dock. The ice was making tiny cracking sounds under him. He looked back at the resort and his friends.

Against a white snowbank, they were two stick figures waving their arms, cheering him on. "Dwyer, you crazy bastard!" Their screams seemed very far away and faint. "Give it the heave-ho! Thatta boy!"

His feet kept slipping out from under him, and Pete realized that to get back to shore he was going to have to crawl on his hands and knees. Wrapping an arm around the piling, he took a flintlock pistol out of the plastic bag and threw it toward the blue hole in the center of the lake. The whole dock shuddered under him. The pistol bounced twice, spinning across the ice, and skidded into the water.

Pete felt all his problems emptying out of him. *He'd throw them all into the blue hole in the middle of the lake!*

Pete turned and waved at his friends. He could imagine them telling this story to all of their friends. Pete took the binoculars and reared back and threw sidearm. The entire dock shook again, the boards groaning and cracking. The binoculars spun across the ice. Hugging the piling, Pete closed his eyes, as the beautiful high thin whine went faster and faster.

Like You Used to Do

ON FRIDAY MORNING the Pepsi truck came first. The Piggly Wiggly always stocked up on pop for the weekend. Across the street Lorraine Glustich sat in her kitchen nook watching Gerald get out of his Pepsi truck. Pulling at his sagging pants, Gerald walked up the loading dock steps. Lorraine liked Gerald but not as much as she liked the Coca-Cola driver, Brother Len. While Gerald was inside doing some paperwork, the Coca-Cola truck pulled in next to the Pepsi truck. A couple of stock boys yelled out that Brother Len was here. Lorraine's kitchen nook window was halfway up, so she could hear what the guys said. Everyone on the Piggly Wiggly loading dock called him Brother Len, even though his name was Lenard and was spelled that way on his red Coca-Cola shirt. Gerald was about done with unloading when Brother Len began taking cases of Coke off his truck. Brother Len kept saying it was Friday and he was feeling good. He kidded Gerald about having a long face.

"What's the matter, Gerrrrold?" Brother Len said. "That Poopsi-Cola getting to ya?"

That always cracked Lorraine up—the way Len said Poopsi-Cola.

Gerald left, and Brother Len finished up with his Coke deliveries and then drove the red and white truck away.

Lorraine shut the window and put her tea cup and saucer in the sink. On the calendar Lorraine saw that Jim had penciled an X in this Friday, today. She had no idea what for. Perhaps a shipment was coming in at the lumberyard. He sometimes did that, marked the calendar, but he never wrote down words, only an X. Lorraine never knew what those Xs were for. Probably a reminder of something important that she didn't know anything about.

Opening the door, she stepped into the garage. Through their window she could see the neighbor's garage window, which was identical to theirs. Both houses were built on the same plan. Lorraine walked around the garage, glancing over at the neighbor's empty window. Then she stopped by the washer and dryer at the back of the garage. She looked at the neighbor's window, but only a reflection of the beige corner of their house showed. Lorraine returned to the kitchen and washed the breakfast dishes.

In their bedroom Jim's pajama bottoms were on the rug beside the bed. She picked them up and hung them on the back of the closet door. She took down Jim's old high school letterman's jacket and put it on over her house dress. She walked to her dresser, bringing up the yellow leather sleeve and sniffing it. Lorraine loved the way it smelled. Then she sat down before her mirror and began to brush her hair, liking that every time she moved her arm the leather smell of Jim's jacket sleeve passed her face.

After a few minutes, she put down her brush and opened the top drawer of her bureau. Inside were several fliptop packs of Marlboros and a woman's cigarette lighter. With her sharpest fingernail Lorraine speared a Marlboro by its filter and lifted it out of the pack. As she brought the lighter up to the cigarette she watched herself in the mirror. She stopped, lowered both the cigarette and lighter, then brought her head up with a toss of her hair, before bending slightly to accept the filter with her lips, and then a small flame flared. She inhaled, holding the lighter steady, watching in the mirror as the center of the tobacco glowed a bright red, and then the flame spread out to the paper. She studied the way the smoke came out of her mouth.

Lorraine thought about herself as if she were in a book. For some time now she had been imagining herself in the third person, as if when she regarded herself, she was reading about what she was seeing. *Lorraine studied her face in the mirror*, she thought, *her cigarette smoke curling up past her chestnut hair.*

PETE DWYER WATCHED Hubie Cooper and Dean Haganbarth on the front step of Hubie's house. Mrs. Cooper was teasing them again. As Hubie joshed with his mom, it was easy to see that something had gone out of Hubie. It made Pete sad. The old Hube wasn't there anymore, inside. Pete was happy that Hagenbarth was along. Dean was good-natured enough so maybe Hubie could relax a little.

Pete took a prescription vial out of his shirt pocket but then put it back as Hubie and Dean came down the front walk. Hubie's mom waved to Pete, and he smiled and returned the wave. He looked up at the roof of the Chevy and thought, *If this turns out to be a bummer, I can always go see Cheri tonight.*

Dean had his arm around Hubie's shoulders. Hubie was talking loud as he opened the door to the car. "That's right, going to Guam. My old man can't believe it. He's proud of me. Got me a job driving a colonel's jeep. No lie. On Guam."

WHEN THE PHONE RANG, Lorraine was in the bathroom. She finished wiping off her hands and strolled into the living room. As she walked out the front door, the phone was on its fourth ring. Through the open door she could hear the phone ring two more times and then stop. Lorraine saw that the maple tree behind their neighbor's house was budding. She was feeling funny shivers on her arms, as if warm and cold air were spiraling around her skin. *It's a spring day.*

It fascinated Lorraine that their house was exactly the same as their neighbor's. She had never lived in a house that was identical to someone else's house. She had never even been in a house that was the same as any other house, and the idea seemed so strange and modern. She often wondered what their neighbors had done to their house inside to make it different from Jim and Lorraine's house. But so far Jim and Lorraine had never been invited over. She guessed it was because Jim's dad owned both of the houses and their neighbors were only renters.

When they first moved in after the wedding, Jim and Lorraine joked about coming home some night and walking into the wrong house. They had spied on the neighbors coming and going and had imagined what each of them might say when it happened. Of course, that was months ago — they had stopped doing that.

Lorraine walked across the street to the back of the Piggly Wiggly store, strolling past the loading dock. The door was open, no one in view, only a stack of empty strawberry flats.

Inside the supermarket, Lorraine took a shopping cart and began to go up and down the aisles. She picked out a can of Campbell's tomato soup for Jim. He might like a can of tomato soup for lunch on Saturday. Sometimes he liked soup after he finished playing basketball with the guys at the playground. At least he had once. Lorraine stopped by the produce section and saw the new strawberries there. She got a carton, feeling as if it really was spring.

Back home, she put down the paper bag by the phone and dialed. Her mother answered. "I just called," she said.

"I was out shopping," Lorraine said. "The strawberries are in."

"Oh, how lovely. Why don't you and Jim come over this evening? I'll get some whipping cream and shortcake."

Lorraine walked into the kitchen, dragging the extension cord behind her. "Love to, Mom. Oh, wait." Lorraine ruffled the calendar pages loudly. "Darn, Jim's already made a dinner date for tonight and Saturday. I don't know if it's with his dad tonight. That may be tomorrow night. Sure. Maybe some other time."

Lorraine looked at the penciled X for Friday on the calendar and listened as her mother concealed her disappointment and began to talk about her church. Something had happened last Sunday after the service. Lorraine cradled the phone on her shoulder and walked back to the paper bag. She took out a strawberry and ate one, the steady buzz of her mother's chat muffled in her collar.

In downtown tacoma, Dean and Pete remained in the car while Hubie went in the state liquor store. After Hubie disappeared inside, Dean and Pete talked about how much he'd changed. Pete said that everyone who came back on leave was that way. Besides, Hubie's girl, Pia, had dumped him with a Dear John letter, and Hubie must be feeling that. Dean thought Hubie was bothered by more than Pia.

"Something's bugging him. He's not the same old Hube. Talking about hammering people. What's this hammering crap? Hubie never hammered no one. He was always the guy who ducked out of fights."

"He used to say to me in football practice, 'Now, Dwyer, just tell me which way you want me to fall—you don't have to hit me.' "

Dean said that he'd finally worked up his nerve and taken a writing class in winter quarter. Once Pete transferred to the U. of W., he'd have to try it. "You're always reading books. You'd like this prof. I wrote about Tacoma, some of the crazy stuff we did."

"What could you write about this dump?" Pete said, waving at the Tacoma harbor.

Along the newer cinder-block warehouses leading down to the pulp mills were FOR RENT signs. Abandoned cars and stacks of old oil drums lined the streets. Along Pacific Avenue the older brick warehouses were boarded up with weathered plywood. Between the scattered apartment houses on the hill were gouged-out holes and ruins. From Puget Sound the wind was blowing inland, driving the red haze from the smelter and the blue-gray smoke from the pulp mills south up the Puyallup River, an acid fishy smell.

LORRAINE TURNED on the radio. It was only two o'clock, so all they played was country music. The rock came on at three o'clock, when the kids got out of school. Lately Lorraine listened to the last hour or so of country music, to have something to do. She felt a little ashamed, since she had always called it hick music in high school. But she found that the songs after three o'clock seemed awfully immature. When Lorraine listened to country music now, she heard the words. She liked to fix Jim's dinner then. She was using the leftover aluminum trays from her parents' TV dinners. Jim liked that, since he could watch the Friday night fights and eat off the trays. Only, Lorraine did not actually fix him TV dinners. She put her own food in the little slots, filling them up with much more meat than the regular TV dinners had. Then she covered the top with aluminum foil. All she had to do was pop them in the oven whenever Jim came home.

Lorraine put the two homemade TV dinners in the refrigerator and took out the half-gallon of Christian Brothers Vin Rosé. It was only about a quarter full. She liked to drink a glass in the afternoon now. Jim's dad always dropped a few half-gallons by on Monday after work. He restocked his liquor cabinet after the dry Sunday, and he'd pick up something for them. He was a kick. Lorraine liked Mr. Glustich a whole lot.

A honky-tonk tune came on the black plastic Motorola, and she turned the volume down. She didn't like that kind of country music. It reminded her of where she grew up, out in the boonies. Lorraine looked out the kitchen nook window at the Piggly Wiggly loading dock. The back door was open, but no one was around. The place looked deserted.

> *My hair is still curly,*
> *And my eyes are still blue.*
> *Why don't you love me*
> *Like you used to do?*

IN SHONE DUNNIGAN'S APARTMENT, Dean and Hubie sprawled on the bed, and Pete slumped at their feet on a rolled sleeping bag. Beside a quart of orange juice and an empty vodka pint on the floor sat Shone Dunnigan. Everyone had a Dixie cup.

"Last month Jim Glustich came over to the university with his dad's team for a winter league basketball game," Dean said. "Hey, Gluey and me, we hoisted a few."

"Naw, not Gluuuueee," Hubie said. "Mr. Clean hoisting a few? Naw."

"Yeah, he did. In fact, we got a little buzz on, you know? He told me all about how Lorraine couldn't get enough," Dean said. "I said 'Come on.' You know, I thought Gluey was full of crap as usual. But no! Once Lorraine got a little, why, she was wearing poor Gluey out. He complained that she was right on him the minute he came home. At first, I thought, *Oh, sure.*"

"Trouble with Gluey is, he never did like anyone to get too close," Hubie put in. "Mr. Straight Arrow."

"I can believe it," Pete said. "Cheri said Lorraine married Glustich mainly to get out of her mom's house. Cheri said he was a big step up. She stopped seeing her friends from the Midland boonies once she moved into Parkland, hobnobbing with the Glustichs."

Shone sniffed once. "I saw Lorraine the other day."

"You sneak. Whatta ya mean, you *saw* her?"

"I just ran into her at the Piggly Wiggly." Shone shrugged and reached over to fill up his Dixie cup from the orange-juice quart. "When did Gluey come over to Seattle and talk about this?"

"About a month ago. Gluey was complaining. He asked me, 'Does it ever get sore?' "

Hubie kicked the bedstand. "*Glustich* said that?"

Dean laughed. "That's really funny, isn't it? Old Straight Arrow Gluey and No-Go Onderdonk getting married, and then Lorraine hopping to it."

"Let's go see him. I'd like to see Gluey in harness, man," Hubie gloated.

"I got a date with Sigrid's little sister, Ingrid," Shone said.

"Robbing the cradle, Shone. What's gonna happen when you run out of young ones?" Pete asked.

"Hey, yeah, let's go over and see Lorraine and Jim," Dean said. "What was funny was Gluey wanted me to fix him up with a date when he was over at the university. I said, 'I thought you were tired?' I think she had him worried, or maybe he just realized what he'd been missing all through high school. I told him, 'Hey, if you need any help, I got the girl for you.' "

"Then what'd he do?" Shone asked.

"Look at *him*," Hubie crowed, pointing at Shone. "Look at him. Flatfoot buzzard—that's what Shone is, taking out everyone's little sisters and cleaning up after the busted marriages around Parkland."

"Come on, lay off." Shone pretended to be hurt. "I was just curious. So what'd Jim do?"

"Ah, we both were drunk."

"Okay, but what'd Gluey say when you said you'd get him a date?"

"Ah, you know. He said sure. But he didn't mean it," Dean said. "I gave him her number, but I don't think he did call that girl. Gluey's a good guy. Let's get some beer, and then let's go see Gluey and No-Go Onderdonk."

ON THE FRONT PORCH, Mr. Glustich winked at Lorraine. "Look, wine with dinner. Before dinner. *After* dinner, hey?" He pushed the paper bag into Lorraine's chest. "Take it. I'm making your husband work late. Give him a drink, rub his shoulders, be a good wife to him. He's been looking tired. You come over tomorrow night. Dinner. Okay? *Hey, I said, 'Is it okay?' Hey?*" He bent over and looked in Lorraine's face as she stared off at the neighbor's house.

Lorraine snapped out of it. "I was just thinking. Okay."

"And I gassed up the Plymouth. You might like to take a drive. It's spring, hey? You could drive out to American Lake. Pick up one of your girlfriends and go for a ride." Mr. Glustich pointed at the oxidized green 1955 Plymouth in the driveway. "Jim'll be taking you guys' car tomorrow, and you should get out in the country."

When Mr. Glustich drove off, Lorraine went back in the house, took the two wine bottles out of the paper sack. She had never seen those two kinds of wine before. One was white and called Chenin Blanc. The other one was a Crackling Rosé. Lorraine tried to remember her high school French. Dog White? Why would they call it Dog White? She couldn't remember what the French for *dog* was. It sounded like *Chenin*.

She tried to remember her French again as she washed the dishes from lunch. Lorraine was happy that Mr. Glustich had stopped by with the Plymouth while his wife shopped. He made it a point to do that every other week so Lorraine could get out if Jim was using their car. It had been fun talking to Mr. Glustich. Lorraine hoped that eventually Jim would be more like his pop. Right now, Jim was almost exactly the opposite. The way Mr. Glustich said *"Hey!"* She loved that. She laughed as she poured herself a half glass of wine. He was so crazy sometimes. Lorraine went into the bedroom and took out a cigarette from the pack of Marlboros in the drawer. She lit it and looked at her books on the bottom row of the bookshelf beside their bed. Her French book from high school wasn't there. Lorraine picked out her home economics book. She opened it up. With the wine relaxing her, she dropped into a reverie about her old home-ec class. That had been her favorite.

Whenever Lorraine thought about being happy, she remembered sitting around in home ec and talking with the other girls. One Sunday Lorraine had accidentally run into Mrs. Glaubinger at church. Normally Lorraine didn't go to the Parkland Lutheran church. Her mother was Baptist, and Lorraine had stopped going to church once she left home, but one Sunday Lorraine had gone when Jim was in Seattle for a Rec League basketball tournament. She'd had a chat with Mrs. Glaubinger and told her that she had learned so many things in the first few months of marriage. When Mrs. Glaubinger had expressed interest, Lorraine had even said she would consider coming in sometime, when Mrs. G. wasn't busy, and giving the junior girls a few tips on homemaking.

Lorraine hadn't heard from her, but then Mrs. G. herself had gotten remarried and wasn't even going to church much any more. Lorraine had been to church twice again but Mrs. G. was nowhere to be seen. Lorraine had asked why, and they hinted that Mrs. Glaubinger was still on her honeymoon.

With her home-ec book in hand, Lorraine watched herself smoke in the mirror. In her mind she went over the speech she was going to give if she was ever called in.

Lorraine sat on the edge of the desk and surveyed the home-ec class. She held up two TV-dinner trays and pointed to them. "Don't expect your husband always to pay attention. Sometimes he just wants to relax in front of the TV set. Let him. You don't always have to have a sit-down dinner. Learn to adapt."

IN THE PARKING LOT of the Park'n'Shop, Pete and Dean listened on the radio to "Cheri, Baby," by The Four Seasons. As the song ended, they saw Hubie come out, a half-case of Olympia under each arm. Hubie put the two half-cases in the back seat of the Chevy.

"You still going with Cheri?" Dean asked Pete.

"Yeah, we're still together."

"I got a girl now," Dean said to Pete. "She's great."

"No kidding?" Pete said. "Hey, Hube, Hagenbarth's got a girl."

"What's her name?" Hubie said, climbing in back.

"Elsie," Dean said. "She's tough. Blond. She's graduating this spring, then going on to her fifth year of teaching."

"Where is Cheri tonight?" Hubie said over the seat to Pete.

"She's with some people from work, I think."

"You don't know? Man, if I had a woman like Cheri, I'd *know*," Hubie said.

"Yeah, but then, you lose women right and left," Pete said.

"Hey, lay off me. I've got a broken heart." Hubie punched Pete playfully on the shoulder. "I knew it was coming."

Pete drove out onto Pacific Avenue. "We're not like that. Cheri can do what she likes. She's got the job—and money. When I go to the University of Washington this spring, she'll be transferring her work to Renton. First I got to get in the university. I petition to wipe my record clean down in California, for a special admission. It's a drag."

At Hubie's house, Hubie and Dean put the beer in Hubie's mother's 1961 Nash Rambler station wagon. Pete drove back to his house and dropped off his mother's car. Hubie and Dean picked him up in the Nash. Hubie asked Pete if he was going to marry Cheri.

"I don't know. When I had my football scholarship and Cheri had her job, it was like we were equal, but now I've lost it, seems like things have changed." Pete brooded on this a bit. "I've been back from California a month now, and all we do anymore is sit around and watch TV."

Hubie turned off Pacific Avenue and took a swing around O'Rourke's Carpet Shop, to check if Rob and his dad, Big Rob, were around. Hubie pulled the Nash Rambler up to the O'Rourke house behind the carpet shop. "Well, what is it? Do we go see Gluey and Lorraine, or drink this beer in the car like old times?"

LORRAINE WAS ON the side of the garage, putting the empty wine bottle in her neighbor's garbage, when she saw the 1961 Nash Rambler pull up. She dashed back into the side door of her house. She opened the back bedroom windows to let the smoke out, then checked her face in the mirror. *It can't be. I only saw him a few days ago.*

There was a knock on the front door. Picking up a quilted potholder, she pulled open the oven door, exposing the two foil-covered TV dinners inside. With the second knock, she walked into the living room and opened the door with the potholder still in her hand.

"Hey, Onderdonk," Hubie said, "thought we'd drop in. Jim around?"

"No, he's still at work," Lorraine stepped back and let them into the house.

"You look startled," Pete said.

"Oh, I saw the Nash, and I thought that was Shone's car. He said he'd stop by sometime."

"I bet he did." Hubie grinned. "Naw, he used to borrow it. That's *my* mom's car. Hey, nice place, no lie, Lorraine."

"Thank you. Jim'll be home any minute now." Lorraine waved

them toward the couch. "He'll be really surprised to see you. What are all you guys doing together?"

"Oh, I'm the only one legit," Dean teased. "Hubie's AWOL from the Marines, and Pete here's been bounced out of college down in California. He *says* he'll be coming to the University of Washington with me, but I think he's bulling again. Cheri's going to marry him. You mind if we drink a beer, while we wait for Jim?"

"No, oh no. I was about to have a glass of wine myself. Jim's dad left some for us."

Hubie looked at Pete and raised an eyebrow as if to say, *Do tell.* Dean went outside to get the Oly out of the Rambler. Pete and Hubie sat on the couch and looked around the house. Lorraine followed their gaze. As they looked at each thing, she felt as if she were seeing it anew.

There was a knock on the door. Lorraine got up and let Dean in. He had both half-cases of beer. "Mind if we keep this other one cool in your fridge?"

"Hey, Lorraine, did you know Hagenbarth's got a girl now."

"Really?" Lorraine laughed when she saw Dean blush. "Don't be shy. Tell me about her."

"She's an older woman, too," said Hubie.

"Aw, she's only a couple years older than me," Dean said. "She'll be doing her fifth year at the U. this fall for her teaching credential."

While Dean put the beer in the fridge, Lorraine chatted with him about his girl and poured herself a glass of rosé. Dean took three cans of Oly out to the living room. Lorraine followed him and sat in Jim's big easy chair. Hubie took out a pack of Marlboros and asked Lorraine if he could smoke. She said sure and handed him an ashtray.

As Hubie bent over to take the lighter out of his pants pocket, he held the pack out toward Lorraine. She started to shake her head no, when her left hand slid a cigarette out of the pack. She put it to her mouth, not looking at the others, and Hubie flipped the top off a big Zippo Marine Corps lighter and sparked a flame for her.

ONCE THEY GOT settled down with their beers and cigarettes, the guys began telling stories. Hubie and Dean got into it, kidding each other about how Hubie lost his girlfriend, Pia, and Dean finally got one. Dean got all flustered.

"The look on your face just slays me," Lorraine said, and when Hubie offered one, she took another Marlboro.

The guys had another round of beer. Dean told a funny story about a professor at the University of Washington who was so absent-minded that he walked into a telephone pole. Then Hubie imitated their old social studies teacher, Mr. Cupat. Everyone joined in remembering Q-Tip, the way he stuck his thumbs in his sweater and how he used to tap his empty cigarette holder on the chalkboard and stick it in his mouth like Franklin D. Roosevelt. Lorraine had a story about when Jim was first driving truck for his dad's lumberyard and a load of plywood fell off his truck in the middle of an intersection. Pete talked about his first week of college football in California and how he got a concussion. His headaches lasted for weeks after that, until the team doctor gave him some pills.

Hubie and Dean joked around some more. Pete got up and went into the kitchen. After a few minutes, Lorraine went in the kitchen too, and she found Pete holding a half-empty glass of water and standing in front of her oven—the door was open—staring at the two TV-dinner trays. He looked sort of embarrassed and went back in the living room. Lorraine wondered if something was wrong with the way her homemade TV-dinners looked.

Before she returned, she got herself another glass of rosé. She recounted the time that Jim got lost outside of Olympia during his first week of deliveries. Everyone got a big kick out of imagining Jim driving farther and farther out in the tule bushes around Olympia. Jim got lost a second time, Lorraine said, but that was outside of Puyallup. Apparently Jim and his mom and dad never went for Sunday drives like her family did.

"It's funny how you find out things like that once you're married," said Lorraine. "I thought everyone knew their way around Puyallup, for God's sake. I never realized that Jim hasn't been anywhere. Mr. Glustich is such a kick—he *says* he wants to go places, but he never does. He's just like Jim that way."

Hubie offered Lorraine another Marlboro, but she said no thanks. She was feeling a little giddy already from smoking in her own living room for the first time.

"It's been such a big day, first the guys on the Pepsi and Coke trucks were kidding the heck out of each other, and then Mr. Glustich came over, and then you guys."

"That's a big day?" Pete laughed. "Well, maybe it is." Dean handed Pete another beer. "One more, one more," Pete said, feigning weariness.

"That's two for Dwyser. One more and one more. Give him two!" Hubie yelled. "You get what you asked for. That's what we say in the gyrenes."

Pete protested that he wasn't in the Marines, but Dean got Pete another Oly. So then Pete chugged it, and Hubie timed him on his watch, even though Pete told him not to bother because he never was a good chugger.

Then they all talked about high school and how happy they were to graduate, what a drag it had been, and how no one they knew had gone back for a visit. Lorraine was going to mention that she was going back to lecture the home-ec classes, but instead she said even Jim had not gone back. Of course, he had been busy learning the lumberyard business from the ground up. His dad started him driving truck, the lowest rung on the ladder. Jim was saving money so they could move to their own place in the country.

"To the country?" Pete said. "Where?"

"Up by Mount Rainier. He wants to get away from all this," Lorraine said.

"All what?" Pete said, looking out the window at the loading dock. "The delivery trucks?"

Lorraine was about to say that she had never lived this close to anybody before, being raised out in the boonies herself. Then she realized that she hadn't thought things through, because when they moved to the country, she would be back in the boonies and wouldn't even have Gerald and Brother Len any more. She laughed, and the guys looked at her funny. "Well, I just thought that if we don't know the neighbors anyway, how can I miss them?"

Hubie and Dean both laughed too, but Pete only looked down into his beer. "Hey, what's the matter, Pete. Don't you think that's funny?" Hubie turned to Dean. "Pete's passing out on us, Deaner."

"Hey, come on, Pete!" Dean grabbed Pete as he began to weave to the side. "Hey, lemme take Pete over to Kreech's Drive-in, get him something to eat."

"Screw off, man, I'm okay," Pete said. But when he stood up, he almost fell over.

Dean helped Pete to the door. Hubie followed them and stood out on the porch. "I'll stay here in case Jim comes in," Hubie called after them. "Take him in the Nash. Here." He threw Dean his keys.

"Dwyser had more of that vodka this afternoon than any of us did. He got into drinking at that school down south. He did real good on the team, though. That's what he said. I think he just got homesick. That's why he got thrown out of school. And Cheri—he missed her." Hubie sat back down on the couch, taking out his Marlboros and offering one to Lorraine. Then he lit her cigarette and his own and looked around. "Lemme police up the place a bit, okay? We don't want Gluey coming home to a mess."

Lorraine protested, but Hubie picked up all the beer cans and took them into the kitchen. Lorraine followed, showing him where the garbage can was. Luckily she had just emptied it. Then they came back to the living room, and Lorraine sat down in Jim's easy chair. As Hubie lapsed into silence, they both became aware that they were alone.

"Hey, what time does Jim get in?"

"I don't know. I mean, his dad said he'd be working late. He doesn't like me to call." Lorraine leaned forward and tapped the ash off her cigarette into the ashtray. "So. Where you stationed?"

"Oh, uh, I'm about to be...you know," Hubie said. "See, they give you leave before you're transferred. Guam. They're sending me to Guam."

"Is that like Korea?"

"What?"

"Guam. Like Vietnam or Korea? I just know them from seeing those shiny jackets around. You know, with dragons and maps. You used to see them around."

"They're *fighting* in Vietnam."

"I guess I haven't followed any of that in the news. I've been so busy."

"Yeah, sure." Hubie stared down into his beer. "Busy, huh?" He took a swallow. "So what keeps you busy?"

Lorraine waved at the house with her cigarette. Hubie looked at the living room. "How can you keep busy with a little place like this?"

"Well it's not...horrendous or anything, keeping this place up."

"So what do you do? I mean, everyday?" Hubie drank the rest of the beer and set the empty can down. "I don't know what the hell women do, myself. Can't just sit around all day. You're looking good—no, I mean it." Hubie tipped the beer can over and lightly karate-chopped it. "You want to know where I'm really going?" He laughed and plinked his Oly can with his fingernail.

"I'm not going to Guam. It's just a stopover. I'm going to Nam." Hubie looked out the window at the back of the Piggly Wiggly. "You know?" He took a deep breath. "You don't know," Hubie said, picking up his empty and going into the kitchen. Hubie came back in with an Oly in one hand and the bottle of white wine in the other.

"What's this stuff?" He held it, label out, to Lorraine. "I never heard of this stuff. It any good?"

Lorraine took the bottle from him without looking in his eyes. She glanced out the window as a car passed, hoping it was Jim. Hubie was making her uncomfortable. "It's Chenin Blanc," she said, turning the bottle around so she could read the back label. "*Blanc* is *white* in French, and it says here that *Chenin* is the name of a grape."

"Look, Lorraine, hey, no lie. Sorry about the…" He waved, at everything. "You know, this may be the last time I'm home." He regarded his Oly can and shrugged. "You know…well, maybe you don't."

"Can't you stop by and see Pia? Maybe that would help."

Hubie shook his head. "No, it's not women, or Pia. It's like…you know, would anybody miss me if I'm gone—for good, I mean. No one seems to—I don't know." Hubie drew his hand down in front of him as if he were erasing a chalkboard. "Everybody's acting like it doesn't matter. You know? No, not that it doesn't matter but that they know, you know, what everyone's going through, and they're all acting so cool. That's what gets me, no jiving lie. But they're missing everyone. They don't know anyone. And I can't talk to them, because I *know*." Hubie sniffed. "I can't talk."

"I know," Lorraine said.

"This could be it for me." Hubie choked back a sob. "Goddamn it."

"I know, Hubie," she said, "I really do. I'm alone too. All day." Lorraine picked up her glass of rosé and sipped it. "I thought when we got married, I'd really get to know Jim. I thought if we had our own house, if I got away from my mom, then I'd really get to know him—and his friends. The guys. And…and…that's not what hap-

pened." Lorraine blinked back a tear. "You don't want to turn out
like your parents, but then you find out...I don't know what you
find out. You get in a house, and what you think of doing is what
they do all day. But you tell yourself it's different because you don't
think the way they do. I'm not going to end up that way. I'm not.
It doesn't *have* to be their way."

Hubie raised his head slowly. "I'm not talking about marriage,
I'm talking about dying."

"But you can die a little at a time, too," Lorraine blurted out,
starting to cry. "You *can*."

"Oh, yeah, sure. Hey, sorry about that. I didn't mean to come
down so hard." He put out his hand. "Let me get you another drink
of wine, okay?"

Lorraine shook her head no. Then she went in the kitchen and
poured herself a small amount of rosé. The second bottle of rosé
was now almost halfempty. She wondered if maybe Pete had some
too. He was in the kitchen an awfully long time there and seemed
to get drunk so fast. Lorraine couldn't forget the look on his face
as he stared in the oven at her two TV dinner trays. He seemed almost furious. *What is happening?* Lorraine thought. *We were all so
happy.*

"I've got to go," Hubie said when Lorraine came back in. "Hey,
lemme, uh..." He shrugged apologetically. "The guys might want
the rest of the beer."

He walked toward Lorraine, and she stepped back to let him pass
by. She turned her eyes away from him and felt a breeze as his body
passed her.

AT THE PICNIC TABLE in the back of Kreech's Drive-in, Dean
pushed a hamburger and a bag of fries closer to Pete, and he
shoved them back. "She says we tried it my way and it didn't work.
Going to school. I got bounced, losta...lost my scholarship," Pete
had difficulty saying *scholarship* and he laughed. "Can't even say it,
no wonder why I lost it. So now we have to try it her way. Her way!
Get married. She'll work, put me through school, see."

"What's wrong with that? That's what me and Elsie are planning
to do once she starts teaching," Dean said. "Then I can start writing, too."

"I'd rather blow my brains out than live like that. Did you *see*

Lorraine? No, I mean really see her?" Pete grabbed Dean by his neck and pushed his head toward Lorraine's house. "That's a god-damn coffin, not a house."

"Hey, ease up on the neck—you're choking me." Dean tried to duck out from under Pete's hand, but Pete held on.

"I'm not going to end up that way. Might as well let your god-damn brains drain out your toes as live like that." Pete stood up and pointed at his heart. "I'm not dying! Not here inside, not me." Pete grabbed the picnic table and flipped it over. He hit a tall white gar-bage can by the phone booth and sent it flying into the fence. "I'll kill myself before I end up in some pissant place like that!"

Dean snagged his left arm, and Pete jerked free, picked up the garbage can, and threw it at the phone booth. The can hit the side-walk, whacked into the aluminum side of the booth, and bounced into the parking lot. Pete swung at the phone booth, his palm smacking against the glass, the booth shuddering under the blow.

Dean grabbed Pete's shirt collar from the back with both hands, trying to bulldog him down. Pete fell onto the little fin on the Ram-bler fender. He twisted around, banging his head against the sta-tion wagon. Stunned, he sagged into Dean's arms.

Dean opened the car door, putting one hand on Pete's back to hold him up against the side of the car. Pete collapsed onto the back seat. Dean shut the door, locked it, and then leaned against the car.

After catching his breath, Dean checked on Pete. He was think-ing about what to do, when he saw Hubie coming out of Glustich's house with the half-case of beer under his arm. Hubie gave a little wave as he crossed Park Street. He opened the Rambler door and put the half-case on the front seat.

"Pete just went nuts," Dean said. "He's too strong for me. I barely got him turned around. He's having trouble with Cheri." Dean shook his head. "Damn, I've never seen Dwyer like this. He just goddamn exploded."

"Hey, you remember that Auburn game when he got pissed off and broke that guy's leg?" Hubie leaned over the front seat and reached into Pete's shirt pocket and eased the prescription vial out. "Codeine and aspirin, that's a painkiller."

"Remember Pete said he got a whole jar of it from the team doc-tor? Suppose he's on pills?"

"Naw." Hubie read the label. "This is from California. I don't think you're supposed to mix this stuff with the booze." He laughed and put the vial back in Pete's pocket. They decided to take Pete up to Rob O'Rourke's new house, dump Pete in Rob's bedroom, and drink the rest of the beer there. When they drove around in back of the carpet shop, they saw both Rob and his father were still on a job. They parked the Nash alongside their garage and decided to leave Pete in the back of the Rambler, rather than wake him up for the move into the house. Hubie and Dean took the beer and walked around to the swimming pool.

The sun was setting in the firs behind the house, streaking the dark waters of the pool a bloody red. They drank some more beer. They talked about some of the good times they used to have at O'Rourke's old house during high school, how the guys all used to meet there. After a while, Hubie walked out on the diving board and sat on its end, staring down at his reflection in the dark red water.

"Be careful there, Hubie," Dean joked. "Don't want you to roll off there and drown now."

"Oh, no, don't want that to happen here," Hubie said. "No use anything like that happening here. Not here."

Dean talked about his girlfriend, Elsie, back in Seattle. He told Hubie how they met at a jock's party at the university. Dean was scared at first that she'd come there with some jock, and she had played along with that for a little bit, and Dean had been nervous, expecting some big guy to show up and chase him off. She loaned him some great books to read, and he'd started writing, and she was a musician, too, and used to sing "Summertime" for him.

Hubie kept telling Dean how great it was that he was in love for the first time. "I really hope you two make it through. It's tough," Hubie told him, "but if you can make it, I really hope you do."

"Hey, Hube, what about you, man? We've got to get you a girl. You need one."

"Not where I'm going. I don't think I'll need one." Hubie stared down at the water. "Not like I used to."

VACUUMING IN FRONT of the couch first, Lorraine did the whole rug next and then the kitchen too, noticing that an ash off of Hubie's cigarette had fallen under the kitchen table. Then she opened the front windows to let the room air out. Lorraine still felt a little sick from too much tobacco. At least, she hoped it was tobacco and not the wine. She had never thrown up from alcohol, and she hoped she never would. But she'd heard Jim talk about it.

When she came out of the bathroom, it seemed as if nothing much had happened, what with the room looking so clean and all. Lorraine went into the kitchen and closed the oven door on the two TV-dinner trays. She didn't feel hungry. She called the lumber-yard, but no one answered the phone.

Then she had a cup of tea. She sat in the kitchen nook and looked across the street at the dark loading dock. She pushed her teacup to one side and took down the three-by-five yellow pad from the knickknack shelf. With a red ballpoint pen, she wrote quickly across the pad from corner to corner, making it look as if she were in a hurry. "Had to step out. Put the oven up to 450. Lo—"

She taped this to the oven door and then got her purse and the keys to the Glustichs' Plymouth off the counter. She locked the front door and went back through the kitchen to the garage door. As she stepped into the garage, she reached into her purse and took out a handkerchief and blew her nose once. Then she walked over to the washer and opened the top and put the handkerchief in.

She was busy rearranging a load in the washer when the garage door opened. Lorraine was startled. Her husband, Jim, was standing there. She said something about not hearing the car drive up. Jim smiled and said he had coasted up with the engine off. He just felt like doing that. He got back in the car and drove it in. Lorraine went back to adjusting the load and glanced down at her reflection in the chrome. Her hair was slightly disheveled. Jim got out of the car and closed the garage door. He was smiling, said he'd come home early, nothing doing at the yard. Lorraine punched the button to start the washer. She stepped to the side and glanced at the neighbor's garage window across the way. She thought she saw the flicker of someone's face in there. The machine began to shake just as Jim came up behind her. He was wearing his letterman's jacket and put his arms across her shoulders, the scent of his leather sleeves surrounding her face, and as he moved up close to her, she saw his hands coming in to cover her eyes.

Crème de la Crème

THE HOUSE WAS WHITE with a long porch with green framed windows. The glass sparkled in the sunlight, reflecting a privet hedge. Red clay pots of poinsettias lined the porch rail. A smooth gray walk cut through the middle of the lawn and stopped at the sidewalk between two fluted columns rising out of mounds of manicured ivy.

"You and me, Dwyer, see—we were the tops," Peter Dawson told Pete, as he parked his 1958 Plymouth in front of the house. "We were the only two to get out of that high school with four-year rides. We were the dudes."

"Oh, sure," Pete said. "But no more for me."

"Naw, don't say that. You can make it back. Look, Dwyer, you gotta meet this chick." Dawson popped his fingers and began to sing "So Fine." "*My baby's so doggone fine, chills run up and down my spine, oh yeah, oh yeah, so fine.*"

"How could you have any trouble with your grades, Dawson? I thought the U. of W. football team selected all your classes, gave you a tutor, too."

"That old witch never did squat for me. She wrote me some papers, but then, eh—I stopped going over there when she got on my case," Dawson said. "Lookit, isn't that one bitching house? Her old man's one of those assistant deans."

Peter Dawson got out of his Plymouth, the dented door cracking loudly as it swung open. He stood up and pointed his index finger at the front door of the house. "Ka-pow! Man, I am going to nail that chick. Trudy—you like that name? Trudy."

Pete followed Dawson up the walk. "But what's happening with you and school?"

"Coach says all I got to do is drop out, pick up a few credits at a junior college, and then I'm back for fall quarter."

"Yeah, but you lose your free ride then, don't you?"

"See, this is the kind of class of people you get to associate with," Dawson said, stepping up on the porch and gesturing at the side garden with its half-circle of laurel hedges.

On the front porch, Pete looked at the painted white wicker couch with the deep red cushions under the big green-framed windows. A brass lion's head decorated the door. Growing out of its mane were daffodils.

"See, I told ya," Dawson said, diddling the daffodils with his fingers. "Some joint, eh?" He pressed the white button next to the leaded window panels framing the door. "You gotta meet Trudy's old man, Pete. He's a kick. I told him about some of the wild shit we did in high school, you know, jerking out highway signs with those chains hanging down off Rob's old truck. Man, he *laughed*. One of the guys, Dean Sommerall."

Inside the house the buzz of the doorbell faded away. Dawson pressed it again. "And this broad is so fine, man. My baby's so dog-gone fine."

The Sommerall house was only a few blocks from Volunteer Park on top of Capital Hill, and through some shrubbery Pete caught glimpses of Lake Washington glistening a dark blue in the chill March sun. Pete looked back at Dawson's 1958 Plymouth parked in front. The left fender was crumpled, one headlight pointing out as if the car were walleyed.

Dawson knocked on the door. "After your transfer comes through, Dwyser, babe, I want your ass out for spring practice. You got our honor to uphold." Dawson peered in through the leaded glass window.

"What honor? I'm not playing any more football, Dawson," Pete said. "It's a waste of—"

Dawson tried the brass door handle. A small precise click—and the door swung open. He stepped in. "Trudy?" he called. Dawson motioned Pete in. "Come on, she's probably around here somewhere."

Pete looked in at the cream white hallway with the long green strip of rug leading down to a stained glass window with ferns under it. "Uh, how well do you know this Sommerall guy?"

"C'mon! Get *in* here!" Dawson said, grabbing Pete's arm and pulling him in. "You come out this spring, you're as good as on that team!"

"How many times have you met Trudy?"

"A whole lot. She hangs around jocks. You know that kind of a bitch." Dawson strolled down the hallway, pointing at the framed prints on the walls. They were all of manor houses in England or France. "Isn't this too much? I told ya. Me, I'm going waterskiing, none of my sweat on those blocking pads this spring. Making time with the chicks. You shoulda never gone down to California. Man, if I only made third fucking string on the frosh team, you coulda made first. You always kicked butt. So you are coming out for the team. I'll introduce you. They're a buncha animals. You'll love em."

Dawson turned left into a dining room. A long polished table reflected the light from the windows looking over a rose garden. All the roses were pruned back severely, their thorny branches short and blunt. "Had dinner right here, no bull." Dawson closed his eyes and sniffed, as if he were smelling the meal again. He walked over to a walnut cabinet and opened its doors. Inside, bottles of liqueur gleamed.

"Hey, hey, Dawson, let's get the hell out of here," Pete said. "Jesus, this is breaking and entering."

"Relax, the Dean'll remember me."

"*Remember you?* Did you call this Trudy, let her know we were coming?"

Dawson bent down and started to rifle through the bottles. "I don't know what all this yellow and red colored shit is," he said. "Maybe you oughta have a souvenir, eh, Pete?"

"Dawson, I'm walking back out that door."

"Relaaaax. You should have been here that night," Dawson said, waving his hand back at the table as he went through the bottles. "Silver plates and wine glasses—the whole works. It was the Cadillac of dinners. Eh, there's no real booze here, no Scotch. After-dinner crap. Hey, look at this. You ever have any of this?" Dawson put a bottle of crème de menthe on the table. "This is the shit you get after dinner."

"You can't drink that stuff straight," Pete said.

"Yes, ya can. They did. Got it in these little old glasses." Dawson laughed, pointing at Pete's face. "You're really fucking panicked, aren'tcha?"

Dawson stood up and took the crème de menthe bottle off the table. He unzipped Pete's windbreaker and jammed the bottle under his arm. "There, take that. I don't know what that other gunk is. But we can drink that. Let's go over to the park, get a buzz on."

Pete took the bottle out from under his arm and put it back on the table. "That's it, I'm gone."

"Hey, Pete, wait!" Dawson sat down in a chair, uncorked the crème de menthe bottle, took a taste, and pointed at the molding around the ceiling with its patterns of roses and interlacing leaves. "This is exactly where I sat, across from that rose. Exactly."

Dawson stood up and poured the green liqueur over the table top with a slow serving motion. "See, this is the crème de la crème. You know what that means? It means this is the kind of joints you get to eat at if you're on the team."

A 1957 Ford

UP PACIFIC AVENUE the ground fog turned the oncoming cars into colorless hulks. Pete only recognized Cheri's car when the car behind turned left, and in the headlight's passing glare he saw the familiar hump of her 1957 Ford top.

With his small suitcase in hand, Pete waited at the curb. Cheri's blue and white Ford slid behind a Yellow cab, and Pete reached for the door. He was halfway in, lifting his suitcase over the seat to drop it in back, when he saw what Cheri was wearing.

"Hi," she said. Then she bent her head and looked in her side mirror to pull out into traffic. Pete dropped the suitcase and looked at the plastic scarf on her head. Underneath were pink plastic curlers. She had on a pair of old pants and a sweater Pete could remember her wearing sometime two years ago.

"Hi," he said. He waited until she wheeled the Ford back out into traffic. "Friday night," he joked, "big traffic jam in Tacoma."

Cheri leaned forward and squirmed, pulling her sweater down with her left hand. Turning right off Pacific Avenue, she circled the Greyhound station. "Yeah," she said.

Pete looked at his knees up against the dashboard. All of a sudden he wanted to tell her to stop and let him out. He would go back to the Greyhound station, get a bus to Seattle.

"We stopped about every five minutes from Seattle," Pete said. "It was a local."

Cheri smiled and turned on the radio to the news station that she listened to on her way to work. She didn't turn it to the rock-and-roll station.

"I'll never do that again," Pete said. "Take the local bus."

Cheri stopped at the corner, and Pete looked out to the right and then glanced to the left. Cheri was looking to the left. "It's okay on your right," he said.

She pulled out into traffic without looking in his direction. Pete waited until she had to stop at the traffic light in front of the train station before he tried again. "I got in," he said. "I start this spring." Then, "They're on quarters at the university."

"Good." She glanced up at the stoplight.

"There was no hassle about me being kicked out of college in California. They acted like it was no big deal. I had the grades."

Pete looked at Alphonse's Italian restaurant on the left side of Pacific Avenue. He remembered taking Karen Skaugstaad, one of the sosh girls, there once on a date. During a few weeks of their senior year, Cheri and Pete had broken up because they were getting too serious. Feeling adult because of the mature decision that he and Cheri had made, Pete decided to take Karen to dinner. He thought it would make a big impression on Karen: no one did that in Parkland. The night was a disaster because she had been scared of the food. Pete had ordered spaghetti for her since that was the only thing she knew on the menu. Karen had picked out the tiny clams and eaten very little.

As they drove by Alphonse's, Pete looked behind Cheri's head at the restaurant sign. On the back seat of the car his suitcase looked small.

"So I'll be going to school in Washington again." Pete waited for Cheri to say something. "It was a good week for me in Seattle."

She downshifted into second for the climb up the Pacific Avenue hill. "I'm glad for you," she said.

"Did you want to go some place tonight?" Pete said.

"No," she said.

Cheri's place was in the Palisade Apartments two blocks west of Pacific Avenue in Parkland, a U-shaped complex containing mostly single bedroom units with small living-room-kitchen arrangements. For the last few months, Cheri had gone on a furniture buying spree and, in her apartment everything was new except for a couch from her stepmother's house. When Cheri moved away from home, Cheri's stepmother had asked her if she wanted their living-room couch, and Cheri had said no, she'd take the one in the guest house. Pete and Cheri had laughed about that then. "I wanted to say that we about wore hers out," Cheri had said. Now it was the only old thing in her place.

Pete put his suitcase inside the door and sat down on the couch, while Cheri went into her bedroom. Pete could smell something cooking. He got up and walked over to the pot on top of the stove and lifted the lid. Inside was spaghetti and meatballs.

"Leftovers tonight," Cheri said from the bedroom. She had heard him lift the lid. "I got home early from work, and I decided to do my hair for tomorrow's regional luncheon, and I got too tired to cook."

"Work been hard?" Pete asked.

There was no answer from the bedroom. Pete looked around the apartment at all the gleaming new furniture. He had the sudden sense that something else had changed. He inspected the kitchen and then the living room. His framed picture was gone.

"Sure you don't want to go someplace tonight?"

Cheri came in the room. She had changed to an old dressing gown, her head a mass of pink plastic curlers. "No, go ahead and eat," she said. "Don't wait for me. I'm going to watch some TV first."

THAT NIGHT, Pete found his graduation picture face down on the bedroom dresser. He took off his pants and folded them and placed them across the chair. He tried to remember if he had ever spent such a dull evening with Cheri. Outside of her mother's house watching TV, he decided no. Pete hated TV. And Cheri had laughed all night at the TV. They had laughed together only once.

Pete got into bed. Cheri came out of the bathroom and turned off the bedroom light. Then she got into bed. She was wearing her pink flannel nightgown. Pete felt it against his naked thigh. He took a deep breath.

"What's the matter?" he said.

"Nothing."

"Cheri." Pete moved his arm a little and touched her arm. "This means I'll be in Seattle. That's not an hour away from Renton. When you move to Renton…" And then he did not know what to say. "When you get an apartment in Renton, we'll be close." He raised his arm and put it over her shoulder, and she slid closer to him. He kissed her cheek.

"What's wrong?"

"Nothing," she said. "Are you going to go home in the morning?"

"I don't have to. Mom still thinks I'm in Seattle."

"Well, maybe you better," she said.

Pete felt as if he had just taken a big deep breath of cold air, there was such an aching in his lungs.

"Cheri."

"Yes?"

Pete was getting scared. He could tell that she was expecting him to make love to her, but it was as if she were impatient. He began to feel that this was going to be for the last time. Yet he could not stop himself from doing it. He pulled her to him, but she felt almost dead in his arms.

"Well?" she said, and she pulled her nightgown up.

Pete put his nose in her flannel shoulder and stared across her breasts. In the dim light from the overhead blinds, the pink flannel had turned gray. She reached down and started to pull her nightgown up higher, sliding it over her waist. Pete felt her bare leg touch his, as her legs opened a bit. He closed one eye so he couldn't see her face, only the rough gray landscape of her nightgown.

WHEN HE WOKE UP, Cheri was sleeping, snoring lightly. Pete felt so alone that he could not believe Cheri was next to him. He wanted to get out of bed, but he was afraid that if he did, he would never get back in. He had to go to the bathroom, too, and he knew he wouldn't get back to sleep unless he did that first. But if he got out of bed, that was it—he'd leave for good.

Pete slid one leg out, feeling the cool air on his skin. And then he sat up. Cheri didn't stir. Pete went into the bathroom and closed the door before he turned on the light. After he took a leak, he stalled for time by washing his hands, letting the water run slowly. Once before he had tried to guess how it might end, but he had never guessed this.

He turned off the light, and he began to cry. The memory of their first night at Cheri's old house came back to him: how he'd waited in the bathroom for the bedroom light to click off, suddenly shy about stepping out naked, and then he'd come out to Cheri sit-

ting up in bed and smiling. He turned on the light and wiped his
face with a towel. He ducked his head away from the mirror and
cried again. Then he turned, looked at himself in the mirror, and
washed his face with cold water. He didn't let the water run full so
it would wake up Cheri. He didn't want her to see him like that.
He stood there, looking at the trickle of water sliding into the drain.
Her house, her furniture, her Ford, her food, her TV.

With a twist he shut the water off. When he had left to register
at the university in Seattle, he no longer loved her. He should have
broken it off then. But he had come back. For sex, really—he had
to be honest with himself—and instead, she took it from him until
she was pleasured, and then she acted as if he wasn't there. Pete
breathed deep and looked down at his legs. Going up on his toes,
he straightened his back. Looking down again, he tensed his body,
as he had been taught to do in sports before he did something
smooth, something graceful and swift. Watching himself in the
mirror, he tried to think exactly what he was going to do and how
he was going to do it. Then he flicked the light switch down, waited
in the dark until he could see, and opened the door.

Above the bed the venetian blinds sent meager lines of light up
to the ceiling. Pete waited until his eyes adjusted to the light, and
the scene under the blinds came in clear: the bed with the covers
to one side, Cheri's face on the pillow asleep—all the same, slightly
fuzzy gray. Pete stepped around the bed, picked up his pants and
shirt and shoes and socks and shorts, and then began to back out
of the bedroom. When he felt the edge of the open bedroom door
touch his back, he sidestepped and backed all the way out.

He turned and walked into the living room, and sat down on the
couch. He put on his socks. Then he stood up and slipped on his
shorts, buttoned up his shirt, pulled on his pants. He sat down and
tied his shoelaces, left foot first. He wondered what he would say
if she came out and found him like that. She hadn't left him anything to say. There was only one reason why he had come back,
and she had taken care of that.

Standing up, Pete took his coat off the back of the couch and put
it on. The tears came again, and Pete had to sit down. He turned
the TV on, making sure the sound was off. A late night car dealer's
ad blinked on. Pete walked over to his suitcase and picked it up.
He watched the light from the TV flickering across the empty
couch.

He had watched TV with her and everyone in her family: her sister, her mother, her stepmother, her stepfather, and her dad.
Sometimes, during their senior year — always after her dad and
stepmother went to bed — they made love on a couch with the *Tonight* show on, while listening to the snores from the other room.
In the bedroom he could hear her soft breathing. One at a time,
he thought about each of Cheri's relatives watching TV. He imagined each of them watching TV alone and then getting up and going into the bedroom and closing the door — her mom, her dad, her
sister, all of them. When all her relatives were in the bedroom with
her, Pete watched the bluish light bathe the couch beside his leg
until it was only light, not something he hated.

Pete turned and went to the front door, opening it slowly and
softly, so there was no click, and then he felt the cold damp air pour
in over his left hand as he touched the outside doorknob. Thick
ground fog covered the parking lot. Pete could barely see the front
end of Cheri's car. He looked behind him at the soft light from the
TV flickering on the couch corner. *Let her wake up to that.*

Pete took the first step out, holding his suitcase up to his chest
with his right hand, and then he brought the door closed behind
him with a click. His eyes began streaming again, his tears turning
cold on his face. He walked, the tears fanning back across his
cheeks, growing icy on his chin. He turned around and went back
to the front door. He tried the door handle, and the door opened.
Pete reached around inside and pushed in the button on the door
handle. Then he let the door click shut, locking himself out.

He started across the gravel again, shifting his suitcase to his left
hand as he passed the Ford. He let his palm touch the top of the
fender, and then he wiped the cold dew off on his pants. Beyond
the apartment parking lot, the line of Pacific Avenue streetlights
glowed a cold white in the thick mist. He could barely see the other
wing of the Palisade Apartments. He walked over to the passenger
door, and with his finger he traced a line on the chrome lip of the
roof, then made a curl in the mist on the hump of the roof itself.

He tried the car door. Locked. But the wing window was open
a crack. Pete pried it wider, reached in, and got the handle for the
window. After rolling down the window, he unlocked the door and
got in. The seat was cold to his touch, the dashboard cold on his
knees. Pete reached down and hit the lever to move the seat back.

When Cheri had first got the Ford, it was a sunny July day. She

was so proud: her own car bought with her own money from her
first job. When Pete had driven up, she had been washing the Ford
on the lawn in front of her stepmother's house, white suds in big
clumps all over the green grass. She was in her cutoff jeans and a
floppy sweatshirt. Excited, she turned around and waved at him,
her hands big bubbly mitts of white foam.

Pete stared at the glove compartment. They had probably made
love more in cars than anywhere else, even on her stepmother's living room couch. They had never made love in this car. By that
time, she was living in her own house, and she only used the Ford
for going to work.

Pete reached over and touched the steering wheel. Then he
looked back toward the apartment. In the fog he could barely see
the outline of the roof. He tried to imagine Cheri in there, but he
couldn't imagine her any more. He climbed out of the Ford, closed
the wing window, and moved the seat forward. Pushing the door
lock down, he shut the door and stared at the Ford until it became
someone else's car. As he walked backward, the Ford's blue and
white faded into the gray closing around it.

The Second Pete

WHEN PETER DAWSON called one Sunday night in April, Leigh and Pete Dwyer were playing Scrabble. They were living in a one-bedroom house on Spencer Street in Monterey, waiting for their first child to be born. Dawson said he was at the Monterey bus station and asked if Pete could pick him up.

On the drive down to Monterey, Pete thought about the last time they had met in Berkeley. A year earlier, Dawson had called from Washington to say that he was hitchhiking to California to tell Pete everything he had learned on his first acid trip. Although Pete didn't say anything to him, he had already heard from a friend who was with Dawson. Peter had dug a grave and had tried to crawl into it.

When they met in Berkeley, Peter insisted that they get high together. Rather than argue, Pete split a sugar cube with Dawson and nothing much happened — weak acid. Dawson was writing poetry, and he insisted that he was about to do something great. At a bar on San Pablo Avenue, Peter showed Pete a poem he'd written in a barn while hitchhiking down the coast. The poem was about the udders of a cow.

Dawson said that he had not been free before, but now he was free, and he could write many more poems like these.

"What do you mean, free?"

Peter had grinned, as if Pete were testing him. He put some money in a cigarette machine and then backed up against the buttons. "See?" he said, holding his pose. "It doesn't matter to me."

Then Dawson turned around and looked in the tray to see what brand of cigarettes he got. A pack of Larks.

Peter was still dressed as he had in Seattle: frat-boy ski bum. But out of his mouth came talk about freedom and intuition. Pete had probably said those things to Dawson up in Seattle when he was dealing. Pete was happy that he had never sold any acid to Dawson, but he was uncomfortable hearing those notions again. Pete wondered if what he believed now was that much different. When Dawson said them, the words became a weird echo of his present beliefs.

Before they parted, Dawson said, "You know what finally freed me? How I became a new Pete?"

"How?" Pete said.

"I pissed in my bed," Dawson said. "I just let it go, man." He flicked his fingers out and closed his eyes. "Pssss," he said.

IF PETER DAWSON hadn't been the only civilian at the Monterey bus station, Pete would have walked right past him. Dawson had lost about half his weight, his face was gaunt, his clothes were faded, and a bright orange sleeping bag was rolled up under his backpack.

"Hi, Dwyse," Peter said. Pete's old nickname was the only thing he said at first.

Pete led Dawson out of the bus station to his 1950 Chevy panel truck. As Pete drove down Lighthouse Avenue, Dawson didn't talk, leaning into the dilated nod of an acidhead, the bass pump of the blood and the high whine of the nervous system. Pete asked him how he got his phone number.

Dawson didn't say anything. He only smiled.

"My mother?" Pete guessed.

"Going to Sur," Dawson replied. He nodded at his pack in back. "Going to see Henry Miller, man."

"He doesn't live there any more." Pete got irritated by that. Instead of going to the Playboy Club, digging Cannonball Adderley, and buying Head skis, Dawson was now shopping Henry Miller. "He's been gone for years," Pete added.

"That's okay, too." Dawson smiled. He could tell that Pete was irritated, and such things amused him.

"You're passing through then, Peter?"

Dawson smiled again, nodding.

"You can sleep in your bag on our couch, unless you want to sleep out on the porch."

When they got to Spencer Street, Pete hurried up to the house ahead of Peter. He told Leigh that Dawson was only staying overnight, and she continued to stare at the Scrabble board. When Pete returned into the living room, Dawson was standing on the porch, looking out at the lights ringing Monterey Bay. Pete tapped him on the shoulder and pointed at the couch. Then it occurred to Pete that Leigh hadn't said anything.

He walked back into the kitchen, and Leigh was staring off into space. Pete looked at the Scrabble board and saw that she hadn't made a word while he was gone.

"The contractions have started," she said. "They're about four minutes apart."

Pete felt a cold rush inside him, and for a moment he could feel the evening air from the open front door moving across his skin. Then he gathered himself up inside, ready to do everything as precisely and perfectly as he could. Without replying to Leigh, he walked into the bedroom and took the clock from beside the bed. Putting it next to the Scrabble board, he leaned over and stared into Leigh's eyes.

"It's your turn," he said softly. "Make another word." Leigh nodded, but she didn't do anything. She seemed a million miles away, listening for the next tightening. "Make a word, Leigh," Pete said again.

In the bedroom, Pete called the hospital, and the staff nurse told him all the things he had already memorized. He walked back and looked at Leigh. She was still staring down at the Scrabble board, completely oblivious to him.

Pete paced back into the living room. Dawson was sitting on the couch, staring at his foot, so Pete turned around and went into the kitchen and sat down at the table.

For a few hours, Leigh and Pete pretended to be playing Scrabble, while they timed the contractions. Leigh couldn't make any words. She was moving further and further away from Pete, only seeming to see him from time to time. At midnight the contractions began coming closer and closer together. Pete called to alert the hospital. Then he got Leigh's travel bag. Helping her up from the chair, they walked past Dawson, who was still sitting on the couch and staring at his foot.

At the truck, Pete eased Leigh into the front seat, and she looked up as if she had just remembered that he was there. "I forgot a nightgown," Leigh said. "I mean, for myself." She smiled at the humor. "I only packed one for the baby."

And then it hit both of them that she was really going to have their baby.

All of Pete's control evaporated, and in a panic he went scurrying up the stairs to the house. As he came through the living room, he stopped in front of Peter, who was still staring at his foot. "Leigh's going to have our baby," he announced, making his recent discovery down at the truck public. "I'll be back for sure by morning." Pete looked at Dawson's face. No sign. "I have a job to do then," he added, as if to reassure Dawson he was a responsible adult and wasn't lying about their baby coming.

"I could feel it," Peter said without looking up.

"Feel what?"

Dawson smiled faintly. He did not answer.

That pissed Pete off. He didn't want to share their baby with an acidhead. "Look," Pete said, heading for the bedroom, "if you want some food, it's in the fridge."

"I only eat nuts and raisins now," Dawson said. He looked up at him with an amused look, as if Pete should have known that he was a vegetarian now.

By morning, Leigh was still in labor. The doctor told them it would be hours before birth. Pete had a hauling job, so he went back to the house for some tools. When he stepped up on the front porch, he saw Dawson through the front door window, sitting in the same position as the night before, looking like a scarecrow propped up on the couch. His sleeping bag was unrolled on the floor. Pete walked past him into the kitchen and made some sandwiches for his lunch.

"Would you mind feeding Cowtrail?" he said. There was no answer. "Cowtrail is our cat," he explained. There was still no reply. "He will be around looking for food, so could you feed him." Pete listened. Still nothing.

Then he went out the back door to get a shovel and a pitchfork.

As he walked around the house with his sandwiches and tools, he looked in the window at Peter. Dawson hadn't moved. Pete stood there for a long time, watching him, and Dawson only stared down at his foot, smiling every now and then.

After Pete did the hauling job, he went to the hospital. Leigh had planned to have a natural birth, but the labor had gone on too long, exhausting her. The doctor recommended a saddle block. Both Leigh and Pete agreed. The doctor had okayed Pete to be in the delivery room. Pete would be the first father in the hospital's history to be present at the birth.

But when Pete walked into the delivery room, the nurse became very upset and territorial. A short, older woman with a very self-important way about her, she was the boss in that room, and she did not want Pete there. Pete ignored her. Pulling up a stool next to Leigh, he held her hand. The nurse made grumbling noises every time she had to step around Pete, as if he were in the way.

The doctor showed him when the presentation of the baby's head took place and then sent him back to comfort Leigh. Pete was feeling wilder and wilder, his anguish at Leigh's suffering flowing into an amazing and crazy high. And when the purple wet being was delivered from Leigh's womb, Pete was so joyous—he had never felt the joy that he felt then. That baby girl became the star of his being.

Pete stared at the child as the doctor set it on Leigh's belly. "It's a girl." His voice came from a very long way away.

Leigh seized the baby so fiercely that Pete tried to stop her. "What are you doing?"

Leigh stuck her left elbow out to ward Pete off. She pulled up the baby's hands and felt her fingers. "I'm counting her fingers," Leigh said. Then she held up the baby's feet and counted her toes.

The ferocity of the gestures stunned Pete. It was the most purely animal thing Pete had ever seen Leigh do.

She's a mother, he thought. Then he realized that this made him a father. The idea seemed so huge and heavy, Pete sat back down on the stool beside Leigh. *A father, I'm a father.* For a moment Pete felt dizzy. After kissing Leigh, Pete got up from the stool. It was as if the work were done and he had to go off and think about it. But he could not stop smiling.

Confusing joy with fainting, the nurse thought that he was

about to pass out. She jammed her fingers in his armpit, almost lifting him off the ground, and cracked an amyl nitrite under his nose.

Pete didn't pay any attention to her. Shaking her off, he said, "I
think I'll sit down in the corner." He went over and sat down on
the delivery-room floor. He had never felt so wonderful. The tile
floor was cool, and he put his palm down on it. Then he discovered
the amyl nitrite the nurse had pushed between his fingers. *Hey*, he
thought. *Dope! Why are they giving me dope?* Then he thought, *It's
over. I'm a father. Why not?*

He sniffed the amyl and waited to go up. Instead, he came down.
He looked at the capsule to make sure it was amyl nitrite. That was
another first. Sniffing amyl nitrite and then coming *down?* Ex-
perimenting, he sniffed the capsule again, and this time he went
up. "Oh, amyl nitrite," he said, as if greeting an old friend.

The nurse shot nasty looks at him. Not only did she have a father
in the delivery room, she had a dope fiend too.

Pete wanted to say to her, *Hey, I'm not supposed to enjoy this or
something?* But, instead, he got up, walked over to the nurse,
winked at her, and dropped the spent capsule at her feet. *Baby*, he
kept thinking, *it's a baby.* He could not get over it. *Our baby.*

WHEN PETE got to the house, he was still flying high. He paced
around the front room, describing the scene over and over: the
nurse, the doctor, the way the baby had looked when she came out
of the womb. "I mean, Leigh had all these little clothes, but I never
thought there'd ever be a real baby inside them. Erin, her name's
Erin!"

Pete couldn't stop talking while he marched around the living
room. On the couch, Dawson sat staring at his foot. Finally some
of Pete's energy rubbed off on him, and Peter began pacing around
the room with Pete, the two of them going around in circles.
Dawson even started talking.

"That musta been something," Dawson kept repeating after
each new volley of chatter from Pete. "That musta been
something."

THAT NIGHT, when Pete came back from the hospital, he explained to Peter that Leigh and the new baby, Erin, would be needing

the house all to themselves when they came home in the morning. Pete wasn't sure that Dawson understood: by that time, Dawson was back on the couch staring at his foot again. Pete tried to point out the effect of this on Dawson's upcoming future, "so think about where you want to go, and I'll drop you off, okay?"

There was still no response. Dawson continued to stare at his foot, but something must have got through, because in the morning his sleeping bag was rolled up, the bag of nuts and raisins was gone, and Dawson asked Pete if he could get a ride down to Big Sur. The hospital was just off the Big Sur highway, so Pete told him he'd take him that far. He was relieved that Dawson had some plan of action.

Just before they left, Pete put the breakfast eggs back in the refrigerator, and he saw a can of tuna fish open on the bottom shelf. Dawson had fed Cowtrail tuna fish rather than cat food. Pete wondered if Peter could tell the difference any more.

Just before Pete turned into the hospital entrance, he pointed out Highway 1, going south to Big Sur. Then he turned off into the hospital parking lot. After Pete got out, Dawson stood beside the truck.

"You'll go that way," Pete said. "I'm going a different way." And he walked off toward the hospital.

It wasn't until Pete was checking Leigh and the baby out of the hospital that he thought that Peter might have wanted to come in and see the baby. Pete felt bad about assuming that Peter wasn't human enough to want to see a baby. But then that night Pete thought that Dawson wasn't human enough to use words and ask.

TWELVE DAYS LATER, Pete came back home from a job, and he found Leigh standing in the kitchen doorway with a terrible fragile look on her face.

"What happened?" Pete moved toward the bedroom. "The baby?"

"No, you better sit down."

Pete sat down on a kitchen chair and Leigh told him that his father had died that afternoon, dropping dead on the third floor of the mill.

All Pete could think was, *There should be more.*

He reran what Leigh said, and the words dissolved, and then he heard them again inside himself. He felt himself open up, taking in everything that he could see or feel or think, until it seemed as though there was so much inside him, nothing could ever end. *But there should be more.*

The next night, after the funeral in Tacoma, Pete was resting on his childhood bed upstairs in his mother's house. When he closed his eyes, he saw his father on a dim round screen. His face was confused, as if he weren't sure what he was doing there. His lips moved. But no words were coming out. Then he faded.

And Pete thought of his new daughter, and of Peter, and of words and why you want to live. He thought about them, one after another: of his daughter who was new and had no words, and of Peter who was losing them, and of his father without them, and how he connected them all together. Then he thought about them again, of words, of Peter, his daughter and his father, until he fell asleep.

III

TEN YEARS LATER

Over and Under

HE WAS SORRY he told her about the slug. "Look, there's no reason to do that," Dean said. He looked up in the fir tree and shook his head. Then he shifted his over-and-under rifle around, so it was pointing down the slope at soft, loosely packed duff. The slightly bitter scent of the dry pine needles drifted up the slope on the breeze.

"Come on," Valerie said. "God, you're the one who said you had one."

"I know. I wasn't thinking. I'm not even sure that a shotgun slug will kill it."

"Of course, it will," Valerie said. "My uncle Phil shot a young one just like that with a .410. Bigger than that." She looked up in the fir tree and nodded. "God, don't tell me you're scared. Give me the gun. I'll do it."

"No, no," Dean said. He looked down at his parka vest and fingered the shotgun shell in the pocket. "But it's just that we only have one chance."

He looked over his wife's head at the tree. From where they stood on the slope, they were only about twenty feet under the treetop. Up in the crown of the fir was a black bear. Small, not very large at all compared to some Dean had seen, it clung to the tree trunk, looking down and eyeing them.

"It's meat," Valerie said.

"Val," Dean said.

"And it's money. The company will give us some bounty money.

And with you going on leave, we'll need both. Oh, god, Dean, give me the gun."

"I just don't believe in…" Dean said.

"Don't start that. You'll shoot deer, you'll shoot this. The company's taken us out in the tree farm, and I've seen how many sprouts they've eaten. It takes a crew half a day to do one hillside, and a young one like that could mow down a whole slope." Valerie put her hand out. "Give it to me. I'll do it. Besides, I'm a better shot than you are."

After Dean unloaded the .410, taking the bird-shot shell out, he put in the shotgun shell with the slug in the lower chamber of the over and under. Even though he knew it was almost useless, for a backup emergency round he took a .22 Long Rifle shell, and with his knife whetstone he filed down the bullet until the tip was flat, then notched it with his knife. He loaded the shell into the upper .22 chamber. A dumdum bullet wouldn't stop a bear, but it would blow a good hole in it, slow it down if it came after him.

Checking the safety again, he began to climb down the slope, holding the rifle up and out to the right, so if he slipped, it'd be aiming away from him. On his left, Valerie watched him from the top of the slope. At the base of the fir, he moved back until he was clear of the lower branches and had a good angle. He checked for a good escape route, and he found one up the side of the slope, heading off toward a creek. Taking the safety off, he stepped back a little farther.

He aimed for behind its ear and pulled the shotgun trigger. The black bear seemed to jerk, as if it were scooting up one more step on the tree trunk. A dark clot sailed up off its head, and then it was dead. The dead bear fell, tumbling backward, hitting limbs. Turning sideways, it smashed into a bough, broke it, and then flopped off and dropped, arms outspread, facing up to the sky, crashing through the limbs, until it hit the snow—a big black ball of fur.

THE DUSTY BACKYARD smelled of wet fur, blood, hot mufflers, and gasoline. Behind the Durn's Honda three-wheeler trailed a blood-clotted hank of rope. A hoist had been formed by roping two four-by-fours to either side of the top beam, which extended out four feet from the side of Durn's cinder-block garage. Under the beam, a block and tackle hung from a heavy rusted chain. The black bear was hooked to the tackle rope, slung up by his back feet.

When Dean came out with two Rainier beers, Hank Durn was busy sharpening his butchering knives. A dark-stained butcher block stood to one side of the four-by-four. A big green fifty-gallon drum was on the other side, smelling of blood.

"Just got to bring in the paws to the company for the bounty," Hank said. "Val can take them in when she goes to work in the morning. The hide'll go to the Boy Scouts if you want."

"Gimme it. I'll tan it, put it in my new study for a rug," Dean said. "You want some of the meat, neighbor?"

"Naw, I'm partial to venison, myself."

"I've never eaten bear meat before," Dean said.

"Like horse or fatty pot-roast beef," Hank said. "Bear's best in stews."

"I've never eaten horse."

"It's good," Hank said. He smiled. "Frenchies eat it." He winked. "But then they eat goddamn near anything."

On the chopping block Hank laid out a long skinny knife that had been sharpened so many times, the blade now curved in just above the handle, along with a short squat knife with an upturned tip on it. "Now this here one," Hank said, holding the short one up, "is for flensing the hide. I'll do that first, after we lug the guts into that barrel there."

"I forgot, I've got to make a phone call," Dean said. "I'll be back in a few minutes." He handed the knife back to Hank and shrugged. "What with me taking leave for a year, everybody thinks of stuff they never had to know before. Go to old Hagenbarth—he'll know. It'll just be a minute."

"Well, this won't take long," Hank said, testing the edge of the knife with his thumb. "Hurry back, or you'll miss it."

The phone calls to his office took longer than Dean thought they would. When Dean stepped out on the back porch, Hank was just finishing with the first part of the butchering. As the hide was stripped off, Dean saw with horror the naked body of a fat uncle emerge from under the fur, streaked with blood and yellow slabs of fat. The bear, stripped, looked truly human.

Dean hesitated, then ducked back in the house. He felt ill, and he walked back across the kitchen and opened the refrigerator door. The cold air felt good, and he leaned in farther and breathed

it, staring at the neat packages of food inside. He reached for a
Rainier beer, thinking hard about the body outside, hoisted up beside the garage. After a while, he found himself staring at a package
of ground beef, a mottled red and white mound. Under the shining
plastic wrap, the meat looked okay, like nothing human, and Dean
had to remind himself that's how the bear would come out, once
this was over.

Feeling less sick, Dean opened the beer, sat down at the kitchen
table, and made a few more phone calls to the Human Resources
Department, checking up on some details. Sitting with his back to
the window and talking to a caseworker, he heard *wok, wok, wok,
wok,* as Hank chopped something four times.

He came down the back door steps into the smell of freshly
butchered meat. On the dusty ground under the bear's stripped
and opened body was a thick congealed pool of blood. A few maple
leaves had fallen and drifted into it, their pointy yellowed edges
dyed a black red. Flies were beginning to land around the edge of
the pool, and the rim of the fifty-gallon barrel was thick with fat
bluebottle flies, a cloud of them rising and falling in the mouth of
the barrel. On the wide blue and white fender of the Honda three-
wheeler were the four chopped-off bear paws.

GETTING UP from his typewriter, Dean pushed open one of the
small windows that lined the bottom of the north wall. He was looking through the larger upper windows at the snow on the pine
bough outside, when he heard the back door of the house open and
the faint sounds of Valerie talking low. "Daddy's working in his
study. Karl, you go outside. Don't play on your dad's side of the
house." The back door closed. He waited until the sound of his
son's boots went crunching down the packed snow of the driveway.

Dean picked up the coffee cup beside his four lucky books on the
corner of his desk: *On The Road, Crime And Punishment, In Our
Time, Sons and Lovers.* Those were the only books he kept near his
own writing—the books he was reading in his hotel room that
summer, the same summer he was writing about now. Four portable library bookcases were stacked next to a cork bulletin board,
the top case empty. Dean put his four lucky books in it and slid the
inch-high stack of manuscript next to them and pulled down the
bookcase's sliding glass door. Then he walked slowly by the bulletin

board, reviewing the four typed sheets with the outline for his book. Dean continued out of his study down the long hallway toward the door to the kitchen.

Dean's study had been originally built separate from the main house, but then he added the hallway, thinking it would raise the value of his property if it was connected. But he had put in a thick solid-core door with soundproofing around it, so no domestic sounds filtered down the hallway to his room. In the kitchen, he went over to the Mr. Coffee machine beside the sink, as Valerie came in.

"Hi, hon, how's it going? I sent the boy outside to build a snowman."

"Great." Dean added some cream to his coffee. "Got in a good morning."

"Are you done for now?"

"Well," Dean shrugged, "sorta. Taking a break."

"I want to show you something I found. A letter from you." Valerie went into the living room. "I was going through some old letters you wrote me when you were working on the freeway that summer." She came back with some lined notebook paper, folded over once.

"Wow, that looks like a manuscript almost," Dean joked, hefting the paper. "I was prolific in those days. With letters."

"It was when you decided to be a writer," Valerie said. "I thought it was so brave of you."

"Which time was this?" Dean joked. He looked warily at the first page. "I remember making up my mind over and over."

Valerie took the big blue roasting pot out of the refrigerator and put it on the gas range. She came back over and stood beside his chair, looking down at him. She smiled. "Aren't you going to read it? Lord, I was so proud of you — and myself," she giggled. "Some country girl from Centralia with a real writer for a boyfriend. I told everyone in my dorm."

"Well, I was only nineteen. I hadn't written anything," Dean said. "Still haven't."

"Well, don't say *that*. You've started. You're really doing it now."

Dean tried to read the first page, but it was so full of posturing and references to great works of literature that it was too embarrassing to read it with Val staring at him. "I am in top form. With these books for fuel and a fresh pack of cigarettes…"

Everything he wrote in the letter appalled him. None of it was true. The letters didn't even mention the dingy cheap room, the stink and racket of the Seattle skid-row hotel. He claimed he rented it so he could save money from his construction job, but actually he was trying to imitate Jack Kerouac. He could remember sitting in a robe and smoking cigarettes and writing in a journal and playing writer.

"I'll look at it in my room." Dean pointed at the roasting pot. "What's for dinner?"

"We're having stew, using up the freezer meat. I didn't mean to pry. I just thought it would help, now that you've got such a good start," Valerie said. "You know, to look back and see how far you've come."

DEAN LOOKED BACK from the blooming apricot orchard and the waves of yellow mustard flowers under them. He shrugged at Val seated across from him at the patio table."It's just that…No, I don't want to do that," Dean said. "I'm not looking back. Not while I'm rolling like this." Dean regarded the wine bottle shaded by the patio umbrella. He tipped it to its side, holding it outside in the sun to check how much was left. "Val, it's just that's the way it's gotta be."

"Where are you now?"

"I'm on the part where the construction crew goes to the religious guy's hotel apartment. That's the middle part." Dean thought about what he had said. "See, the hotel—that's where the hero finds out he really doesn't fit in with all those guys. So it's important." He pushed the wine away and stood up. "I better get back."

"Honey, we were just talking about it. You don't have to run off."

"Well, it's just that I don't like talking about it, Val. It ruins it. I'm not looking at what I've written, I'm not talking about it, I'm just going on. See," Dean held up his hands and looked at them, "I don't know how to say this. When I'm rolling like this, they feel…like they're on their own."

But when he returned to his study, Dean couldn't concentrate, his hands only lay there on the typewriter. He had never imagined there could be such a distance between the two, between paper and the typewriter. And between what he had held in his mind for so long and the words that came out. Whenever he started thinking about the hotel room and the guys in it, he ended up telling himself what that scene meant to the novel, not what was happening. The real stuff didn't come out real. And he was no longer there any more in that room. In that hotel room.

Getting up from his typewriter, he paced around. He put his four lucky books back inside the polished oak bookcase, laid his pages beside them, swung the door down, and stared through the glass at them. Maybe some of that old feeling that he had for those books would rub off on his stuff. As he circled the room, the only sounds were the soft *shish-shish* of his feet as he passed over the bear rug. Picking up his mug, he sniffed the the cool cream and coffee, the coffee now only a faint burnt brown smell.

On the bulletin board next to his chapter outlines hung his old letter to Val. Dean started to read, but it didn't have what he wanted. The letter was just words. That wasn't what his life was like then. "My mood is probably one of a little more quiet nature." Ugh, what crummy language. Confessing crap like that, what had he been thinking about then, *really*?

He had to get it down, how his whole life had changed *in that hotel room*, but it had to be right, exactly how it felt. Let the scenes flow over him. How the hotel room looked, how it smelled, how the closet smelled, the way the guys sprawled there, talking, their yellow hard hats on the floor. But nothing was coming back. He wasn't there in the hotel room any more, and all that was left was his dumb letter—crap about what he was reading, when the whole time the real life was right there, and he was in the stew of it, and it was so much better than that letter written when he was actually living in that hotel room. Dean wished Val had never dug out the letter. It upset everything, put a huge hole under his hopes for what was on that stack of paper. He was afraid now to go back and read what he'd written, frightened that it was going to be just as fake as that phony letter.

Dean stood looking out at his orchard in his backyard. The apricot trees were blooming, red and white blossoms. The apple trees were budding, not quite blooming yet. Five years ago, two days after Val gave birth to their son and was still in the hospital, he had stayed up, planning his study away from the main house. Karl was going to be their only child, and Dean decided it was now or never for his book. He had to make plans. Val had been in his corner every minute, even helping lay the concrete for the foundation.

From his study he couldn't see the garage, the driveway, only the

back yard with its trees and then the barbed-wire fence and the pasture behind that, a level green sea almost as high as the fence, and
the line of firs behind that, the old rotting stump in the corner, next
to the bleached white granite rocks. In the nearest corner of the
pasture stood an old weathered shed with a new corrugated aluminum roof. Dean stared at the shed and the roof that he put on
about a month before Val got preggers. One window was knocked
out, blocked with a yellow rusty Pennzoil sign.

When he and Val first bought the property, he'd held the roman-
tic notion of turning that into his writing room. But after Karl was
born, he got serious. He'd need his room warm enough for winter.
Building the study, he thought, would take two years, and by then
Karl would be old enough for baby-sitting. Dean had been wrong.
His room had taken five years, but he had done it on his two-week
summer vacations and weekends, had set everything up so it was
perfect, and it was perfect—he knew it was. Then he'd taken a
year's leave from work.

Stepping over to the side window, Dean slowly pulled back the
blinds. Through it he had a view of the main house, and it provided
his only access to his household except by the hallway. He watched
Val in the kitchen moving around. Dean was always pleased how
sure she was—how even the sounds of the dishes touching, the
pots being emptied by a wooden spoon, the swift click of the egg-
beater tines, all seemed so right. *Serial intelligence*, he thought.
*That's what she has. Never gets too deep, never too high, one thing
at a time.*

And suddenly Dean wanted to go back there, in the kitchen
watching Val, and be like he used to be, before he started in on this
dream of his, before he tied himself to something he was afraid to
look at, afraid to finish. Dean stared at Val and felt a sudden surge
of bitterness, as if things were somehow her fault. Now, cutoff
without sound or smell and framed in the kitchen-window pane,
she was more an actor on a defective TV set, no less perfect, but
unaware that she was no longer getting through.

DEAN HAD JUST FINISHED reading his manuscript all the way
through for the first time when the blatting exhaust of Durn's
Honda came down the drive. He put the pile of pages alongside his
four lucky books, stacked on the corner of his desk. He located two

long tan rubber bands, and, lifting the manuscript again, he put both rubber bands around the paper and put the manuscript back alongside the books. He sat there listening through the open window, as his son jabbered and yelled in the driveway and the three-wheeler revved and revved. Hank had taken his boy for a spin. A cloud of dust and exhaust drifted over the browning grass and under the fruit trees, between the poles propping up the apple limbs, sailed over the barbed wire fence, and dissolved on the front of the shed.

For years his story had been under all the other stuff. He could feel it there inside him. The way Dean had always thought about it, he imagined that once out, then it might be hurt, maybe even to the point of dying, and he'd been frightened of that, worried about who was going to see it first, whom to send it to, things that seemed pointlessly remote now. But because he had felt it in him for so long, he never imagined that his story could die inside him, before it ever came out. That's the one thing he never considered: that when it came out from under all the other stuff into the light, it would be lifeless—that it would be stillborn.

"THERE HE GOES, one more week before he's back at the office, jawing with those unemployed jar-head loggers, and he's still steaming out there to work on that book of his," Hank Durn laughed. "Remember, Hagenbarth, all your neighbors are rooting for you." He turned to Val who was at the gas range. "That guy of yours is spending every minute out in there, isn't he?"

Dean paused as he opened the door. Val didn't turn around from her work. "Oh, yeah," said Val. "But it's about over."

"Can't even hear him typing out in that shack of his. Howdaya know he's not doping off?" Hank said. "Just funning—don't mind me. He's going to let us read it when it's done, ain't he?"

"No one's read it yet," Val said to the pots and pans. "I mean, he's read it, but he's letting it sit for a few months, and then maybe…"

Dean shut the door and walked down the hallway to his room. His desk top was bare except for the quarter-inch of typing paper and the stack of four books. After opening the top window out, letting in cold air, Dean watched the fruit trees shake in the wind, leaves shuddering and then spinning off, the leftover leaves turning perfectly still as the gusts subsided. He took his four lucky books off his desk and walked toward the library bookcases. Lifting the glass door, he shelved them, looking once at each: *On the Road, Crime and Punishment, In Our Time, Sons and Lovers*. As each book was eased into its place, Dean thought about what was in them, how much he had wanted to tell someone how much they meant to him when he was nineteen, because that was part of his story. But he had only taken care of the books themselves, he hadn't cared for what they meant — *inside, back then*.

He slid the glass door down and thought about the afternoon when he had bought the bookcases at the grade school auction. When he brought them home, he stacked each glassed shelf one on top of the other in the driveway, the oak and glass and brass fittings all shining in the sun. He showed Val how each little glass door still worked, and he said, "One more piece is in place. These are my four lucky shelves for my four lucky books." He had been gloating about how his plan was moving so surely toward that thick pile of typed paper. Of course, over the years the book shelves had filled up with junk from his job, files and case loads and memos, so he ended up keeping his four lucky books on the top shelf, but even then he had reserved space beside the lucky books for his own book.

Dean picked up the manuscript for his book and put what there was beside the four books in the top shelf, closed the glass door, locked it with the little brass key. He turned as a breeze rattled the windowpane, feeling a gust of cold air on his neck, and he tossed the key out the open window. Over the rustle of the wind-blown plants he imagined the click as the key was lost under the high dry grass.

Jesus Christ and
The Plaster Squirrels

A FEW YARDS off the main road, the lane to Ray Steen's house plunged down. The asphalt narrowed, and rhododendrons crowded in, rubbing on the car and pushing a damp heavy smell through the open window. On the other side of the thick green leaves, the overhanging alders obscured the lane with gray and black blotches, and the car seemed to glide down into shadows. Then the lane turned up out of the dark, and Pete Dwyer drove into the mottled sunlight of a circular driveway.

He parked beside a beige 1968 Chevrolet station wagon in front of a closed garage and got out to have a look around. Built long and low and set into the ridge like a bunker, Ray's dark wooden house blended in perfectly among the alder and fir trees. The front of the house was barely visible behind banks of rhododendrons.

An old woman stepped out from behind a rhododendron bush, and for a moment Pete thought she had been hiding. Wearing a pale blue skirt and coat and a white blouse, she held her hand in her purse. "Who are you?" she said.

"You're Ray's mother," Pete said, remembering. "I'm Pete Dwyer, from high school? Just stopping by before the reunion."

She turned away from him, as the sound of footsteps came toward them from inside the house. Ray's mother stared at the carved oak front door with its big brass knocker.

"Some place Ray has," Pete said. "A real hideaway."

Ray's mother didn't reply. She stood there, staring at the door, until Ray opened it.

"Hi, Mom," he said. "I thought I heard two cars." Then he saw Pete. "Oh, Jesus. It's Pete!"

Pete stepped out from behind Mrs. Steen to say something, but he stopped when he saw that Ray's mother was not moving.

"She's gone?" his mother asked.

"This morning," Ray said.

Pete waited beside Mrs. Steen, as she stepped forward and raised her hand out of her purse. In it was a Colt Cobra pistol.

"Here."

Ray took the Cobra in his left hand, holding it so the barrel pointed down and the black handle stuck up. Ray's mother brushed past Ray and stepped into the house. Pete stood there looking at the Colt. It was an ugly squat gun.

"Come in," Ray said. "Hey, long time no see." He let the hand with the pistol drop to his side. He put out his right hand. "Welcome."

They shook hands. Inside Pete could see Ray's mother standing by some polished wood banisters that led down to the bottom floor, craning her head this way and that, as if inspecting the hallway. Then Pete walked past Ray into the house. "This is some place."

From the hallway he could see a bank of windows in the living room overlooking the alders and the jungle of blackberry vines on the bank opposite the house. It seemed like a tree house, with only limbs and leaves and dark shadowy tree trunks visible. To Pete's right, Mrs. Steen moved behind the kitchen counter, peering at the cupboards and the sink and the electric range. A counter divided the rec room from the kitchen. Both rooms were clean and shiny. Everything seemed almost new.

"Well, hey," Ray said. "Uh, you came at a...odd time." He shook his head and shrugged, as if he couldn't do anything about it.

"What did she do?" Ray's mother said to him. She looked closely at the large oven in the wall and peered in through the glass window at the gleaming racks inside.

"The papers were served this morning, Mom. End of the line this morning," he said to Pete. He held out his right hand, palm up, as if to say, *What can you do?* Pete looked at the hand with the Colt Cobra in it. With the cylinder hidden in Ray's hand, he couldn't see if the gun was loaded.

"The neighbors found out this morning, and they came over and told me what she'd been doing," Ray said to his mother.

Pete looked out the living room windows. *What neighbors?*

In the kitchen, Ray's mother was eyeing everything, fiercely ex-amining every object and then turning to look at something else. "They did, did they?" she said, inspecting the cabinets above the counter.

Pete stepped around the stairway banister and walked into the living room. He thought he should leave the two of them alone for a second. On the rock fireplace there was a cardboard box with a gross of cassette recording tape. The top was pried open. One of the tapes was sitting next to the stereo equipment on a bookcase. On the rug alongside the bookcase were six other cardboard boxes. They were filled with record albums, all in worn, scuffed sleeves: Peter, Paul, and Mary albums, Harry Belafonte, the Kingston Trio, Chubby Checker, and Herb Alpert albums. Flipping through them, Pete could see many duplicates.

"That was one of her projects. Just before we moved out of the old house," Ray said, coming up behind Pete. "You remember Eva, don't you, Pete?" Ray gestured at the record boxes with the butt of the Colt. "Project," he said. "Another project."

"I was at your wedding."

Ray acted as if he hadn't heard Pete, and he stood there staring at the albums. "She was going to tape all our friend's records. She borrowed these from our neighbors, back in our old neighborhood. After we moved, when one of them asked for them back, she told them they were all boxed up. That was six months ago. Now I'm the one who's got to take them back to our neighbors."

"She's not getting the house, is she?" Ray's mother said, standing in the hallway. "You built this. It's yours."

Ray turned to his mother. "No," he said, "not our little retreat. I'll give her anything else." He seemed as if he were discussing the weather. "She didn't believe me. Then this morning the sheriff came with the papers." He laughed. "She thought I was bluffing again. She can only have half of it now. She had all of it before. Hell, I didn't *live* here."

"But what did she do?" Mrs. Steen stared hard at Ray. "She had to do something. What...did she do?"

"She wouldn't let my mother visit us the last six months," Ray said to Pete. "Can you imagine that?" He laughed. "She wouldn't let my own mother visit us." Ray looked up at the ceiling. "I still can't believe that."

"But what did she do?"

Ray ignored his mother. He walked back into the hallway with Pete and pointed at the sliding glass doors to the rec-room patio. It was dark there, the light blocked by huge rhododendrons. "That's hers, too. Project. Another project. She bought rhodies." His voice went up in its amazement. "More and more rhodies..." For a moment, Ray stared at the rhododendrons, then he turned to Pete. "Prize rhodies. Do you know how much prize winners cost?" He laughed again. "Up and down the lane. Every time I drove home and knocked off a goddamn leaf, I thought, *I wonder how much that leaf cost me.*" Ray shook his head as if baffled by his own stupidity. "You know, when Mom came over for the last time, she had the kids dress up as waiters. I thought it was funny, until I noticed that she had told them not to speak unless spoken to while serving dinner. I should have thrown her out then, but I didn't. I didn't. Jesus, I didn't."

Pete was trying to remember Eva and what Ray's mother was like when Ray was in high school. All he could recall was Ray's mother sitting in front of a picture window painting a landscape. Pete could remember all kinds of things about their house, and he felt embarrassed that he could only remember one thing about Mrs. Steen, her painting. Suddenly it seemed to Pete as if his past were peopled with phantoms. Eva was only a face, a round face in a white wedding dress. She had acne and an intense smile. He could picture Eva in her wedding dress posing for photographs in the Pacific Lutheran Church basement, full of tables stacked with unopened gifts.

In the living room, Ray's mother was looking at each thing there for a long time, but she wasn't touching any of them. Just looking. For a moment, Pete had the sensation that Mrs. Steen was pricing everything in the house.

"Okay, okay, I'll show you what she did," Ray called in to his mother. "You want to see what she did? I'll show you what she did. She said it was the others—that was the problem. So we got away from them. I built this house out here for that. I mean, hey, what the hell do you work for, if not to get away?"

Pete didn't know what to say to that.

"Come on down to the basement. I'll show you." Ray turned to go down the stairs. "All the neighbors came over today, one after another. They told me the things that she had been doing while

I was at work. And we've only been here six months." Ray stopped
at the head of the banister. "I had no idea." He laid the Colt Cobra
down on the polished wood post with his hand resting on top of
it, staring off as if amazed by his own ignorance. "No idea *at* all."

The gun was pointing at Pete, and he slid around to the other
side of Ray. With Ray's hand covering it, he still couldn't see if the
cylinder held any bullets.

"No idea at all," Ray laughed. "No idea at all. You don't know people. You know that, Pete? You just don't know what people will do.
You think you know people, and it turns out you don't know people
at all." Turning away from Pete, Ray lifted up the Colt and walked
downstairs. "Right this way," he said.

Mrs. Steen trotted in from the living room, and Pete waited for
her to pass him, as Ray stared up from the bottom of the stairs. He
was smiling, acting as if he were a tour guide. "To your right," he
pointed with the butt of the gun, "is another project. Prahjeck!"

Pete followed Mrs. Steen down the stairs. As Ray's mother
moved over behind Ray, Pete looked over where Ray was pointing.
In the long alcove behind the stairs, there were shelves lining the
three walls. On the floor in the middle of the alcove was a pottery
kiln. On the shelves were statues, hundreds of plaster figures. The
two side shelves were filled with unglazed statues, and the shelves
behind the kiln had glazed statues.

There were only two kinds. One statue was of Jesus Christ from
the chest up, praying to heaven. The other statue was of a squirrel.
The squirrel had his paws up, staring straight ahead as if he were
waiting for a nut. Hundreds of painted squirrels and Jesus Christs
populated the shelves at the back of the kiln. The squirrels were
either red or brown or gray, and all the Jesus statues were the same
color combination: brown robe, white shirt, and creamy pink skin,
with brown hair and beard.

"Uh," Pete said, "did Eva plan to sell these?"

"Hell, no. She *gave* them to our friends. You can imagine what
they said. How many goddamn Jesus Christs and squirrels can your
friends use? Hey, that was one more way to keep me in debt. Clay.
Buying clay. Buying glaze."

Ray's mother had obviously seen the statues before. She began
to poke around the basement. She opened the door to Ray's wood-
working room and peered around. It was full of saws and tools and
stacks of lumber.

"Uh-uh, no, not in there," Ray said. "It's not there. In here. I'll bring it out. I'll show you what she did." He walked into the other room. Through the open door Pete could see a washer and a dryer. Ray came out with some torn-up pieces of cardboard in his hands. They were painted blue. He put the Colt down on a step and handed the pieces to his mother, one at a time.

Behind him, Pete leaned over and saw the copper tips of the bullets in the cylinder holes of the Colt.

"Those were...that was..." Ray's voice choked up. He swallowed and tried again. "That was a painting by my mother. But *she* kept it in the washroom."

Ray's mother began to shift the pieces around. She acted as if she could fit the painting back together. She was nodding. "Yes," she said, "yes, this is what she did."

Ray waved at the alcove full of Jesus Christs and squirrels. "Everything else in this house could be bought at a store. Everything. That's what a man does, doesn't he? Provide? And I think just about everything could be got somewhere. Except this..."

Ray's mother continued to shuffle the pieces around.

"You don't know people," Ray said. He began to cry as he picked up the Colt Cobra off the stairs, holding it with its butt up again. "She walked right down here after the sheriff served her the walking papers. She tore this up and walked right out the door. That was the only thing she did."

Ray sniffed, and he wiped his nose with the back of his hand that was holding the Cobra. For a moment, the barrel of the Colt was aimed at Pete, and he moved sideways, but Ray wiped a second time, and the barrel swept across Pete's chest again.

"When she tore that up, then I knew she had to go. It was the only thing in the house that I could not replace."

"I'll paint you another." Turning away from Ray, his mother held up the pieces, spreading them out as if offering them to Pete. "You see? This is what did it. This is what she did."

The Sea Lion

THEIR OLD HOUSE was still there, faded and moldy, its sides turning a seaweed green. The siding of the porch splayed out at the bottom, and the front stairs slumped forward, the first step now reduced to a rotting board. The house looked as if it were nosing into the damp ground.

Franci slowed the car as she came to the intersection, rolling down the window for a closer look. The house seemed so small to her. She checked the corner of the front porch for the mark she had left when, on her tenth Christmas, she'd crashed a new Schwinn bike into it. That scar was still there but only as a dark smear filmed over by mold and dirt. Franci couldn't imagine anyone still living there, but apparently someone did. Off the top step of the porch hung a long twisted roll of dirty white cloth, probably a piece of dropped laundry.

In the back seat of the car Serena's head came up, craning to see. "Why are we stopping here, Mom?"

"We aren't." Franci put the rental car in drive and circled the block, mentally checking off the neighbors' houses — The Puhls, MacQuires, old lady Bester…

Her daughter was staring out the back window. "I like cars when they smell new," she said. "Do you like the car when it smells new?"

"Yes."

"I like it too."

Franci slowed as she neared the back alley. The gravel road was still pocked with dry holes, and a mound of sparse grass ran down its center. She turned the car into the alley; the crunch of the gravel changing to a memory of that familiar *squitching* sound under her bike tires. She stopped the car. The back fence of their old house had collapsed, blocking the alley. Franci put the car in reverse and turned to check for cross traffic as she backed out.

"Why are we here?"

"I used to live here. That green house on the end."

"Ugggh! How could you?"

"I don't know. We just did," Franci said.

She put the car in drive, and it rolled forward slowly. She drove around to the front of the house again to take one more look. Then she could go away. She pulled up to the curb and stared at the twisted white tube of laundry drooping off the porch.

"You mean you *had* to live with your mom?"

"I don't know if I had to. I just did, that's all," she said. "Sometimes you do things, and then later you wonder why."

THE REUNION WAS held at a community center located in a park out at Brown's Point. Franci had never been there before, but over the phone Millie MacDonald had told her how to find it. The center was a large square cinder-block building with a view of the bay and the town of Tacoma. On the right side of the hallway there was a kitchen. The reunion dinner had been catered by Colonel Sanders' Kentucky Fried Chicken, and big red and white cartons were stacked up on the kitchen tables. In the main hall, a tiny bandstand stood by the big sliding glass doors leading to the patio.

Millie MacDonald was waiting at the registration table. Over the years, Millie was the only person Franci had kept in contact with from those days. "Come outside and talk with Shirlee Botterini and Pia Swift, when you finish registering," she told Franci. When Franci walked out on the patio, Pia and Shirlee were laughing while Millie launched into another one of her arm-waving monologues.

"Oh, God, I believed that old hen, Mrs. Glaubinger, when she said that if you were going into politics, it didn't matter what or who you were. You had to get the facts and act on them," Millie said. "That gave me hope—that and the fact that she was in local politics, too. I thought politics was a way out. I didn't want to be

just a housewife. So I did my senior report on Taiwan. They called
it the Republic of China then. I read all the articles I could find.
I combed through the *Reader's Guide to Periodical Literature,* those
big green books. I read everything on Taiwan. Congressional Record, too. And what I found out was that Taiwan was a hole that the
United States was pouring money into. Even people in Congress
said it. I said it in my report. Old Mrs. Glaubinger gave me a C mi-
nus. I went to her and asked her what was wrong with my report
on Taiwan. She said I hadn't used the right sources. I said I used
direct quotes from *Time* and *Newsweek* and the Congressional
Record. She said that I hadn't read them right, and then she got
upset with me and told me I would never work in politics. I was
crushed. She got all up on her high horse and said that I was weak
because I had been fooled by the emotional charges in those
quotes. Glaubinger had a chart of U.S. Senators on the wall. You
remember that? Anyway, she says, 'Millie, look at this man. Look
at that man. They know what they're doing. If they give our money
to China, they have their reasons.' I said, 'But China isn't Taiwan.
Taiwan is a little island and a little island can never be China.' She
said, 'These men, they have a reason. Even if they can't say why
it is, we women have to support them.' Can you imagine?"

AT DINNER, people were curious only about how Franci had
graduated with them. Franci explained that she had finished high
school after completing her last required class in California. Summer school business-ed classes had allowed her to skip the senior
year. But that was about all she was asked. The old Parkland Lutheran clique was there, the cheerleaders and student body
officers, jocks and song leaders, and they took up everyone's attention. Most of them looked less successful than Franci had imagined
they would.

She was feeling slightly out of place. She had dressed for a con-
vention, in a gray jacket and skirt with a blue silk blouse and gray
handmade pumps—perhaps too professional a look. As she circu-
lated through the crowd, other women kept eyeing the blouse and
her gold watch. Some of the women were in evening wear. In the
harsh evening light bouncing off the pewter water, their shining
dresses seemed odd against the gray cinder-block walls, as if during

THE FIRST THING COMING

a shooting session, some local models for a chain-store fashion line had wandered into this picnic bunker to escape a rain. Halfway through the evening, Franci slipped off her watch and put it in her jacket pocket. She had kept looking at it as if she had to be somewhere. This was merely a habit, because usually Franci did have to be somewhere else—but not this night.

Since she hadn't been around Tacoma for over ten years, Franci kept feeling that she was now even more of an outsider than she'd been as a teenager. She couldn't seem to rid herself of the fantasy that she'd been sent here to scout talent for her company, for someone who was only number five on their list. As hard as she tried, she could not shake this image of her role. As people came up to chat, everyone kept grading out on her mental chart, and, except for Millie, every time anyone turned away to go elsewhere, Franci imagined a name being crossed off her list.

AFTER DINNER, Franci was sitting with Pia Swift and Shirlee Botterini, when Dean Hagenbarth and his wife, Valerie, came in late. There was a big whoop-de-do as he was welcomed by his old buddies, Hubie Cooper, Rob O'Rourke, and Pete Dwyer. When Dean came over to talk to Pia and Shirlee, Franci was chatting with someone else and had her back turned to them. As she turned around, Dean was saying something to Pia, and he stopped.

"Hey, it's...Franci," he said, checking her name tag to make sure.

"Hello, Dean." Franci was surprised how large he was. She didn't remember him being so tall.

Dean introduced her to his wife, Valerie, a short dark-haired woman who had a habit of leaning her head toward Dean as if she had trouble hearing him. Drawing up two more chairs, Dean launched into some old story from their junior year, and he kept glancing over at Franci from time to time, as if saying, *You probably never heard this.* Franci had never been a member of the social set at school like Dean and Pia and Shirlee. Dean was quite funny and had everyone at the table laughing, as he described how he forged their class adviser's signature on passes and got everyone out of classes for a solid week.

"Oh, my god, look at that!" Dean said, interrupting his story. Coming in through the patio doors was the band, three white guys and one Filipino, all in red blazers and white shirts with skinny black ties.

"Damn!" Dean said. "I bet that Flip plays an organ. Where do you suppose the committee got *these guys?* Wow, they look like they've been in a deep freeze since 1963 and just got out."

Everyone laughed at that. The band did look like some rock group that never got off the roadhouse circuit from Puyallup to Bellingham. As they set up their instruments, it turned out that the Filipino did play the keyboards, just as Dean predicted. Only it was an electric piano, not the usual electric organ that Franci remembered was a necessity for a sound big enough to fill up the cavernous Tacoma Armory or Spanish Castle dance hall.

There was no introduction. The band simply started playing, opening with "Day Tripper," and proceeded from one bar-band favorite to the next, "Satisfaction" to "Twist and Shout," the lead guitarist alternating vocals with the bassist.

The chairs and tables were pushed back, but since Franci's table was located back by the fireplace, she didn't have to move. When "Twist and Shout" started, Hubie Cooper, who'd been drunk when he got there, raced over and asked his old girlfriend, Pia, to dance. They did the twist together, which Shirlee told Franci was their big number at the high school dances. Since Franci hadn't gone to those dances at the high school, the mythology of who dated whom and who did what when seemed like a half-forgotten song.

Dean danced with his wife, Valerie, but she wasn't a very good dancer. She only went through the motions and tried to keep up with Dean. Watching the dancers, Franci's mind began to float — the old familiar feeling of being left out of the social whirl. She never fit into the system that had operated so strictly, allowing only certain girls to date certain guys. It was the delicacy of this tyranny that made Franci marvel at how easily it could be torn apart, and how it often was, but also how the ones who had the game down pat returned to it with such ease, sustained by its illusions. Looking up Dean in the reunion handbook, she found that his wife worked, which surprised her. Valerie had a dispatching job with a lumber company, and Dean was a social worker in Sedro Wolley, an area in a perpetual economic recession. Franci wondered how that must feel, constantly processing unemployed loggers.

After the song ended, Valerie came back with Dean and sprawled on a chair. "Lord," said Valerie, "I'm pooped."

Dean looked down at Franci and put out his hand. "C'mon. You haven't danced yet."

The band was taking a break, as Franci followed Dean out on the floor. She looked up at the back of his head and his shoulders. She didn't remember him being so broad. When Dean turned and faced her, he winked. "Long time, huh?"

"Oh, yeah." Franci had to smile. "Well," she turned in mock annoyance toward the band, "when are they going to go?"

Without waiting for the band to play, Dean started to dance, and Franci joined in, picking up the beat from his movements. People around them started to laugh a little, seeing they were dancing to imaginary music. When Franci and Dean got into it, they formed a circle around them, clapping in time. Then the band kicked off the song, "Proud Mary," and Franci and Dean stepped right into it together, timing their moves exactly to the back beat.

WHEN FRANCI and Dean came back to their table, Shirlee jumped up and applauded them. "You guys were really great! You had everybody going out there." She laughed, clapping her hands. "God, you two should have danced together in high school."

Franci was still a little winded from the dancing, so she only nodded at that comment. Dean glanced at Franci as she sat down, and he shrugged. "Well, yeah. You can't have everything, right Franci?"

"Ohhhhh, I don't know about that," she said, giving Dean a big obvious wink. "I think you can."

Around the table everyone laughed at Franci's comeback. And then Franci saw Valerie staring at her for a moment, before turning to Dean. Valerie put her right hand on his shoulder. "I never knew you had that in you," Valerie joked. Her hand stroked down his arm and she patted his leg. "Save a little of that, will you?"

Everybody laughed again, and Dean smiled. He wiped his brow with a paper napkin and leaned toward Valerie. "Aw, you haven't seen nothing yet," he boasted. "I still got surprises left in me."

"Promises, promises," Valerie said, faking a tired housewife whine, and Shirlee and Pia both laughed at her tone.

Dean glanced over to Franci, but she was looking out at the bay. The tip of a fog bank was creeping in from Puget Sound, covering the peninsula. Across the water, Tacoma had become a huge hulk nosing down into the thick fog, the downtown lights only dim points in the gray.

THE NEXT DAY at Pia's house, Shirlee and Pia were at the sink, Pia washing and Shirlee drying. Franci remained at the kitchen table, drinking a cup of tea and looking out at Pia's backyard. A cyclone fence bordered the back-yard lawn, and behind it was a large square pasture. A bay mare stood at the farthest corner, looking over the fence at another pasture, a cyclone fence, and a house painted the same tan as Pia's house. The only thing ruining the symmetry of the arrangement was the horse and a metal Sears and Roebuck shed in the corner of Pia's pasture. The white roof had weathered into corrugated rust, and its walls had oxidized into a chalky faded lime green. Above its door was a wooden sign: OUR ACRE.

Pia was talking about her husband, Ron. "And then he told his supe that he wasn't going out there."

Shirlee grimaced. "That probably cut it."

"Well, Ron's such a card."

"When he wants to be," Shirlee put in. Turning to Franci, she made a face. "My Steve's the same way."

"So his supervisor says, 'Well, who's going to do it then?' " Pia snorted. "And Ron says, 'The same guy who screwdle-doodled it up!' "

"Oo-la-la. *Screwdle-doodled*," Shirlee squealed. "He's such a card. Did you get to meet Ron, Franci? He came in late to the reunion."

Franci shook her head.

"Well, Ron's a lot like Steve," Shirlee said. "Except he works at the pharmacy supply, and Steve's with Uhl's furniture warehouse."

Franci went back to watching the horse. It was the most interesting thing about the back yard, and it wasn't even moving.

Shirlee put the dishtowel over a chair and sat down by Franci. "You must have a lot of stories like that. But, of course, not so crazy like that, having to tell people what's what."

Franci turned away from watching the motionless horse. She asked, "Why not?"

"Well, I mean, you're a secretary..."

"No, no, no, Shirl, geez," Pia broke in. "Franci's the director now. *She* tells people what's what—lots now, I bet, too."

"Oh," Shirlee said, "I guess I didn't read your thingee in the reunion handbook."

"Well, I had to fire my boss," Franci said.

Shirlee squinted for a second, then laughed, thinking Franci had made a joke. "You what?"

"How'd you do that, for the love of Mike?" Pia asked.

"I had to fire my boss," Franci repeated. "After I was working there three years, I went to a meeting with the president, and my boss couldn't make it. I had to cover for him, and I was tired of doing that. I was going to quit anyway, so I went over my boss's report—told the president where his report was wrong. When I got finished, the president called my boss and told him not to bother to come in—someone else had his job."

Pia rinsed off a platter and put it in the rack. Seeing that, Shirlee moved away from Franci and picked up a fresh dishtowel from the pile on top of the refrigerator. Lifting up the platter, Shirlee glanced back at Franci. "Um-hmm," she said.

"So after my mother died," Franci continued, "I took the money from selling the house and bought into the company. The firm was expanding our line of sports clothes, and they needed capital. But I couldn't have done that unless I fired my boss first."

"Well, I guess that's how those things get done." Shirlee carefully dried off the edges of the platter. "But I sure wouldn't want my Steve trying that."

MILLIE MACDONALD'S HOUSE was near Ocean City. Millie had inherited it a few years before, left her teaching job, and joined the administration of the local junior college. When Millie's grandmother owned the house, Millie and Franci had vacationed there during their summers. Those were the best times, and Franci always remembered how happy she was at getting away from her mother. On Monday, Franci found the place without too much trouble.

The house was just as she remembered it—only it seemed smaller, while the overgrown jungle of blackberries and alder around it seemed bigger, thicker. Built on a slight knoll, the white clapboard two-story house with its tiny front lawn faced the road and the ocean. A thick stand of alder and pine shielded it from the road. A guest house had been added toward the back, between the old garage and the main house. On the other side of the road, some freshly bulldozed beach fronts were dotted with newer homes, and now Millie's ocean view from the knoll was partially blocked by half-finished condos.

Millie's car wasn't parked at the house, so Franci took a drive around Gray's Harbor and through the town of Hoquiam. She parked the car on a slight bluff and enjoyed the clear light coming off the sharp curls of onrushing waves. She wanted the pleasure of driving up when Millie was there, to see Millie come out and welcome her, as in the old times. Franci wanted to get out of the car then and smell the grass and pine trees and ocean breeze.

Serena was curled up in the back seat, staring out at the ocean and hugging a large purple teddy bear. The bear was homemade, an old toy of Franci's. After her mother died, her aunt had stored it in Seattle until Franci came back up to the Northwest.

Millie had a daughter too, Trish, one year older than Franci's girl, and this excursion to the ocean promised to be a treat for both. Franci and Millie had kept in touch with letters for ten years, and Millie had been telling Trish all about Serena, the same as Franci had talked to Serena all about Trish. When Millie called Franci at her aunt's house to confirm the meeting, the two girls had talked for the first time, and this had excited them. From Serena's serious and thoughtful composure, Franci knew that this was a big event for her. Franci hoped that this could blossom into a friendship as open and easy as Franci had always felt toward Millie.

"So I WAIT two weeks, sure that I'll get by with it, but no. Old Mill's knocked up the first time she tries it. We didn't even *do* it again those whole two weeks. I was waiting to go to the campus doctor and get birth control pills for my complexion. Do you remember that? I keep forgetting that you didn't go to college. A lot of girls on campus had complexion problems in their freshman year, let me tell you."

Millie laughed, waving her arms around. Franci had to laugh too, seeing Millie doing that arm-waving stuff again.

"I mean, the whole thing seems so stupid now. Boy, was I ever dumb, dumb, dumb. Some campus radical I was."

"In high school I did everything to avoid getting pregnant," Franci said. "I was terrified of getting pregnant."

"Who wasn't?"

"That's the one thing I didn't want to happen. I didn't want to end up married to a stranger and then spend the rest of my life watching him go to Boeing every morning," Franci said.

Millie looked down at her mug of tea and tipped it up, staring through the thin brown liquid at the round bottom. "There are worse things." She shrugged. "I can think of some."

"Sure, there are always *worse* things, Mill. That doesn't mean you have to shortchange yourself."

"Well, at least in high school *you* went out and had a good time. I thought you were so brave, when you left town for California and graduated a year early," Millie said. "Old Mill here threw herself into campus politics. What a waste of time."

"I don't know about that, Millie. You were good at that stuff. Well, you were. You wouldn't be working at the college here, if you weren't, right? And you learned about people."

"Oh, I guess. Sometimes I think it's only a safe way for me to get excited."

"Well, I was trying to have a good time, too. I'm not sure that's what I had. God, some of the guys I went out with..."

"Speaking of guys, I met this old classmate at the reunion. I don't know if you ever knew him that well. Anyway, he's coming out to stay in the guesthouse."

"Oo-la-la," Franci laughed.

Millie flushed. "God, I haven't heard that expression in years."

"You remember the Everly Brothers? 'Wake Up, Little Susie.'"

"That's right. '*All our friends will go, Oo-la-la.*'" Millie grinned shyly. "Anyway, we sort of hit it off. I mean, we didn't even stick around. You know how *I* am sometimes. After two marriages in ten years, you'd think I'd learn. But that's me."

"I wondered where you disappeared to. You didn't even stick around for the dancing. Who is he?"

"He was one of the Army brats, came to the school in the spring that you left town, and then stayed to graduate the next year. You probably never met him. He ran around with Pete Dwyer, Rob O'Rourke, Hubie, and Dean—you know, the jock crowd."

WHEN ORIN SLOAT showed up in the afternoon, Franci had gone ahead to the beach with Serena and Trish. Mill promised to bring Orin along, once she got him settled in the guesthouse. Two hours later, Orin Sloat walked down to the beach and Mill was not with him. By then, Franci was ready to take the two kids back to the house, because they were almost completely played out.

Orin was wearing a faded pea-green turtleneck sweater, and old torn jeans. "Hey, now, Millie's taking a nap," he said to Franci. His moon face was flushed from the wind, and he smiled pleasantly.

Franci didn't say anything. She turned and shouted to the kids to get ready to leave.

Orin chatted about a few things, how long the beach was, how fast the wind had come up, how fast the sun seemed to go down at the ocean, and how much fun the kids were having. He mentioned again that Millie was taking a nap, and said maybe he should have brought his parka vest, and then he remarked on the length of the beach.

Franci agreed the beach was long. She called again for the girls to come away from the surf, and she got their beach basket ready to go.

When the girls came back, Orin joked with Trish and produced some striped candy from his pants pockets for both girls. His cheeks were getting red in the ocean wind and he stood with his arms crossed on his chest, trying to stay warm. Franci slowed down her packing, allowing the girls to wander back to the beach. Then she rounded them up again, taking time to play in the surf, as farther up the beach Orin stood by the basket, his fat-cheeked face getting more and more red in the cold wind.

As the girls raced ahead to the path cut between the grass and logs, Orin fell in beside Franci. He trudged alongside until they reached the loose sand, where the going was slower. On the slope leading to the path, he went ahead of Franci and then paused, waiting for her to catch up. When she came up to his level, she looked at him, and he smiled and nodded. "That's okay," he said offhandedly, as if they'd been talking. "You don't *have* to like me. Only Trish *has* to like me."

BEFORE DINNER, Orin sat at the table beside the bank of windows facing the ocean. Wadded up on the window ledge was a *Seattle*

Post-Intelligencer. On the floor under the table were his shoes, and his parka vest hung over the back of his chair. An opened jar of pickled herring on the table was surrounded by red and gold and blue wrappers of cheese wedges. The chair opposite Orin was empty, and when Franci came in, he held out his hand, inviting her to sit down. Franci shook her head and walked over to the French doors, staring up at the layered red streaks of clouds in the sky. From the kitchen, floated in the sounds of Millie and the girls fixing dinner and setting the table.

Orin picked up the squat jar of pickled herring and, with a delicate quick twist of his fork, speared a piece. He looked up and saw that Franci had been watching him. He rested the edge of the fork on the glass mouth of the herring jar and let out a belch.

"Hey, now. Tastes just as good the second time," he said.

"To some," Franci said.

In the cool summer evening, Millie and Franci sat at the kitchen table, sipping tea out of Millie's grandmother's best china. Out the back window they could see Orin Sloat pushing the two girls on the swing set. Behind the garage, the alders and pine trees were a green canopy, shining in the fine ocean mist.

Millie shifted her saucer and cup around and cleared her throat. "He's retired."

"I bet he is," Franci said.

"No, he is. On disability from the Army. Really. His jeep overturned, and he wrecked his shoulder. You should see the big scar on his thigh."

"I'd rather not."

"Oh, God, Franci, you're acting totally jealous, you know that?"

Franci looked down at the steam coming off her tea. "Maybe I am," she said. "I guess maybe I thought this time was going to be for Serena and you and Trish and me."

Millie didn't say anything to that. She only looked out at the kids squealing, as Orin pushed them higher and higher on the swings.

"He told *me* he'd been in far-eastern imports after his discharge," Franci laughed. "With some buddies from Nam. *Nam* — I hate the way some men say that. I can imagine what they imported and why he's retired from it."

"I don't care. Franci, you've known me for ages. I don't go half-

way on things. I never handle new love well, or anything that ex-
cites me, for that matter. I never know when to stop."

"You don't have to be the one who brings all the emotion, while
some guy picks off what he wants."

"I've never done things any other way. Franci, look, I'm not getting married again. If this is the way things have to be, then that's
how it is."

"But it doesn't *have* to be that way."

Turning away from Millie, Franci stared fiercely out the window
at Serena and Trish, flying back and forth on the swings. Behind
them Orin was saying, "Hey, no, that's high enough," and the girls
were screaming, "Noooo, higher!"

From the knickknack shelf beside the window, Millie picked up
a large wooden box marked *Flour*. Under the word was a painted
tulip. Millie took off the lid and inside was a second, smaller
wooden box. She took off its lid, and there was a third box under it.

"I remember that," Franci said. "That was your grandmother's,
wasn't it? From Sweden?"

"You haven't said how things are going with you and Rich. You
haven't mentioned him once."

Franci reached into the box and took the third lid off. Inside,
there was an even smaller box. She held the wooden lid by its
round knob and twirled it once. Then she put it back on. Millie laid
the lid back on the second box, and then she put the biggest one
on. She looked at Franci and shook it, and all the boxes inside rattled a little. She pushed it to one side.

Franci put her hand on top and looked up at Millie. "It was amiable," she said.

Millie put her hand on Franci's hand. "Oh, no...I'm so sorry,
Franci."

"There's nothing to be sorry about." Franci shook her hand off.
"It's not like that. When I get back, then we decide. He's moving
out while I'm here. Don't look at me like that, Millie. We're
both...Rich and myself...nothing's final. I said this is amiable."

"Well, lucky for you."

Franci glanced over sharply at Millie. "Thanks."

"I didn't mean that." Millie looked back out the window at the
swing set. "They're really getting along, aren't they?"

Franci turned her back to the window, ignoring the scene by the
swings. "Both of us thought that maybe it wasn't for us anymore.

But when I get back…" Franci said, and then she reached out and rattled the box again. "When I get back, we'll get — we'll decide, and then…" She started again. "And then…"

WHEN FRANCI CAME downstairs after tucking the kids in, Orin and Millie had gone to the guesthouse. Franci brewed another cup of tea and waited until the fading evening light revealed that no lights were on in the guesthouse.

After her tea, Franci walked out on the front porch and stood there awhile, viewing the sunset through the dark line of condos. Then she returned inside the house to charge a call on her business credit card to her aunt in Seattle. Franci told her to expect them in the morning. Then she put on a parka, walked out of the house, and knocked on the guesthouse door.

"I'm going back to the beach!" she said to the door. Inside she heard someone stir. "Check in on the kids when you get the time."

"Hey, now, will do!" Orin yelled out.

When Franci came to the road, she turned north. She didn't want to walk toward town. She continued up the main road until she came to the access road for the condo development. Millie had said the condos weren't selling. The area was economically depressed, what with the logging and fishing falling off so bad. Several looked abandoned, the windows empty and the yards littered with scrap wood.

A little farther on a painted sign on a Quonset hut advertised a combination rock shop and cabinet maker's studio. In front of the hut, a yellow electric sign was mounted on a trailer. From the back of the sign, an orange extension cord snaked through the uncut lawn and disappeared under the Quonset hut's door. There were no letters stuck to the yellow panels of the portable sign. On the Quonset hut was a peeling plywood FOR SALE.

Franci stopped at a stream flowing under the road. On both sides of the stream, a thick stand of alders blocked access to the beach, and the only road had a chain across it, with a NO TRESPASSING sign hanging from it. Screwed to the bottom of that sign was another: FOR SALE BY OWNER. Franci almost decided to ignore the NO TRESPASSING sign and turn off the road to follow the stream down to the beach, but instead she walked down the road toward the blackberry brambles, and that's when she saw it.

At first she thought a big canvas tarp had fallen off a truck, but then as she moved closer, she saw the puckered crotch of its flippers, half-hidden in the roadside grass.

The sea lion covered the gravel shoulder of the road, turned slightly so the flippers rested in the grass sloping down to the blackberries. The large muddy green body looked flat on top, as if it were deflated. But as Franci drew near, only a faint smell of seaweed came to her. If there was any corruption, it was still inside.

Franci looked for signs of ropes on the body or of a track through the grass showing where the body had been dragged up to the gravel, but there was none. The sea lion was too huge to have been trucked there and then dropped for a prank. That would have taken a crane. Franci stared at the sea lion's back and its flippers, trying to make sense out of it but nothing added up.

She returned to the chained-off road, but it hadn't been used for a long time. The ruts were overgrown with summer grass. She walked back to inspect where the stream passed under the road. If the sea lion had dragged itself up from the beach, then it would have left a trail in the grass or in the gravel beds alongside the stream, but there was no sign of that.

Franci returned to the sea lion and examined it. There were no wounds. From the sea lion's left eye socket, a long white tube of fatty tissue hung out, dangling over its muzzle. Some scavenger had gotten the eye.

In the fading light, Franci stood staring down at the wide flat body of the sea lion, thinking of different explanations for why it would be there like that, but none of them worked. The sea lion was just there, at the side of the road, a tough leathery thing slowly collapsing in on itself.

He Was Reaching
For a Shovel

PETE SAT in the living room, looking out at Spanaway Lake. He had a glass of Scotch in his right hand. He put down the glass and walked over to the bar. He poured himself a club soda and dropped some ice in it. Leaving the glass of Scotch on the bar, he sat down on the couch and looked out at Spanaway Lake again.

Maria came into the room with Hubie's shirt over her arm. She walked past Pete and disappeared into the washroom. He heard the top of the washer open and close. He looked down at his shirt and saw that the bottom button had been ripped off. Maria came back into the living room and sat in a big leather chair opposite him.

"We used to roll cars over there," said Pete. "Behind the campgrounds. I was trying to remember if there were houses over on this side of the lake then."

We lined them up, the whole village, and told them not to move.

"It's been built up in the last few years," Maria said.

"You don't drink?"

"No," she said. Then: "physical problems."

Maria curled her feet up under her legs and scooted back, the chair surrounding her. She was a small dark woman, almost foreign looking. Pete could remember little about her. She was younger, graduated maybe three years after Hubie and Pete, so that meant Hubie got together with her a year after she graduated from high school—after his four years in the Marines.

"This is one of the last houses built on the lake. This was the last empty lot."

"You had it built?"

"No, we got it off the original owner. He went bankrupt. A lot have lately." Maria kept looking out over the lake. "That's a golf course, now, behind the campgrounds."

"Used to be prairie," Pete said. "Hubie and O'Rourke, and Flipper, myself and Ray — we rolled cars there. That was our idea of fun then. Hubie and me and Ray, we were in the back seat when that old Dodge went over." Pete was about to start the story, and then he stopped himself. He took a drink of his club soda instead and then held it up for her to see. "I'm tapering off."

Maria did not say anything to that.

"I'm going to see Ray."

"We don't see him any more."

"Why's that?"

"Hubie said it was his wife. I never knew more than that. Ray is up there," she pointed towards Mount Rainier. "Up where the big money is. He has a big house."

"Maria, I want you to know," Pete said, leaning forward, "we were just having a few drinks. I don't remember what sparked it off. He started talking and then...bang, he was plowed. I didn't know what to do." Pete paused. "I mean, I knew what to do, but I just wasn't expecting that from Hubie." Pete shrugged. "Hubie's the sixth one, now."

"The sixth what?"

"The sixth one of my friends who has told me things like that." *The whole village.* "He was the sixth guy. Six buddies — five into the Marines, Flipper joined the Army. All of them came back and told me stuff like what Hubie said tonight. And I never knew any of them were there. They all said they were someplace else. I thought Hubie really was in Guam. I really did. Driving jeep for some colonel." Pete took a drink of soda. "He always said that he had it soft."

Pete got up and walked over to the window. Down on the edge of the lake, ducks were cruising by. A big V spread out behind them as the ducks swam single-file past the shore.

"He never said he was there. Well, hell, nobody did when they got back. He went in a year after boot camp. By then we'd lost contact," Pete said. He took a drink of his soda. "I guess that's sort of a pattern."

"What is?"

"Never saying they were in Nam when they came back." Pete tried, but he couldn't remember when he saw Hubie after he came back.

Maria stared past Pete at the lake. Pete could not tell if she was upset or not. The room was getting darker, evening coming on over the lake, turning it a metallic black. *He was reaching for a shovel.*

"Does it bother you if I talk about it?" Pete said. "I'm doing all the talking."

Maria shook her head and leaned back in the chair. She waved her hand for him to go on talking. Pete paced back and forth in front of the window.

"Six, now that makes all six of them have said things like that to me. I thought Hubie got away. Goddamn it. All six. And it always happens the same way. We have some drinks. And then they break down."

Maria shifted around and reached behind her. There was a click, and the lamp on the table lit up, the light weak and soft.

"He has dreams," she said. "Not so many any more."

Pete stopped his pacing and stood by the window. "You better check on him," he said. "He might bring up some more while he's sleeping."

Maria nodded. She had turned gray as the light behind her put her in the shadow of the big chair.

"I didn't go," Pete said. "My friends came back early from the war, and I knew what was going on there."

He was reaching for a shovel. I thought he was reaching for a gun.

Pete walked over to the bedroom and opened the door. Inside he could hear Hubie's slow breathing. "I don't mean to barge around here." He shut the door. "He was my best friend, you know." Through the door Pete could hear Hubie breathing. He walked back to the window. He didn't like the sound through the door. In the failing light the lake had calmed into a still black sheet.

"All of them, that makes six." Pete looked at Maria. Her face was almost indistinct, her small body curled up in the chair. "Boy, I thought Hubie got away. I really did. I'm glad you're living with this guy, I really am. I haven't seen those five guys again. After they broke down. You know. That was it. You know what I mean?"

Pete walked back to the bedroom door and stood there, head inclined, listening to Hubie's breathing again. *That much is alive,* he thought.

"I mean, someone's got to forgive them. I get so angry I can't forgive anyone. No one should have to do it. I want to apologize to you for coming here." Pete looked at her, to see if she understood. She seemed to be barely there, now only a small bundle in the chair. "But I get more angry, and I can't apologize or forgive anyone. You know what it is? I'm pissed off at him. He didn't tell me. Maybe I came on all righteous to him. I was like that then. I'm still angry at him for not telling me. Do you get that? I wasn't even there, and look at me."

Pete stepped out and looked directly at her. She shifted in the chair, and her entire small body was in shadow, only dim silver slits where her eyes were. It was as if she were only watching. Watching. A fury rolled up in his throat and Pete felt a backward pull on his head, and for a moment the glass window behind him dissolved, and he saw her dissolve too, and he felt himself floating up backward over the lake. In front of him, she seemed to become the gray smoke of a woman.

The Fort

PROPPED ON THE BACK SEAT were the last three shopping bags of food, and Kristan was looking through all of them. She found a canister of Quaker Oats and shook it. As the station wagon went around a corner, a cardboard box tipped over and a plastic-wrapped frozen turkey began sliding around in the cargo area behind Kristan. She whooped and, leaning over the back seat, trapped the slippery turkey and put it back in its box.

"You know, Mom, when I was a little kid, I used to feel sorry for people who had to eat oatmeal," Kristan said.

"Why is that?" Cheri said.

"Because it wasn't Cream of Wheat." Kristan waited for her mother to say something else. "So then I found out all those things are like the same, nutritionally. I really thought some were more high-class than the others. But they're almost all the same, nutrition-wise."

Cheri turned the station wagon up a steep street. In back, the cardboard box spun around and tipped over once again. The frozen turkey skidded across the floor and crashed into the tailgate. Lunging over the back seat, Kristan captured it, but this time she carried the turkey into the back seat with her and wedged it between two of the shopping bags. Then she picked up a black portable tape recorder off the car floor. "Lucky I didn't put our old stereo back there or it would've been *mashed*. That turkey weighs a ton. When you gonna remember to drop this off at the church, Mom? We gotta get rid of this thing."

"After the weekend."

"God, I'm sure glad this is our last delivery. That turkey has been in a track meet back there all day long. At least this one's going to be tenderized."

THE LAST ADDRESS turned out to be near the edge of an industrial district, a two-story pink stucco with apartments upstairs and a beauty salon on the bottom floor. The upper windows had black wrought-iron balconies. The name of the beauty salon was Arabian Nights, and in its picture window a Venetian blind slouched behind a peeling decal of a woman peering out from a swirling burnoose.

Behind the Arabian Nights, a long high wooden fence enclosed the back yard. A door had been cut in the fence, and beside it was a black slot for mail with the address painted above it in green.

"This is the one," Cheri said, nodding toward the numbers by the mail slot. "Thirteen twenty-two B."

"Uck, what a dump," Kristan said.

"Shush," Cheri said. "Can you carry the turkey?"

Kristan got out of the station wagon, cradling the turkey under one arm. She held the car door open, and Cheri hoisted the heaviest paper bag, carried it to the fence, and leaned it next to the door. After Cheri got the other two bags out, Kristan walked over to the fence, opened the door with her free hand and stepped aside to let Cheri pass. After lifting the heavy bag inside the door and setting it down, Kristan ducked in behind her mother.

The yard was much larger than it looked from the outside. At the back of the lot was a small blue-gray house with a white door. Two neat garden plots lined either side of the path. A few winter garden cabbages, chard, and brussel sprouts rotted there from the recent cold rains.

Behind the house was a metal foundry and concertina wire coiled across the top of the high wooden fence. Rusting metal junk was stacked above the wire, and on top of one pile a truck cab tilted to one side, its windshield a sagging crater of smashed glass.

On the front porch, Cheri slid one of the bags down her hip and let it slump against the door frame. After she fished a plastic identification badge from her purse, she knocked.

"Who is it?"

"United Church Thanksgiving Fund," Cheri said.

"Okay," and the door opened on a blond woman in a soft green cotton jogging suit. Her left cheek had a small purple bruise under the eye, and when she smiled at Cheri, its irregular shape made her face seem lopsided. She stepped back to let Cheri come in.

"Happy Thanksgiving," Cheri said, looking around for a place to put the paper bag.

"On the table there," the woman said.

Kristan came in behind Cheri, holding the turkey under her arm like a football. "Hi."

"I'm Cheri, and this is my daughter, Kristan Fisher," Cheri said, setting the bag down on the table top.

"I'm Mary Lou Lang."

"Geemanee, are you going to be able to cook this turkey in that?" Kristan pointed at the apartment-size gas range.

"Oh, I'll be roasting this at a friend's house," Mary Lou said.

"I thought I recognized you," Cheri said. "I'm Cheri Evers, remember?"

"Oh, well, *yes*," Mary Lou said. "Cheri. Well, now, I'll be."

Cheri hurried over to pick up the second bag outside the door. As she struggled with the bag for a moment, Mary Lou steadied it by grabbing the top. They both laughed. Then Cheri ferried the bag across the room to the table, with Mary Lou still holding on.

"They fill these things to the top, I don't know why—we have all kinds of paper bags at the church," Cheri said, turning to Kristan. "Mary Lou and I went to the same high school," she explained.

"They fill them so full so they don't have to make more than three for each family," Kristan said. "Lazy butts."

"Get the other bag out by the fence, Kristan," Cheri said.

"I'll get it," Mary Lou offered.

"No, let her do it. She's younger than us."

Kristan went back outside and retrieved the last bag. Mary Lou and Cheri both watched.

"You have kids?"

Mary Lou nodded, pressing a hand on her bruise. "My ex-husband picked them up today."

"Ah," Cheri said, looking away. She pointed at the bags. "Well, they should enjoy this. Now, there's some pie crusts in here, so if you're not going to use them right away, you should freeze them."

Mary Lou watched Kristan looking around the house. In the living room was a small couch with a faded flower cover. In front of the couch, a footlocker doubled as a coffee table. A deck of cards was on top of it, with three cards laid out face up.

"We've got to be getting back home," Cheri said. "We're packing for a visit with my husband's parents on the holidays."

"Well, it's nice seeing you again. And thanks heaps for all this."

"Isn't us — it's the churches all getting together." Cheri was about to go into the regular spiel, but she caught herself. She patted Kristan on the arm, signaling it was time to go, and Kristan turned away from the living room. Mary Lou followed them outside.

"You garden?" Cheri said.

"Yes." Mary Lou looked down at the garden plots and smiled. "It really makes me happy. It's something I can do really good. And I get a lot of our food from these, too. Do you garden?"

"I wish I did," Cheri said. "We have the land for it, but I don't have the time."

"Well, if it isn't one thing, it's another," Mary Lou agreed, following behind Cheri. "You have a job?"

"Yes, for DeFroe Chemical."

Kristan was staring at the back of the beauty salon. Iron grilles protected all four windows, and inside, the glass was covered with faded posters. Bleached from the sun and warped from the damp, the smiling faces of the models peered out from under 1960s bouffant hair styles, their long black eyelashes dripping milky gray tears.

As Kristan held the fence door open, Cheri stepped outside. Kristan touched Mary Lou on her arm. "Hey, you wouldn't want our old ghetto blaster, would you? We were going to give it to the church anyway, for the rummage sale, but we forgot to drop it off."

"Oh, I don't think…" Cheri started to say.

"Do you have a stereo?" Kristan asked Mary Lou. "I didn't see one in there. Look, let me show you."

Mary Lou put one foot outside the fence and held the door open as Kristan crossed over to the station wagon. Kristan held up the black portable and pointed to its back. "It plugs in and everything. So you don't have to have batteries."

Mary Lou looked at it and shook her head. "I'd just have to buy tapes for it."

"You sure? God, I don't know how I could live without music,"

Kristan said. "We're just going to dump it at the church anyway, and you might as well have it."

"No, but thanks." Mary Lou waved to Cheri. "Thanks, Cheri, great seeing you again."

Cheri poked Kristan in her ribs, and got in the car. Cheri waved to Mary Lou and eased into the front seat. As she fished around in her windbreaker pockets for the car keys, she saw that Mary Lou was still standing in the open door, watching them.

"You didn't have to force it on her like that," Cheri said.

"I didn't."

"Sometimes people don't want charity, not like that. You didn't have to make the stereo sound so decrepit. It was embarrassing enough for her, you know."

"God, I was just trying to get rid of it. Was she your friend or something in high school?"

Cheri started the car and reached for her seat belt. "No, not really," she said. "Mary Lou was the first one of our class to get pregnant and leave school. I just knew her. No one saw her after that."

"I bet," Kristan said, "if she was living in this dump."

IN THE REC ROOM, Ben blocked the door to the garage with his arm. "I don't want you to worry about it. I told my brother Jake to dump the stuff. I'll take care of it. Goddamn it, I didn't know he was going to bring all his junk over today. I said you weren't going to lift a finger this trip, and you aren't. So anyway, we're going to be a little late getting out of the chute-ola here, because moving my brother's crap delayed me and Randy."

"Oh, Ben, it's okay," Cheri said. "It won't kill me to *look* at the stuff."

"Promise you won't get all depressed. You're looking a little tired or something."

Cheri sighed and gently pushed his arm down from the door-jamb. "Let me look."

"Me and Uncle Jake made a fort out of boxes, Ma. The secret door's on the side," Randy shouted as he ran past. "Dad, we gotta put on the bikes *now*."

"Wait a minute, willya, son? Just one thing, Cheri, honey, do you know where the hell we put the Coleman lamp? No, don't go get it—tell me."

"Under the sink."

"And the gas canisters for it, too?"

"Daaaaad, we gotta put on the bikes *now!*"

Cheri nodded yes, and Ben followed their son into the front yard, where their big beige and white Americruiser RV was parked. On the sidewalk, their bags, camping equipment, and boxes of food were piled in two long lines. Mounted on the front bumper were Ben and Cheri's mopeds. An aluminum boat was tied upside down to the roof rack of their RV, and behind it a huge yellow and blue canvas covered the kids' raft. Two bicycles leaned against the RV's back bumper below the spare tire.

Cheri opened the door to the garage and turned on the light. Covering almost the entire floor was a big jumble of white U-Haul cardboard cartons, with FISHER written in purple marker pen on their sides. With so many boxes, there was barely enough room for Cheri to walk around. At one corner of the jumble, her son's fort was constructed in a square, four boxes high, with a tower of smaller boxes stacked up in its middle.

There was a pounding on the garage door. "Maaawm! Open up in there!" Randy shouted.

Cheri hit the automatic door button. Before it was halfway up, Randy had scooted in, grabbed a tool off the bench, and run out to the RV.

As the door opened all the way, Cheri saw her husband standing by the rear bumper with the pieces of the bike rack in his hands.

Cheri looked at the boxes. *Well, he picked one heck of a time to turn our garage into a warehouse,* she said to herself. *And no way to get even one car in the garage, even if they restacked it.*

That meant every morning all winter long she would be walking out on a rainslick sidewalk to her car. When she and Ben were first married, living in a ratty old house by Green Lake with no garage, she always had to race out to her car in the rain. Walking to the front of the garage, she turned and stared at the boxes, remembering her first winter with Ben.

"You got two calls from work, honey!" Ben yelled at her. "You leave one day early, and that place falls apart. Those people don't know what the hell a vacation is. I told them to stuff it! You're on vacation. I said you weren't even packing the RV! They loved that.

You'll hear about what a good hubby I am when you go back to work."

Cheri walked to the side of the boxes, looking at the large purple letters. Mary Lou's face came back to her, and she saw that livid splash of her bruise again.

There was one box turned out, showing the entrance to the fort. Cheri squatted down and stared in. Getting down on her hands and knees, she crawled in and turned around and drew the box back in, blocking the entrance. The cardboard boxes smelled new and clean. Inside, she could see how Ben's brother and her son had arranged the smaller boxes on top at angles, leaving little cracks for light to come in. Cheri looked down at her hands, and she made fists.

"Mom, Maaaaa-aaawm!" Kristan's voice came screaming out from the rec room. Steps came closer, and then Cheri heard Kristan run outside down the driveway. "You know where Mom is, Dad?"

"No, she must be somewhere in the house."

"Well, I've *got* to have the blue one. And she knows where it is."

"The blue one what, kitten?" Ben shouted.

But Kristan had already run up on the porch, slamming the front door as she went back in the house.

Through a crack in the boxes, Cheri watched as Ben and Randy argued about the right way to put the bicycle carrier on the RV's bumper. Then a part on the carrier broke, and Randy howled that he wasn't going to the lake without his own bicycle.

Cheri slumped back down, looking up at the shafts of light latticed above her head from the openings. In each of the dusty beams were thousands of specks. She watched their restless movements and remembered a game she used to play under her grandfather's big walnut dining room table.

Her mother had just divorced her father, and they had moved into an unfurnished apartment with only a skinny chrome-legged kitchen table for Cheri to play under. At that time, too, her grandfather was dying, and one of her mother's jobs was to give to him his medicine. He lay propped up in his big high bed between carved posts, his skin looking so old and woody that he seemed like part of the furniture.

Under the safety of her grandparent's walnut table, Cheri pretended that each mote of dust was her secret medicine, and that each speck was a little pill of emotion. Each time she breathed them in, she'd feel all the different emotions, a rainbow of them. She'd imagine herself majestically angry, then woefully sad, and then really happy. Just by breathing, she was mixing up all those emotions inside herself. She knew that she was breathing them in and that they were inside her for a second and then she was breathing them out.

Yellow Rock

WHAT HAPPENED WAS that Ripolla passed by the old water tower that afternoon. Ripolla worked for the county roads, and he didn't get out by the yellow-rock tower that often. It was just over the county line, and any job calls went to the other district. He drove past the tower and up the hill to the yellow rock. The grass around the rock was beaten down by the cars, so kids were still using it for necking. There was writing all over the rock: who did what and who loved who and when. But the names were all new. What was underneath was gone.

Turning his CB off, Ripolla looked across the dying summer grass at the water tower with the blinking red light on top. He remembered. He decided to go home that night instead of going to Rainier Corners. He turned his squawk box back on and started the truck. He thought he would talk to June. About old times. Maybe even get friendly for old time's sake. If it came to that.

But when Ripolla turned into his driveway, June's car was gone. Ripolla kept driving up the lane and parked the county truck to the side of the carport. A call came over his CB radio. He listened—it wasn't for him—and then he turned it off. Ripolla sat and stared at the empty carport for a while. Then he got out of the truck. In the evening light, he could see that the house really did need paint. "She's not wrong about that," he said.

Then he looked up. There were five pine trees in his yard screwing up the grass underneath with their needles. He noticed that a lot of the lower limbs had died. Some limbs had big loads of needles resting on them. One more big winter wind and they would be gone, dropping down to kill some more of his lawn. Ripolla felt like he hadn't had a look around lately, so he walked out on his lawn and stood on what was left of it, the ground bare and hard in patches. Ripolla examined his house. The stained decorative wood strips under the windows were splitting, weathered beyond repair.

He walked around back. The back window screen was ripped up. *Wind.* He tucked it back into its slot. Then he thought, *Might as well do it right.* And he went around front, got a hammer and nails out of the toolbox in the back of the county truck, came back, and hammered the screen in place. Then he went inside.

The house was neat. The only thing not tucked away was a *TV Guide* open on the couch. Ripolla touched the TV, and it was warm. *She must have just left. Maybe she was coming back. Probably not. Why would she? Friday night and the Rip's holding court at the Corners.*

Ripolla opened the refrigerator and looked in at the purple and blue and white milk cartons. He couldn't remember if those were new or if he had just not noticed them before. He remembered red milk cartons. So maybe she'd gone to a different store lately. The new ones were kind of pretty next to the white wall of the fridge. "Kind of pretty," he said, and he shut the door. He wasn't hungry. He went into his workroom, got a beer out of the little refrigerator there, and walked back in the kitchen nook, where he stared in at the front room.

In another house Ripolla had seen a different arrangement. He'd been called in about some overflowing county ditches one day, and he'd seen that arrangement when he was in this guy's house talking about the overflow. He had the same house as Ripolla had—same floor plan, only things looked different. Ripolla almost asked the guy who built his house, but since Ripolla did not know who had built his own house, he didn't ask. He'd brought it up to June that night, but she didn't think anything around their place needed changing. That was as far as it went.

"Well, shit," he said. He drained his beer and walked into the bedroom. He decided to get dressed up tonight, go to the Golden Slipper. The hell with Rainier Corners. He opened his dresser drawer and took out the pint he kept there, and that's when he heard a scrape in the bathroom.

Ripolla put down the pint. He left it on the dresser with the cap off, drifted out to the kitchen table, and picked up the hammer. He came back into the bedroom and stood to one side of the bathroom door, listening through the wall for any sounds. Then, with his right leg up, he rocked back and kicked the door open. A form fell down behind the frosted glass doors of the bathtub.

"Come out with your hands up, or I'll whack you out."

The figure behind the frosted glass got out of the tub. The door cracked open, and a man peered out at Ripolla with fear in his eyes. He was dressed in an old sweatshirt and jeans, looking like an old bum.

"Come on, *slow*. That's right." Ripolla was breathing hard with the hammer up, ready for business.

The man stepped out of the bathtub, but before he could get his back foot out, Ripolla had him by the neck. He twisted him out of the tub and threw him against the bathroom cabinet, kicking the legs out from under him. The bum fell, his chin hitting the cabinet top, and he let out a yelp.

"That's right, right there." Ripolla checked him for any knives or guns. Then he stepped back. It was the first time Ripolla could remember any of his old Army MP stuff coming in handy. "Now you just stay there, hear?" he ordered. Ripolla wished that he had put the phone in the can like June had said. He didn't know what the hell to do next. He didn't want to let the guy up.

"Thought you'd slip in here while the old lady was gone, right?" Ripolla was still breathing hard, and his heart was racing. He took a deep breath and tried to think of some way to go call the police. Ripolla looked down at the man's face reflected in the bathroom mirror. The man had his chin down on the cabinet top, looking up at him.

"Say," Ripolla said, "say." He let the hammer down a little. "Say, don't I know you?"

The man lifted his head off the cabinet top very slowly, his eyes on the hammer in Ripolla's hand. He nodded once.

Ripolla tried to think where. "Oh, Jesus," he said.

The man was watching the hammer drop down, as Ripolla remembered. Ripolla raised it up and used it to point at the man's reflection. "Danny," he said, "Danny Conley?"

The man nodded again and his mouth moved, but only a dry sound came out of it.

"You take anything?" Ripolla watched Conley shake his head.

"Just came in?" Conley nodded again. "Jesus," Ripolla said, "did you know this was my place?"

"No," Conley said. There was a silence, and he made the dry sound again, clearing his throat. "I just got into town."

"Yeah?" Ripolla said. "Well, you look like shit." He fluffed Conley's pants leg with his boot. "Crap all over your pants. What have you been doing, sleeping in a bog?"

Conley looked back down into the sink. He took a deep breath. "I've been..."

"Yeah?"

Conley shrugged, as if it was a waste of time to talk about it.

"Get up," Ripolla said. "Get up. You must be goddamn broke to break into this house."

Conley stood up, his legs wobbling a bit as he turned. "I heard a radio," Conley said. "I thought it was the cops. Otherwise I would've run for it, if it wasn't the cops. You can get one in your back with the cops."

Ripolla stood there looking at Conley. Then Conley wiped his mouth and nodded toward the sink. Ripolla stood back a little, and Conley turned and ran the tap. He drank out of his hand before he washed his face. He stooped over the whole time, as if he expected to get hit any moment.

Ripolla went out to his dresser, picked up the pint, and had a drink. "Jesus Christ," he said again. He looked back at the bathroom, and Conley was running more water. Ripolla took a second drink, thought about what he could do for a bit, and when he looked back, Conley stood in the door.

"Come out." Ripolla pointed at the bed with his hammer. "Sit."

Conley sat down, and his hands crossed in his lap. He seemed to be used to sitting. He stared at the floor heater beside the wall. Over his head, the window was up a crack. Ripolla saw that he was wearing new black soft shoes, like deck shoes. They had red rubber soles.

"What's it been?" Ripolla said.

Conley thought. "About twelve years."

Ripolla turned and took the bottle again and drank. "I used to beat the shit out of you down at the bus stop." Ripolla waited, but Conley didn't say anything. "You had those knuckles." He pointed at Conley's crossed hands. "Sharpest goddamn knuckles in school."

He waited again, but Conley didn't say anything back to him. He sat there like an old man. "When'd you leave?"

"Tenth grade."

"You had a car. A 1939 Ford."

Conley shrugged.

"What happened after that?" Ripolla waited. "That's right, reform school. Chehalis." He drank more whiskey and checked the bottle. "When'd you get out?"

"Graduated, same as you."

Ripolla did not know what to say to that. He didn't know that people could graduate from the joint. "They always said I was heading that way," he said finally. "You know, at school."

Conley looked up and began to stare at Ripolla's pint.

"You hungry? You eat?" Ripolla waved him toward the front room, and Conley got up and walked by him into the kitchen. He didn't look up once.

"There," Ripolla commanded.

Conley sat down at the kitchen-nook table. Ripolla put the hammer on the refrigerator and opened the refrigerator door. Taking out a carton of milk, he put it on the table. Then he located a plastic tube of cheese and got some crackers down from the cabinet above the refrigerator. From a drawer by the sink he took a butter knife and handed it to Conley. While Conley was spreading the cheese on the crackers, Ripolla got him a glass.

"I always heard of burglars eating at your house, but this is the first time I heard of the burglaree setting the table for him."

Conley ate, smearing the cheese on one cracker at a time, eating it, and then doing it over again, while Ripolla watched. Then Ripolla went back to the bathroom and got his pint. He expected Conley to be gone when he returned, but he was there, eating one cracker at a time.

Ripolla got a little mad about that. "Jesus," he said again. He was disgusted, but he watched Conley eating as if that was all he had on his mind.

Conley looked up from his meal and pointed with his knife at a picture of June on the knickknack shelf. "You married her?"

"Yeah," Ripolla said.

Conley nodded.

"So?" Ripolla said.

"Nothing." Conley looked around the kitchen and regarded the front room, before he went back to smearing more cheese on a cracker.

"I suppose you'd like to change places with me," Ripolla said. "Like right now."

"No," Conley said.

Ripolla looked down at him in amazement. Then he laughed. "Well, Jesus, the balls of a burglar, I guess. Of course, it's the balls of a bad burglar, so that's not so much."

Conley shrugged and poured himself some milk. Then he drank it, his eyes staring off at nothing, without looking at Ripolla.

"Get up," Ripolla said.

"What?"

"Get up."

Setting the glass down, Conley stood up, and Ripolla walked toward him, taking the hammer off the refrigerator.

"We're going out." Ripolla stopped and brought the hammer up to Conley's face. "I don't want any trouble. Got that?"

Conley drove, but he didn't have the knack of the truck and handled it badly, as Ripolla watched him, thinking that probably Conley had been out of circulation for some time.

"You get those soft shoes in the joint?" Ripolla asked, pointing the hammer at Conley's feet.

Conley shook his head.

"Where?"

"Rehab exercise class," Conley said.

"Where? Where'd you get those?"

"Parole halfway place. They're Chinese."

"Great, just fucking great," Ripolla said. "They give you the perfect shoes at the rehab joint for breaking into places, and they don't even buy American."

Conley didn't say anything for about a minute. He cleared his throat. "I got bad feet," he explained. "They fit."

"Turn here."

Conley turned the truck into the road for the Yellow Rock. In the gray evening mist, the red light on top of the water tower was blinking. Since it was early, there weren't any cars parked out by the rock yet. Conley drove the truck up to the rock and parked it.

"Turn the light on the rock. Not that light—the one on top."

Conley turned the spotlight on top of the cab so that it was facing the rock. Then he flicked the switch, and the spotlight lit up

the names scrawled all over the yellow side of the rock. With the
wind tossing the grass around, casting shadows on the rock, the
names seemed to be moving, shifting in and out of focus.

"I used to come up here," Ripolla said. "I used to come up here
a lot. Did you come up here?" Ripolla looked over at Conley. Conley stayed frozen. "I used to envy you that Ford. I couldn't work after school because I wanted to play ball. You got a job and bought
that Ford."

"I come up here, too," Conley said.

"You know who I laid up here?" Ripolla said. "I screwed as many
times as they put names on that rock."

Turning and looking at Ripolla once, Conley shrank back in his
seat, hugging the door. Nodding as if in agreement with Ripolla,
he put his left hand down on his knee next to the door handle.

Ripolla was staring out at the yellow rock. "I laid Shirlee.
Remember her? And I nailed Doris and little Missie and Dawn and
what's-her-name, the Crispin girl. I turned on my headlights one
night, and Louise, the cheerleader, Louise did her own little dance
for me. She went down right there."

Ripolla touched Conley on the knee with his hammer. "I bet
you'd want that now, wouldn't you?"

And Conley went for the door. He got it open and fell backward
out of the truck just as the hammer hit the cab where his head had
been. The door slammed shut, and Ripolla sent the head of the
hammer through the window. It caught there, the shattered glass
radiating out around it in a star. Ripolla still had his hand on the
hammer. Through the cracked glass he saw Conley running
around the yellow rock, disappearing in the tall grass.

Ripolla was breathing hard. He tugged on the hammer handle,
and the head moved in the glass. Little chunks of glass crumbled
and fell, as he worked the hammer around. He did it almost gently,
breathing easier. He twisted the hammer head free from the glass
and laid the hammer down on the seat. Then he leaned over a little
and looked through the hole.

We Have Another Ape

WHEN PETE and his daughter, Erin, went north to visit his family, his wife Leigh stayed home. She didn't want to see her parents any more. She knew that she would have to see them if she came along, and she liked to keep any contact reduced to letters. So Pete got the duty instead.

Late on Christmas day, he drove his daughter over to the Neilson house near Puyallup. At first, when Pete and Erin walked in, there were only old women and young girls there. Then, hearing the greetings, Leigh's father, Floyd, and Uncle Henning came out of the music room to see what was up, watching from the hallway door. Pete's mother-in-law, Erma, took his daughter away the moment they came in, and that was it for Pete. He got introduced.

While Erin opened her presents on the floor by the fireplace, Pete stood off to one side by the dining room table. Leigh's father circled through and, cocking his head toward Pete, made a drinking motion, before hurrying back into the hallway. Pete looked at the women surrounding his daughter in the front room, checking that there were no more presents to open. He had memorized all the presents and who had given them, so he could bring back a report to Leigh. Pete turned and walked toward Floyd, who was standing in the dark hallway, peering in at the women.

Uncle Henning slipped past Floyd and disappeared down the basement stairs. Floyd held open the basement door and motioned Pete to follow. After Floyd eased down the first step, he gave Pete a big wink. Pete trailed along behind Floyd's broad back. With the door closed behind him, the sounds of the Christmas party faded away. As they descended into the basement, the musty scent of dust, laundry, and heating pipes rose up around them.

Uncle Henning, a bald crane of a man, was waiting for them by the washer, nodding and smiling. "Eh-yup," he said, "we have another."

"Eh-yeah," Floyd said. "We have another." He expelled a short laugh, as he leaned over the washer and brought out a bottle of Old Crow from its hiding place. Then he took down a water glass from the shelf above the dryer. "Wouldn't you know," he said. Floyd poured a drink, about half a glass, and Uncle Henning drank it. Then Floyd poured another, and Pete drank that. After Pete set the glass back on the washer lid, Floyd poured one for himself. Nothing was said, and only Floyd's breathing punctuated the silence. As soon as Floyd had downed his drink, he poured a second one, and they each had another in turn. Then Floyd hid the bottle behind the washer, and they started toward the stairs, Uncle Henning leading the way again.

As Floyd heaved himself up on the first step, Pete caught his arm. "Say, do you have a circle saw around here somewhere? I'm helping my mom build something."

"Hell's bells, I don't know," he said. "There's one around here somewhere. I never can find anything around here." He flung his fat arm out at the basement, dismissing it. "One's sure to be around here somewhere. When I need anything, Pete, I go out and buy it. It's easier than finding it around here.".

Pete waited until Floyd was gone. Stacked up all over the floor were paper bags filled with canned food, in some places four or five bags high. Most of the bags leaned against the wall to the right of the stairs. To the left, the central heater sat in a square hole, with more bags lined along its side. Pete began to move the bags of canned food away from the wall.

Judging by the sales slips taped to the front of the bags, most of it was from the PX. Floyd was retired, but as an officer he still held PX privileges. As Pete unstacked the bags, he began to uncover tools under them. Some of them were new, still in their boxes with the sales slips stuck to the tops with yellow or red tape.

It was slow work. Mostly the bags were full of cans, and they were heavy. Between the dryer and the wall, under paper bags filled with deviled ham and sardine cans, Pete found two electric drills, both without the cartons. One had been used at least once. It had the drill bit still in it, sawdust curled up in its grooves. Under the bags of food stacked beside the back door, Pete found an electric hacksaw, an electric jigsaw, and three sets of Sears ratchet wrenches, all half-inch drive, with some socket heads missing from each. There were various hand tools, all looking as if they'd been used once and abandoned.

Pete laid the bags of food back on top of them. There didn't seem to be a circle saw around. As he climbed the stairs, he stopped to peer into the square hole around the central heater. A bag of canned hams had fallen there and spilled out. Poking up between the hams was one end of a shiny new carpenter's square. Pete decided there probably wasn't room for the circle saw under the hams.

Walking back down the hall, he could hear the high happy chatter of the women in the living room. Pete continued into the music room. Opening the door, he saw that it was gray in there. No lights were on.

In the corner of the couch, Uncle Henning was hunched over beside the French doors. Out on the back lawn Pete could see a gray ghost of a half-built boat up on sawhorses. The weathered plywood on the cabin had separated, and its sheets had curled toward the stern, as if some fierce wind had peeled them back. Its faded sides had thin black stripes of mold where rain had drained down its hull. A forest of tall dead gray thistles hid the keel.

To the right of the French doors, Floyd sat in an easy chair in the darkest corner. He seemed to be staring out at the boat, but Pete couldn't tell because he could barely see him.

Pete sat down in the chair beside the piano, and Uncle Henning began talking about second-string basketball guards for the local Lutheran college team. Pete remembered some. He had played against a few during high school, and on his high school team he had even played with some of the college's first-string guards. Pete brought their names up, but it was clear right away that Uncle Henning did not want to talk about first stringers. He only wanted to talk about the college's second-string guards. Uncle Henning continued to reminisce about how one almost had a good jump shot, about how one had a particularly tricky dribbling motion and should have played more.

By then, the whiskey was working on Pete, and he found it

strange listening to this history. The names of those second-string guards began to attach themselves to faces drifting through Pete's mind. He found that he could imagine a face to fit any name Uncle Henning said. Pete heard himself agreeing that he had known them, and he even described them.

"The blond guy, crew cut," Pete guessed.

"Eh-yup," Uncle Henning said. And he went on talking about this phantom's foul shooting.

Over in the corner, Floyd seemed to be smiling at Pete. He hadn't said anything for a long time. Pete wondered if Floyd had been afraid that Pete might not fit in, might not go down in the basement to sneak a drink with them.

The fading afternoon light filtering through the French doors got dimmer and dimmer. In the shadows Pete could barely make out Floyd any more. He had become a gray lump. Every now and then, the door would open, and a woman's face would poke in. Then the door would close. One time a girl's voice said, "They're just sitting there in the dark."

Whenever Uncle Henning stopped talking, they heard the murmur of the Christmas party going on in the living room. Uncle Henning worked his way back in the past to second-string guards who had been Pete's P.E. teachers in grade school, men Pete could remember trying to teach him two-handed set shots.

When it got so dark that Pete couldn't see Uncle Henning's face, he decided that it was time for him to leave. He stood up without saying anything, and Uncle Henning interrupted his monologue to look up at Pete. "He wasn't *that* tall," Uncle Henning said, motioning Pete to sit down.

"Well," Pete said, his voice sounding very remote to him, "did you ever play?"

In the corner Floyd cleared his throat. "Henning," he laughed, "Henning…first the Depression, then the war, right, Henning?"

Uncle Henning nodded. "Eh-yup," he said.

"Eh-yeah," Floyd agreed.

"Eh-yup," Uncle Henning added.

"First, food on the table. Right, Henning?" Floyd said, still chuckling. "No time for playing."

Then he stopped chuckling, and Uncle Henning sat silently. Then: "Eh-yup."

"We've got to go." Pete's voice sounded strange to him. And he didn't move. He waited for them to say something.

"Sit down," Floyd said to Pete, as he stood. "I've got something to show you." He left the room.

Pete sat back down, not knowing why he did it. He wanted to leave so bad he felt sick. Pete waited for Floyd to return, the smell of the basement dust rising up off his hands. He looked at the piano stool and then at the upright piano. He tried to imagine music coming out of it. He imagined throwing himself against it and the whole piano collapsing, a stunt piano. He saw himself smashing through the French doors and laying a cross body block on the boat outside. He saw the old ghost topple over, its separated plywood sheets waving helplessly.

"I would have played," Uncle Henning said.

Floyd entered, carrying a powder-blue package. He was chuckling as he set the package on the floor and sat down next to Uncle Henning. "Done so pretty, I left the original wrappings on," Floyd said. Then, with a grunt, he leaned forward and began to unfold the wrappings.

The music-room door closed softly, the sounds of the women's Christmas party fading away, and the withdrawal of the hallway light made everything fuzzy and dim in the room again. Pete had to lean forward to see what Floyd was doing.

In the faint light from the French doors, Pete could make out that the package had been gift-wrapped by a store. The top of the heavy wrapping paper came up in triangles, the sign of a professional job. As Floyd lifted each triangle, the wrapping flowered open nice and neat, and then the flaps of the cardboard box under the paper opened up neatly too. Floyd pulled the piano stool closer to him and put the box on top of it. With a rustle of tissue paper, he took the present out, set it in front of the box, turning the present around so it faced Pete.

Against the powder-blue wrapping paper, Pete could see from its silhouette that it was some kind of a potbellied statue, one with a round head. For a whiskey-addled moment, Pete thought it was a statue of Buddha, but then Floyd took hold of its right arm and, with a racheting crack, raised its hand above the statue's head.

"The fellows down at the plywood plant gave it to me for Christmas." Floyd ran his hand over the arm and down the head, feeling the statue's shape. Then he pulled the arm down and laughed again. Reaching in the box, he took out something small and fitted it into the statue's hand.

Pete shifted around so he could see the statue better in the last rays of evening light. The statue now had a miniature airline liquor bottle in its hand. Pete reached out in the dark and touched the statue's face. It was an ape.

Floyd laughed as Pete touched it. "Wait. Watch. Watch this," he chuckled. "That's not all. Let go." He paused until Pete withdrew his hand, and then he reached behind the ape. There was a click and then a grinding sound began. The arm of the ape began to move.

In the dim light Pete could now make out its face. The ape was grinning. With a mechanical hum, the arm circled around in front of the ape's face and rested in its lap. For a second or two, the gears whirred, and then with a swift jerk the ape brought the bottle up and hit himself on the head.

The same whirring sound followed. The arm lifted the bottle off its head, went down, went around, and rested in its lap for a second, and then the ape's arm jerked up and hit its head with the bottle again. The arm got halfway down, when the mechanical sound stopped.